Katherine B. Guthrie

My Year in an Indian Fort

Volume 1

Katherine B. Guthrie

My Year in an Indian Fort
Volume 1

ISBN/EAN: 9783337272371

Printed in Europe, USA, Canada, Australia, Japan

Cover: Foto ©Andreas Hilbeck / pixelio.de

More available books at **www.hansebooks.com**

MY YEAR

IN

AN INDIAN FORT.

BY MRS. GUTHRIE,

AUTHOR OF "THROUGH RUSSIA."

THE FORT DITCH, WALLS, AND BASTION.

IN TWO VOLUMES.

VOL. I.

LONDON:

HURST AND BLACKETT, PUBLISHERS,

13 GREAT MARLBOROUGH STREET.

1877.

PREFACE.

IN the following pages I have nothing to tell
of Eastern magnificence. In the works of
God, rather than in those of man, lies the interest to be found in the somewhat primitive
part of the Western Deccan where, for the time
being, my lot was cast. Tempered by the sea
breeze, its climate is the most equable and delightful in all India. Its high table-lands are
fertile and well timbered, its protecting ghâts
afford mountain scenery of the wildest and
most beautiful description, and it is very rich
in its fauna and flora. The charms of nature
are scattered around with a beneficent hand,
and its strange and ancient people were to me
a fertile source of interest.

Such were the attractions which combined
with the fulness of my family life to make
up the happiness that I experienced during
"My Year in an Indian Fort."

Belgaum Fort, July, 1876.

CONTENTS

OF

THE FIRST VOLUME.

CHAPTER I.

CHAPTER II.

CHAPTER III.

CHAPTER IV.

CHAPTER V.

CHAPTER VI.

CHAPTER VII.

CHAPTER VIII.

CHAPTER IX.

CHAPTER X.

CHAPTER XI.

CHAPTER XII.

CHAPTER XIII.

MY YEAR IN AN INDIAN FORT.

CHAPTER I.

Voyage to Bombay—The *Hindoo*—Unpromising Com-
mencement of the Voyage—Three days in Torbay—
Sunday on Board—Across the Bay of Biscay—The
Sierra of Cintra—Gibraltar Passed—The Mediter-
ranean — Algiers — Carthage — Tunis — Pantalaria —
Port Saïd—Perilous Position of the *Arabia*—A Day
on Shore—Land of the Pharaohs—The Suez Canal—
Pilgrims—Ismailia.

A START for a far-distant country must, even
under the most favourable circumstances,
be accompanied by some emotions of sadness.
There was certainly nothing exhilarating in our
departure for India. Up at daybreak on a foggy
January morning, a hurried breakfast, a crush
into the family omnibus, a tedious delay in a
narrow street where gas-pipes were being laid
down, a tramp through long lanes lined by bales
and boxes, a climb up a greasy ladder, and we
stood upon the dirt-begrimed deck of the *Hindoo*,

a steamer of four hundred horse-power, bound for Bombay.

Our first impulse was to count heads, and these, consisting, in addition to M. and myself, of three children, three nurses, two Irish setters, a terrier, and two goats, were happily found all right. Our next step was to descend and see what our cabins were like, and having satisfied our curiosity on this point, we felt ourselves at leisure to mount to the upper deck, and survey the scene presented by the various groups assembled below, our companions to be for the next five weeks.

All had a subdued manner, and some looked just slightly cross, as I have no doubt we also did; but the appearance of all improved under more favourable circumstances, and we trusted that our visages also lighted up. The scene upon the lower deck, and alongside on the crowded wharf, was dismal; poverty and squalor, dirt and disorder, reigned supreme. Everything seemed to have a leaden hue, and a stifling smoke-laden atmosphere enveloped all. My memory dwells but on one bright speck, the cheerful scarlet of a petticoat worn by a woman who was waving a tearful adieu to her friends.

The ship was by no means ready for sailing. She had only been in dock thirteen days, and the bedding was damp. In my cabin I found a broken cart and ninepins, belonging doubtless to its former juvenile occupant. To make matters still more deplorable, the weather, after we had started, was almost as bad as it could be. We made scarcely any way. The captain passed two very anxious nights on deck, and the narrow vessel—only thirty-eight feet wide by four hundred long, built to pass through the Suez Canal—rolled terribly. The ornamental part of the upper deck was carried away by the violence of the sea, and the berths being all more or less wet, we were very miserable, added to which I had a private grievance of my own. Dogs not being allowed in the saloon, my poor Bustle was ruthlessly ordered off to Mr. Needles, the butcher, under whose care he was placed. How I used to struggle over the wave-washed deck to feed him, and impart a little comfort to my desolate favourite, no one but a lover of dogs can imagine. The poor creature I really believe would have died, had not the captain allowed him to come below, in order to enjoy the sport of hunting the rats which infested our cabins, impudently eating our biscuits, and nibbling holes in our clothes.

It was not long before Mr. Bustle became quite a favourite with the good-natured passengers,

who called him Monsieur Tourneur, and other
pet names. We lay three days in Torbay, into
which a number of other ships ran for shelter,
among them a fine P. and O. steamer, also
bound for Bombay. Having sailed a day in
advance of the *Hindoo*, she had been roughly
handled by the waves, and was obliged to put
back. With the exception of the captain, no
one went on shore, and he paid two shillings
for a boat to take him there and back. Owing
to the stormy condition of the sea, he had to
choose the right moment to jump in, and afterwards told us that he reckoned the distance between the top of the wave and the trough of the
sea to be at least twelve feet. The sight of the
elements at war, the flashes of lightning and
the peals of thunder, were most exciting. When
the white squalls came on, a small part of the sea
would be suddenly covered with foam, a torrent
of rain would pour down upon the spot, and, as
it spread, gradually obscure land, sea, and sky,
leaving us in all but complete darkness.

Torbay, I understand, is very dangerous when
the wind blows from the west. Captain Cousins
(our captain) told us that once when, with forty-
seven other ships, he had to run in for safety,
the wind suddenly veered round in the night,
and all the vessels, with the exception of two,

were either stranded or more or less injured.

In spite of the gales, Sunday brought with it a young clergyman from Torquay to conduct divine service, and all assembled in the long saloon to take part in the religious duty. Afterwards one Sunday on board was precisely like another. The ladies assembled in fresh toilettes. The gentlemen did their little best to imitate them, with crisp white cuffs and collars, and dandy neck-ties; but it was really a pretty sight to see the Hindoo sailors muster in their stainless cotton dresses, bound round the waist by crimson silk sashes.

At ten o'clock precisely two very handsome copper-coloured Bengalese dived into a cupboard, brought forth a number of Bibles and prayer-books, and began to rig up the reading-desk. First they produced two very large chess-boards, then a couple of bed-pillows were fetched from below, after which the union-jack was carefully spread over the erection, which was further secured by a long thick rope coiled around it. The service commenced with the regulation hymn, including the verse, " I have seen the works of the Lord, and His wonders in the deep," and everyone knows the beautiful air to which those words are set, ending with the refrain,

> "Oh ! hear us when we cry to Thee,
> For those in peril on the sea."

Always touching, this hymn was doubly so when one glanced up whilst singing it, and looked around upon the solitary expanse of ocean. No land, no ships in sight, no human aid to help us in distress. In such circumstances the whole service was felt to be doubly impressive.

We rolled through the Bay of Biscay without seeing anything of the coast we knew so well, and kept clear of Cape St. Vincent, from whence the ship usually telegraphs to her owners. As we pitched and staggered on in the dark night, it was awful to think of the depth of the sea beneath. When at seventy miles distance from Cape St. Vincent soundings were taken by H.M.S. *Challenger*, a depth of two thousand five hundred fathoms was found—nearly three miles.

The first land we sighted was the great headland at the mouth of the Tagus, the Sierra of Cintra, as the Portuguese call it. Here we felt a sensible change in the temperature, and having suffered much from cold in the early portion of our voyage, the increased warmth was now the more delightful. On the tenth day after leaving England we skirted the coast of Morocco, and were near enough to perceive the serried tails of the Great Atlas range. None of its higher peaks, which are eternally covered with snow, were visible. The great mountain range extends in an oblique direction, far inland, and as the morning sun lit up the bold swelling hills, they looked very imposing. Towards evening we had on our right the perpendicular white cliff of Trafalgar Bay; and in the distance was the rock of Ceuta, in the centre of a bay which we appeared to be entering. "The Rock" was hidden from our view by a long range of nearer hill.

As the ship had no time to call at Gibraltar, we passed it late at night, when unfortunately there was no moon. We saw the lighthouse at the point, but that was all. "Gib" is by no means given to illuminations, although its love of obscurity is not so great as it was supposed to be by a Russian gentleman with whom we had once voyaged from Malaga to Gibraltar. He was one of those happy individuals who place implicit faith in their guide-book, and the one he possessed informed him that the garrison being in constant fear of a surprise, all the houses were painted black, and that every light was extinguished at nine o'clock. Algeciras, that paradise of nurserymen, where half the hyacinths and tulip-bulbs which supply Europe are grown, having nothing to defend but her gardens, lay curved along the shore a brilliant line of light.

It was pleasant to exchange the grey waters of the Atlantic for the Mediterranean. It would have been still more agreeable had its blue waves treated us less rudely. Many a familiar face at the breakfast-table disappeared, but M. and I succeeded, after a struggle, in mounting to the upper deck, being anxious to catch sight of our old friends, the mountains of Granada, the snowy peaks of the Sierra Nevada. How we longed for wings to fly over them, to find rest in the green Veda at their feet.

We kept close to the monotonous rock-bound coast of Oran, and when the darkness of another night had fallen, we surged past the light-house, and caught sight of the twinkling lamps of Algiers, and thought of the days when we had searched its strand for shells, and pieces of marble and tesselated pavement on the shore of Cape Matifou.

The next day we passed the high mountains of Kabylia, and caught sight of craggy Fort Napoléon, which looks down upon a hundred villages, the inhabitants of which still make the rude herb-stained pottery of their Phœnician ancestors, and work in silver varied forms of the cross, sole relic of the Christianity which they professed under the Romans.*

The shore became flat before the Tunisian frontier was reached. From the sea there is little to see that reminds us of the bygone glories of Carthage, though the ruins of the re-constructed city, in indestructible masses, still fringe the shore, her columns still strow the strand, and her noble aqueduct, arch after arch, an almost unbroken line, still stretches for fifty miles along the plain. Through a good glass we could just perceive the church which the French have built upon the spot where their sainted Louis expired. The hills above Tunis, famous in story, were dimly visible, and then we lost sight of land, until the Island of Pan-talaria, formerly belonging to the King of Sicily, and used as a penal settlement, came into view.

An old brick fort stood upon the beach. The town is large, and the flat-roofed houses, paint-

---

* Among some pottery which I once bought in Kabylia, was a small jug of peculiar shape. It was coloured with dingy red and yellow, and adorned with slanting lines of black, which crossed one another. It precisely resembled the jug found by Captain Warren, under the temple at Jerusalem, an engraving of which may be seen in his work.

ed white, rose in gradation, like steps, against
the side of the mountain, an extinct volcano.
In spite of its isolated position the place had a
cheerful air, and the public garden, placed in
the old crater, appeared to be a charming spot.
What a splendid sea view it must have commanded! Pantalaria owes its present pros-
perity to its vineyards. It exports large quantities of white and red marsala. The island
now belongs to the King of Italy. Though
there was now but an infant moon, the nights
were made beautiful by the luminous appearance of the waves. Bright sparks illuminated
the prow of the vessel, flickered up the ropes, and
lit up its track with millions of tiny lanterns;
and balls of light came dancing along with the
foam, borne past the sides of the ship by the
seething waters.*

Ships generally call at Malta, but we did not
approach it, although the second-class passengers were short of water, and had to drink that
which had been condensed, and even it was
dealt out sparingly, as every gallon so prepared
costs eightpence. With the captain it was a

---

* It is the Medusa tribe who have the faculty of shedding
light in the highest degree, and it is thought probable that
fish which go beyond the depth to which the light of the
sun penetrates the sea, are endowed with this faculty.

consideration both of time and money, the port dues at Malta being exceedingly heavy. All were on the alert when Port Saïd was sighted. We caught sight first of the tall white light-house, which stands at the extremity of a long spit of sand ; then of the breakwater, made of huge blocks of concrete, piled up, and black with shaggy sea-weed ; and then of the low shore, with the wooden railway-station, the post-office, long grey lines of sheds, and stretching out at the back, the town, with straight streets crossing one another with odious regularity. One row of huts was pointed out as having been built by English soldiers, the place having served as a depôt for some of our troops during the Crimea war. Such, with the burning sky above and the dazzling sand around, was Port Saïd. Before the process of coaling commenced, we had to cover up all our effects. The fine black dust is wonderfully penetrating, and it was weeks before the three friends, Grouse, and Drake, and Bustle, were entirely rid of the shining particles. The passengers made up little parties for the shore, and M. was appealed to for hints as to where to go and what to see. M. was considered a great authority, quite equal to the task of writing a guide-book for Port Saïd.

Only seven weeks previously, the *Arabia*, a Rubertino steamer, on which M. was a passenger, had come to grief in the Mediterranean, two days from land. She broke her screw one night, when the gales were frightful, and was in great danger. A brig was faintly seen bearing right down upon her. The Italian steward explained the situation to M., the only one who understood and spoke that language, and requested him to rouse his companions; and when the passengers rushed on deck, a collision between the vessels appeared to be inevitable. The brig was on the top of the waves, with her bowsprit over the deck of the *Arabia*, which lay in the trough of the sea, when a mighty billow broke in and parted them. The unknown vessel herself, probably disabled, drifted away, carrying with her part of the rigging of the *Arabia*. The steamer sent up rockets as signals for assistance, and at last got towed back into Port Saïd. For ten days did poor M., who was in a fever of anxiety to get home, pace the sands, and torment the agents, in order to know when the ship would be able to sail. At last, tired out, she and eight of her companions in misfortune agreed to take the first steamer which would forward them. It proved to be the *Mesopotamia*, a little vessel of eight hundred tons, bound from the Persian Gulf to Marseilles. In spite of heavy gales, she landed them safely in France. Curiously enough, Captain Cousins knew the *Mesopotamia* and her captain ; he declared that it was a fine boat ; he and its commander were friends, and had served together for some years on board the unfortunate *Cospatrick*.

Port Saïd has a considerable but ever-changing reputation. It is an evil place, full of billiard-rooms, gaming-houses, and low drinking booths, where a man must look to his safety after dark. All the French officials who are able to do so live at Ismailia. It so happened that I and another lady were for the first hour alone together after landing, and found it so unpleasant that we were on the point of returning to our boat, when by good luck we fell in with some of our friends. In the middle of the town there is a melancholy pleasure-ground, with scorched grass, and shrivelled shrubs covered with dust. Being a French settlement, the most prominent object is, of course, the Hotel Restaurant and Café de Paris, a great, rambling, buff-washed building. From this centre radiate several streets, with wooden houses and colonnades, underneath which are the shops. The most prudent of us ran wild amongst their contents, eating very dear cakes, which we did not want, and buying expensive boxes of pink and white hearts' delight, which we knew would be like so much bird-lime in our mouths.

The Chinese and Japan wares were really good, and not dear. We treated ourselves to several small articles, along with a pair of japanned vases, which we designed for lamps, and made a mental note to the effect that we should be well furnished with such articles if we ever visited the place again.

The streets were thronged with disreputable-looking people; the Europeans were chiefly French, and surely there is on earth no vagabond like a French vagabond. He is the sort of individual who would rob you with a *débonnaire* air, and take off his hat whilst stealing your purse. There was to be a masked ball in the town that evening, and the exteriors of many shops were decorated with masks and dominos, tall clannish hats, and highly-glazed calico costumes of every shape and colour. In the middle of one street stalked an all but undraped madman, who was endeavouring to hold three umbrellas over his head—an object of derision to the low Europeans, but of veneration to the natives. As is usually the case in such places, we were unmercifully tormented by beggars and little boys, and had the inevitable quarrel with our boatmen before returning on board.

When our company were again assembled, we compared notes as to what we had seen and done; some, not having had enough of the sea, had taken a steam-launch, and had examined the breakwater and the light-house. Our friends, the M. A——s, had visited the cemetery, in order to see the grave of a young friend, an officer, who had died of fever in this wretched hole. They were quite dejected with the dirt and neglect which they had found. "My dear," said the Colonel to his wife, "if I die at Port Saïd, bury me in the sea. That, at least, will be a clean grave." Dick's goat had died, I fear, of cold and exposure (Dick was the adored baby), and from Port Saïd M. took the opportunity of telegraphing to Suez for another. Coaling went on all night, but at eleven in the morning we steamed off, in spite of the absence of three passengers, whom the warning guns had failed to bring back from too protracted wanderings on the shore. We got quite excited in thinking how they would contrive to catch the vessel, for we soon perceived that a boat was slowly toiling after us, making so little way that its occupants were obliged to change it for another, in which, with some difficulty, they succeeded in reaching the *Hindoo,* which did not stop one moment to take them up. It was somewhat awkward for the ladies, one of whom was stout; but at last they reached the deck, with tempers slightly ruffled; and they were certainly received in a very unsympathising manner. The captain explained that it was impossible for him to wait a moment after the ship was ready to start, especially as another vessel, one of the Ducal line, was anxious to get before him, and it was desirable to have the way as clear as possible. He had once been detained six days in the canal, in consequence of ships in advance having stuck.

It was delightful to sit down in a shady corner and watch the landscape, as the plains over which the Israelites had wandered lay extended before me. The land of the Pharaohs was a dead flat, bounded only by the distant horizon. To the left lay a stony desert, but to the right spread the shallow waters of Lake Menzaleh, the abiding place of innumerable wild-fowl. Ducks, with feathers that shone like silver, floated about in thousands; knots of pelicans, fishing for their noonday meal; red-billed cranes, standing on one leg, profoundly occupied in regarding their reflection in the water. The air was also tenanted. The brilliant scarlet plumage of the flamingos flashed in the sunshine as they wheeled about in the cloudless sky; and stiff-legged storks skimmed along in wedge-shaped battalions, led by some crafty traveller, who had flapped his wings over many a land. Who knows?—he might have supped upon the banks of Father Nile, dozed the night away upon the great pyramid, and the morrow's noon might see him hovering over the highlands of Abyssinia. The mirage is often seen to great advantage from this part of the canal, but on the present occasion the weather was unfavourable to any striking display of the phenomenon. Occasionally we imagined that there was a tree or an island, where their existence was impossible; and there was sometimes a deceptive mingling of sand, hill, and cloud—but that was all.

There were fourteen ships before us, and two or three were in our rear. The regulation speed is four and a half miles an hour. Under certain circumstances the mail boats are allowed to pass ahead. The etiquette of the canal is strictly enforced, and in narrow or winding places—for the line taken is far from straight— there are sidings into which ships can enter and allow others to go ahead; and at the frequent stations, which are also telegraph-offices, signals are run up for the instruction of the pilot. The signals for stopping were very simple; two or three cocoa-nuts strung on a rope, or two gourds and a small flag.

These stations, which are long and low, are built of wood, and their rustic porches were covered with creepers. It was pleasant to see such pretty home-like places, each with its patch of garden and grassy banks, little green oases in the sandy desert.

Occasionally we saw a colourless village, built of mud and straw; and little naked children would run down to peep at us, and scamper off again. Now and then a tall, dark man, draped in an ample burnous of striped black and white flannel, with a formidable bludgeon in his hand, would pass along on the raised footpath, accompanied, possibly, by wife or daughter, huddled up on the back of a camel—simple scenes, which were pleasant to behold. The first large steamer which we met was packed with pilgrims bound from Jeddo to Alexandria. The crowd on her decks was great, and there were groups and figures so remarkable that they fixed themselves in our memory.

Majestic old men, with flowing beards of purest white, with immense turbans, and robes, occasionally of the sacred green, but stained

with travel, leant upon their tall staffs, and
gravely regarded us. Their loins were girded
by leathern belts, to which were appended
gourds of fantastic form for holding water.
There were others—the wildest-looking beings
that it was possible to conceive—who leant over
the side of the ship and grinned at us. They
were Somalis, a people whose habit it is to
keep their heads cool by plastering them over
with chenam, a mixture of earth and lime, which
bleaches the hair, and makes it exceedingly
coarse. Their shaks, of tawny hue, entirely
concealed their foreheads, and formed a pent-
house over their fierce eyes.* Some women
were huddled up in a corner. Untempting
bundles of dirty cotton, pots and pans, and
sacks of grain, were heaped up on the deck, where
there scarcely appeared to be sufficient room to
stand ; and loops of sausages, and other edibles,
were festooned about. Conspicuous among the
crowd were the tall Egyptian guards, stern,

---

* Somali land is a triangular country, containing 330,000
square miles. It is bordered on the north by the Gulf of
Aden, on the south by the Indian Ocean, and on the south-
west by the river Jub, which rises in southern Abyssinia.
The present Somali race were originally Arabs, who landed
on the African shore in the fifteenth century, driving back
the original inhabitants of the country, who had, in early
times, become Christians. The Somalis are Moslems.

dark men, with broad shoulder-belts and girdles bristling with weapons, placed there to keep the peace, and to prevent anyone from landing in the Khedive's dominions, and by chance importing cholera or plague.

Contagious diseases are of frequent occurrence on board pilgrim ships, and they have consequently to undergo a quarantine of forty days wherever they stop. It is most unpleasant to sail in a boat which has ever been used for the conveyance of pilgrims. (Having experienced the disagreeable consequences, I speak feelingly.) They abound with obnoxious insects, which swarm out of the woodwork in legions, and no amount of care can subdue them.

The pilgrim ship was soon out of sight, and shortly after we passed a fine P. and O. steamer —a great contrast to the one with which we had just parted company. She ran up her flag, and the *Hindoo* returned the compliment. With the exception of the men and officers engaged in working the ship, there was not a soul on her decks. A face appeared for a moment at a cabin window, a white hand was waved from a port-hole, and she went swiftly on her way. There was something strangely impressive, almost ghostly, in these silent meetings, where people who had never met before, and would probably never meet again, exchanged unasked-for photographs, possibly to be preserved in the mind's eye as long as life lasted. Before reaching Kontora, some hillocks in the distance were pointed out as the ruins of Migdol (not to be confounded with the Migdol upon the Red Sea). At the station of Kontora, which lies at the head of the great lagoon lake, and is five geographical miles from the sea, the influence of the Mediterranean tide ceases to be perceptible. Steamers are not allowed to proceed after sunset. We dropped anchor as close as possible to the sandy shore. The short twilight was soon gone, but the evening air was delightfully balmy. I sat in a quiet mood, watching the crescent moon, which I fancied to be unusually large and bright. Lower and lower she sank, until she rested like an ark upon a low black ridge of distant sand a moment, and all that remained of her beauty were two brilliant stars, which lingered for an instant and disappeared.

We started as soon as it was light, but had to stop in order to let a vessel pass, the canal in this part being very narrow. Some of the gentlemen took advantage of the delay, and went on shore with their guns. They shot some birds, but brought back no trophies, the game being lost in the scrub which covered the sandy plain. One of the number, however, had collected a few plants, amongst which we found a strange sort of cactus, and some stiff branches, which bore a small white flower, with some resemblance to heather. The learned declared that the plant was a degenerate sort of palm. Once more under way, and the scenery changed considerably. Instead of the boundless plain, we now voyaged between banks of sand, which were upwards of forty feet high ; and the canal was so narrow that a good jumper could have leapt across it. Shut in as we were, the scenery possessed its own peculiar attraction. The clear water was brilliantly green, and contrasted well with the rich light brown sand, spotless, save where the tracks of footsteps were discernible—the print of naked human feet, the hoof of the camel, the buffalo, the ass, and the jackal ; or the paws of the panther, the cheeta, and the wild cat. Occasionally the long tracks of a snake could be traced. To keep vigil on the banks of this stream would not have been agreeable, when all these creatures came down in the moonlight to drink. Occasionally the banks broke down, and disclosed some flat-roofed, sun-scorched village, built of

mud and straw and unbaked bricks ; or we saw
a knot of hobbled camels, tended by some wild
dark man, leaning upon his staff, protected
from the sun by a scarf of coarse striped
woollen. Such a group may perchance have
occupied the self-same spot three thousand
years ago. Shortly before sunset we came
upon a number of men who were at work upon
the banks, which have to be attended to constantly. Some of them, their duty being done,
had laid themselves down to sleep, while others
were grouped round fires, baking the peculiar
flat cake which is the staple food of the country.
The scene was exceedingly picturesque.

Ismälia is generally reached on the evening
of the second day, but it was not so upon this
occasion, our progress being slow. We stuck
no less than nine times. Immediately the ship
ran her prow into the bank, she swung across
the stream. We were never aground for more
than half an hour, having, in consequence of
our slow pace (less than three miles an hour)
struck the side of the canal with feeble im-
petus. On each occasion the uproar was deaf-
ening—such an issuing of orders through
speaking-trumpets, such shouts from the crew,
and such guttural responses from the shore,
where men appeared to spring out of the very

sand, anxious to lend their aid, and gain the expected reward. Sometimes horses and donkeys were pressed into the service. The men were powerful, and their clothing scanty, but a dark skin takes away much of the appearance of nakedness, and the absence of costume passes unnoticed, save when the perfect proportions of some particular figure strike the eye, and you remark, " What a fine form!" as if in a gallery of bronzes.

We entered Lake Taman early in the morning, but were not allowed to land at Ismäilia. We had a good view of the town from our anchorage. It is full of modern houses, inhabited by French *employés* and their families. The Viceroy has a Summer palace upon the banks of the lake—a huge square stone building, standing amidst sand-hills, without any appearance of vegetation near it. At Ismäilia, the fresh-water canal, which was made in order to supply the workmen on the line with wholesome drinking water from the Nile, enters Lake Taman. If I do not mistake, the bed formed part of the ancient canal dug by Sesostris. We were amused by the bumboats which came alongside; they were fitted out with such a queer collection of articles—coarse shoes, black bread, onions, and hearts' delight; but the most attractive part of their cargo were the monkeys, which they occasionally sell to homeward-bound passengers. Some of the little ones were pretty and playful—not so their seniors. One mother was continually pinching her little ones, and pulling faces at them; whilst another, with higher maternal instincts, spent her time in gravely searching for the parasites with which her offspring were infested.

CHAPTER II.

Château Eugénie—Suez—The Wells of Moses—The Red
Sea—Remarkable Coral Reefs—Island of Perim—
Novel Postman—Aden—Arabian Dhowd—Signal of
Distress—Sea-beggars—Socotra—Flying Fish—Arri-
val at Bombay—The Esplanade Hotel—Pamphlets—
First Aspect of Bombay—Equipages—Parsee Women
—Polo—The Native Town.

SHORTLY after leaving Ismäilia, we crossed
the bitter lakes—bitter no longer, now
that they feel the influence of the tide from the
Red Sea, which at Suez rises six or eight feet.
The level of the Red Sea is, I believe, eighteen
inches higher than that of the Mediterranean:
When we again entered the canal, the naviga-
tion became difficult, and many dredging-ma-
chines were at work. The sharp elbows were
frequent, and it was by no means easy for so
long a vessel as ours to turn them, especially
as the sand appeared sometimes to bar all further progress. The captain, and the pilot whom
we had taken on board at Ismäilia, along with
four men, were at the wheel.

At a short distance from Suez stands the Château Eugénie, which was built for the accommodation of the Empress when she came to open the canal. It is a large square wooden house, with verandahs, and bears a considerable resemblance to the grand stand on some racecourse. Seen from the water, Suez is a bright-looking town, but "distance lends enchantment to the view." The tapering spire of the cathedral, the large hotel built by the Khedive, and a long row of substantial, green-shuttered houses, give it an air of false importance and respectability. Its dark houses are very unsafe. It has lost the little trade it once enjoyed, and travellers pass it by. Two or three ancient wells near the town, surrounded by trees, are called the wells of Moses, and at the back rise fine crags, serrated and lightning scathed, a spur of the Sinia range. Some authorities believe the present camel ford close to the harbour to be the track crossed by the Israelites, and we willingly entertained the idea, as it gave additional interest to the scene.

Before we started, our new goat was put on board, along with her little one. The expression and features of animals vary as much in different countries as do those of the human race. Our new acquaintance was a large, gaunt creature, with a Roman nose, and fine long hair of a bluish grey colour. I regarded her with awe —who knows? her fore-mothers might have supplied the babes in the time of the Pharaohs with milk, or ministered to the wants of Joseph. Her ladyship was by no means shy. To the astonishment of the captain, the amusement of the company, and the vast indignation of the pompous steward, she and her kid quietly walked into the saloon during the sacred hour of dinner, calmly surveyed the scene, and not finding it to her mind, marched through and departed, possibly on the search for her late master's hut.

As we slowly steamed round the long spit of land which forms the harbour, we passed a garden, in the centre of which stood a handsome stone pediment, supporting a bust in bronze—a memorial erected by the canal company as a tribute to the memory of the unfortunate Lieutenant Waghorn. The dues paid to the company at first strike one to be enormous. Those of the *Hindoo* amounted, I believe, to fifteen hundred pounds—little enough, however, when the time and money saved by this route are taken into consideration. The distance to India by the Cape is eleven thousand eight hundred miles—by the canal it is six thousand five hundred.

We had now, to my regret, done with the canal. I believe that I was the only person on board who had enjoyed the transit, or taken an interest in the time-honoured plains through which we had passed. We glided into the Gulf a little before sunset. A glorious light burnished the far-stretching range of hill upon the Egyptian shore, but the dark blue mountains of Sinia were in shade. The lateness of the hour was much to be regretted, for in consequence of it we lost a long stretch of beautiful scenery. I was on deck with the dawning day, and the captain was kind enough to show me his charts, at the same time remarking how seldom passengers cared to relinquish an hour or two of sleep in order to see this fine gulf. It is a curious fact that people who would rise with the lark in order to gaze upon a sunrise in Switzerland, or a castle on the Rhine, will scarcely mount to the deck to look at anything remarkable on their passage to the East. The very name of India appears to cast a spell of indifference over those who have touched her shores, or are likely to visit them. The secret may be that the hearts of both the outward and the homeward-bound are full to overflowing with memories of their native land. The point of view from whence a glimpse of the peak of Sinia is sometimes obtained, we had passed in the night, but were still skirting the range. It looked very fine as the mild sun of early morning lit up the great masses and points of rock.

We had entered the Red Sea, and were now in the Straits of Jubal, which are lined with coral reefs; nor is the mid channel free from dangerous islands and hidden spurs, and even in calm weather the watch is doubled. When stormy it is a most anxious time for the ship's officers, and even the captain remains on deck at night. We felt the periodical current which flows into the Red Sea from October to May. From May to October the flow of the current is reversed.* Once more we saw the Egyptian cliffs at sunset. They glowed like copper, richer colouring it was impossible to imagine. As the hours flew by we caught sight of mountains to the right, and far inland, some of which attained a height of seven thousand feet, and shortly afterwards the Elba mountains in Arabia, which are nine thousand feet high, loomed grandly in the far distance. Oh! for the wings of a dove, to have explored them!

Losing sight of land, we encountered a gale, and rolled terribly. The *Hindoo* was too long

------

* Somerville's Physical Geography, vol. i., p. 249.

to ride the waves, but "she cut her bright way through." The skylights were battened down, all loose articles secured, the saloon carpet was taken up, and stout wooden slides, four feet high, were slipped into the doorways. Prostrate forms strewed the sofas, and dismal groans issued from below. Holding tight to the woodwork, I could see what was going on outside this little Pandemonium. Every four or five minutes there was a bang, succeeded by a momentary interval of silence and then a mighty roar. The staggering ship was stunned, and when she recovered herself, quivering and groaning like a wounded creature, the water came rushing along the deck, and foamed away through the rope bulwarks, which caught all the waifs left about by the heedless and the sick—mops, and pails, and camp-stools, books, bits of needlework, handkerchiefs, and stray wraps.

All this time the sun shone brilliantly. The fine spray, hurled high into the air, was tinged with prismatic colours, flickering rainbows of exceeding beauty, and dead white sea-crests, curled and rushed impetuously down into gulfs of deepest indigo. The sight was magnificent, and I felt that I should soon learn to prefer rough weather to the monotony of a calm at sea. When the ocean is perfectly smooth I always experi-

ence a vague sense of disappointment, and the
vast plain of water fails to excite my enthusiasm.
After a few hours the wind fell, and we were
able to resume our seats upon the upper deck,
to mark the distant sail by day, and at night to
watch the increasing moon.

We reached a part of the Red Sea where two
very remarkable coral reefs stand out of the
water. They are so symmetrically formed that
they appear as if they had been shaped by the
hand of man. Their perpendicular sides rise
high out of the water, and their tops are perfectly level. Upon one of them there is a beacon,
and an apparatus for signalling. Ships pass as
far from these islands as possible, for they are
dangerous neighbours. Not many years ago a
fine French steamer was lost upon the smaller
of the two, and all hands perished. In rough
weather the sea dashes completely over them.
At the mouth of the Straits of Babelmandeb
("The Gate of Tears!") lies the large volcanic
Island of Perim. At a little distance from it a
fine mass of red rock rises abruptly from the
water. It reminded me of the Bass rock, and
all the more as it was covered with silvery sea-
fowl. The French tried hard to get possession
of Perim, but the officer who commanded the expedition which was to plant the French *drapeau*

on its shore talked a little too much. The English, consequently, were too prompt for him, and when the representative of "La Belle France" arrived, he found the union-jack floating over the island. Since then a small garrison has been maintained upon it, as its position is important. We saw the lonely row of barracks stretching along behind the tall spectral lighthouse.

I afterwards met with a friend whose husband had commanded this little force of fifty sepoys, who, along with herself and children, a condensing engineer, a native apothecary, and a certain number of Somali followers, composed the sole population of the black rock, which has neither soil nor fresh water. The sole vegetation consists of a few bastard cocoa-nut palms, which bend away from the prevalent gales, and a little scrubby plant, with a tiny yellow flower, which creeps among the sandhills. The family were put upon a small daily allowance of condensed water, which unfortunately will not bear exposure to a hot atmosphere. All provisions were of course brought from Aden, a distance of ninety miles. Fish was good and plentiful, but there was no one to catch it until my friends imported a fisherman, who skilfully threw his nets from the rocks, and supplied their table, while shell-fish also were procured. The position was rendered still less desirable by the tediousness of the postal arrangements. They only received their letters once a fortnight. For some reason with which I am unacquainted, passing steamers were not allowed to convey them. They were brought by land, a six days' march for a man and his camels, along the Arabian shore. When this novel postman arrived at his destination, his duty was to light a great bonfire, in order to attract the attention of the watchful Perimites, who, it may be imagined, lost no time in sending their boat to fetch the precious mail-bags. Letters were opened and answered in hot haste, the little boat set forth again upon its three mile voyage, and the weary camel-driver re-commenced his six days' march over the burning sands. Rare shells strow the shore of this island, and occasionally fine bunches of coral, white and red and black, are washed up. A story is told, which probably rests upon some slight foundation, of an officer in charge of the Perim detachment, who, at the expiration of his term, applied to have it renewed; the request was granted without difficulty; but a similar application, made at the expiration of the second term, so astonished the authorities, that they sent to inquire how the gentleman was amusing himself, and found that he had gone to England.

Long before Aden (a name which signifies Paradise) is reached, the distant Arabian shore is again seen, broken into precipitous gaps and headlands. For hours the great rock is visible, a blue stain upon the horizon, which gradually assumes form and colour. Immediately before reaching Aden, some very curious small volcanic hills and cliffs are passed. The latter are very high, and the strata, which is varied in colour, and strongly marked, almost perpendicular. These heights are so fantastically shaped that it is difficult to believe that they are not an assemblage of ruined fortifications. The base of the cliffs is honeycombed with mysterious-looking caves—and there were many charming little coves. What treasures might not be strown upon their yellow sands! Coral and amber (it is the land of amber), shells and sea-weeds! Alas! they were not for us to gather!

We slackened steam off Aden, but did not stop, passing the mouth of the harbour very slowly. The long lines of the cavalry barracks were before us, but we saw nothing of most of our forces, which are hidden away in the crater of the long extinct volcano. The European town lies at the back of the rock. I am not acquainted with the exact scale either of Gibraltar or of Aden, but the former is certainly far the finest of the two rocks. Aden must be a wretched place to live in for any length of time. The want of fresh water is felt, in spite of the numerous and powerful condensers, and the wells are all more or less brackish. A certain amount of each kind is doled out per head, according to regulation. If I do not mistake, a lady has five gallons of each per diem allowed to her. Cattle also have their allowance. The little Aden cow, unrivalled as a milker, will flourish upon the most brackish quality. The want of green stuff is also distressing, although Government has large gardens thirty miles off, upon the Arabian coast. The great pest of the place are the myriads of insects, which allow of no rest during the day, though at night they fortunately cease to torment. I had always fancied that there was delightful bathing at Aden, but it is seldom resorted to, the shore being inconveniently set with sharp rocks, in addition to which it is dangerous on account of the tides, which rise and fall with violence, and sometimes the wash brings in unwilling and unwelcome guests in the shape of sharks.

As long as we were under the shelter of the

rock, the sea was calm, and great numbers of
sea-jellies vibrated up and down in the clear
green water, looking like lovely pink flowers,
all of the same colour. Borne along by the
same current streamed glossy green and brown
and red sea-weeds. I spent half the afternoon in looking down into this delightful sub-
marine garden. For some time, not one sea-
flower was to be seen, and then suddenly
whole fields of jellies came floating by; but the
charming visions disappeared all too soon. The
crisp waves began to curl, and when we were
fairly away from the influence of the land, it
became very stormy. Before evening closed in
we were passed by an old-fashioned Arabian
vessel, called a dhowd, a strange-looking craft,
with a very high poop, and three tiers of port-
holes. She looked like some ancient galley that
had sailed out of a picture. The dhowds were
formerly almost all either slave or pirate ships.
We were not so fortunate as to observe in this
sea any of that ruddy appearance which, in so
many languages, has procured for it the appellation of the Red Sea. A Belgian *savant*, Monsieur Mossen, after collecting together nearly all
that had been written on the subject of red
water from the days of Moses down to our own,
gives a list of twenty-two species of animals, and

almost as many plants, capable of communicating this blood colour. Some seas are tinged with yellow instead of red. This sea sawdust, as the sailors call it, is of vegetable origin.

As we passed into the Arabian Sea, I strained my eyes to catch a glimpse of the Island of Socotra, which has a somewhat curious history. In very remote times it had an independent king, and afterwards became the seat of considerable traffic. It was used as a kind of storehouse by the merchants who traded between Egypt and the East, and its inhabitants were christianized at a very early period. The lowlands of Socotra are now overrun by a few wandering Arab tribes, but its hills are populated by the families of Bunian traders, many of whom are rich. It exports large quantities of aloes. The island enjoys a busy port, and it is probable that an active future awaits it. It is now thought to be rich in coal fields, and there is even a whisper that it may ere long be occupied by British troops. Socotra is a hundred miles long by forty broad, and is five hundred and fifty miles from Aden.

One morning the monotony of our voyage was broken by the appearance of a distant ship making signals of distress. Our captain stopped his vessel, and the strange barque put off a boat,

which boarded us. It contained five men—an
Arab and four negroes. The Arab, who was
wrapped up in an ample bernous, was a tall,
copper-coloured man, with fine features; the
others were negroes of the true African type.
They had fine limbs and shapely heads, thickly
covered with dusky hair, curled as tight as that
of an Australian sheep. Their skins were perfectly black, and were smeared with oil. They
said that they belonged to a ship with a crew
of thirty men, bound from Zanzibar to Jeddo,
and that having experienced bad weather, they
had lost their reckoning. Their final request
was to be informed as to their position; and
then they prayed for food and water, the latter
of which they declared that they had not
tasted for six days. Our captain was very
kind, and gave them two bags of rice and a
barrel of water, at the same time remarking that
they might have brought with them empty
sacks and a tub. They offered to pay in salt,
which they declared to be all they had; and
this being declined, they rowed off, with small
demonstrations of gratitude. Were they really
in want, or were they sea-beggars? This no
one could decide; and there were various
opinions upon the subject.

The days we spent upon the Arabian Sea

were pleasant, but far from eventful, the only variety being the sight of a few whales playing about—a species of animal, which, though small in this sea, is exceedingly pugnacious. Shoals of porpoises, with an occasional flight of paddy birds, were all we had to divert us; but the morning and evening skies were glorious. The beauty of one particular night is deeply impressed on my memory. The sun, a ball of ardent red, was sinking into the sea, whilst in the opposite direction the full moon, a huge disk of golden pink, rose above the horizon. The grand effect of the mingling lights upon sea and sky was indescribable. I was drinking in the beautiful scene with delight, when my attention was attracted by a small brown object, which emerged from the waves, and which I soon saw was a flying-fish. This was the first opportunity I had of seeing those beautiful little creatures. Afterwards they were to be seen in numbers. It would be pleasant to believe that the flying-fish leave their native element in sport, but, alas! there is no doubt that their object is to escape from some danger which threatens them in the sea beneath. They are able to support themselves in the air only as long as their wings remain moist. If, however, they just touch the water occasionally, they are capable of skimming along for two or three hundred yards.

As evening stole on, the upper deck was now a delightful resort—every spar, every rope was sharply defined against a clear green sky. Surely moonlight upon the sea is one of the most beautiful effects in nature ; still we were almost inclined to wish the Lady Moon could have remained away, the large quiet stars being eclipsed by her light, and the luminous appearance generally seen upon the waves rendered invisible.

In spite of her long detention upon the English coast, and the constant head winds which she encountered, the brave *Hindoo* accomplished her voyage in four weeks and six days. We entered the harbour of Bombay early in the morning. Even with India before me, I felt a pang of regret that the voyage was over. I ran on deck, and saw a great deal of shipping, two or three lighthouses, the rocky shore of a bay fringed with low buildings, a large low fort, with a woody hill rising behind it, and some cocoa-nut trees, the forms of which were seen in clear outlines against the sky. I had scarcely time to realize my ideas of the promised land, when, amidst the bustle upon deck, I saw a well-known form, I heard the kindest of voices, and there was G——, all anxiety to greet his wife and children.

Before we well knew what we were about, we found ourselves at breakfast in a large room, eating phomphlets, a small fish, for which Bombay is celebrated. I did not think much either of it, or of the curry which followed; but a kind of very thin biscuit, served with the latter, and made of fish, which goes by the name of Bombay duck, was novel and good.

The Esplanade is a monster hotel. On the first floor is a large verandah, charmingly arranged with ferns and leafy plants. Part of this was set aside as a kind of bazaar, where merchants spread their wares. There were all sorts of ivory boxes, inlaid with silver, and lined with sandal-wood; besides various articles in black wood, carved in the neighbourhood. (In India each district has its *spécialité*.) There were muslins and silk embroidery from Delhi, and silver ornaments from Cutch; besides English productions. In front of the hotel there was a large green, or rather, a piece of ground which ought to have been green, on which stood some exceedingly handsome public buildings, built of rough-hewn stone. Endless streams of people passed along in gay costumes and large turbans. The carriages struck me as strange, yet still familiar, for among them I saw the bygone cabriolet of my youth, the risky little vehicle which so suddenly vanished to make way for the national hansom. I verily believe that they were the identical conveyances transported from their native land years ago. Then there were shigrams, and buggies, and unpainted broughams; besides the skeleton omnibus, which ran on a tramway, where people, sheltered by an awning, appeared to be sitting upon nothing at all; and, strangest of all, the horses which drew it had bonnets on—not the airy nothing of these days, but the useful coal-scuttle, which no one but a village goody now condescends to wear. During the hot weather the company lost so many animals from sunstroke, that they hit upon this remarkable device.

We had apartments on the second story, large airy rooms, with balconies, very pleasant after our tiny cabins. We sank into some easy rocking-chairs, and then, with delighted eyes, surveyed the curiosities which G—— had collected during his tour. He had been at Aden, and brought from thence black rosaries, inlaid with white dots of silver, rosaries which had touched the Caba stone at Mecca, and various other curiosities.

I longed to go out immediately, but one great drawback in the East is that one is shorn of one's liberty, and I had to wait with all the patience I could command until the sun was low, when we got into an open carriage which G—— had secured, and set off for "the Stable."

No stranger has ever been half an hour in Bombay without hearing of "the Stable" and "the Gulf." Fortunately for me the stable was situated at the very end of the bazaar, in the heart of the native town. Thither we were bound, in order to see a recent purchase of G——'s, a pair of Arab horses, fresh from the Persian Gulf, and he had no unwilling companion in M., who dearly loves a horse. We passed through the modern town, which is full of fine buildings, public offices, and private houses. Handsome equipages rolled along, but the tall black men, with peculiar liveries and naked feet, who stood behind each well-appointed carriage, had a strange appearance. The reclining ladies were such as may be seen any fine afternoon in Hyde Park or the Bois. Far more interesting were the numbers of Parsi women who were walking about in short satin skirts of the most brilliant hues—an exquisite pale cherry and an emerald green appeared to be the favourite colours—flowers were in their glossy black hair, and they wore quantities of gold lace and handsome ornaments. Though very showy, these costumes were tasteless in form. The Parsi men, who are very tall and stout, wear a straight-cut robe of purest white, without a sash, a dress well calculated to show off the rotundity of their persons. They have sly eyes, fat, oily faces, and a well-to-do air. The Parsis, in fact, are the Jews of the East, many of them being very rich.*

We drove past a considerable space of ground

---

* The Parsis claim to be descended from the Medes, who furnished the princely caste of the old Persian Empire. They are refugees, followers of Zoroaster, who refused to adopt the religion which the conquering Arabs endeavoured to enforce at the point of sword, when, in the middle of the seventh century, they invaded Persia under Caliph Omar. After many voyages and adventures, these wanderers arrived on the coast of Guzerat, and were well received by the ruler of that part of India. Before granting them protection, the chief asked them the nature of their faith, upon which the wily Persians declared that they worshipped the sun and fire elements, as well as the cow; that they wore the sacred shirt, a cincture round the loins, a cap of two folds, and that they ornamented and perfumed their wives; upon which they were allowed to settle in India. They were, however, required to dress their females in the Indian fashion, to wear no armour, to perform the marriage ceremony of their children at night, and to wear the hideous Guzerat cap of two folds. All which they steadfastly do now, although it is nearly twelve centuries since the compact was made.

which is set aside for garrison sports. Many
gentlemen on nimble ponies were playing at
polo, a game which requires great quickness of
eye, and is dangerous as far as concerns the
ponies, who are frequently lamed for life. Polo
was originally an Indian game, which was played by certain hill tribes.

When we reached the native town how
changed was the scene. Europe was left behind, and the East was realized—the narrow,
winding streets, the open shops, small, but
highly characteristic, where the owner, Hindoo,
Mahomedan, or Jew, squatted amidst his wares.
Those of the same trade congregated together,
the workers in brass and copper, with bright
vessels of curious shape, such as the lato, with
its narrow neck and bulging sides, the lamp of
many beaks, the little bells, with images at the
top, used in the temples. Then there are the
leather workers, from whom one may select embroidered slippers, turned up at the point,
saddle-bags, and trappings for horses, covered
with gold, and silver, and cowrie shells. There
were rows of wood-carvers, who work upon the
black wood furniture peculiar to the Bombay
Presidency, and fine specimens of their art were
placed about to attract attention. The general
merchant had his small store, heaped from floor

to ceiling with bales of cloth, gaudy shawls, and cottons, with various patterns printed upon them, vases, and griffins, and pagodas, for furniture, and dark but deep-hued checks and stripes for garments. There were little niches where betel-leaves and pungent seeds were sold, and, most picturesque of all, were the shops of the Indian druggists, where one was sure to see a venerable old man with a flowing white beard; probably a learned man, and one who possibly dabbled in magic, his drugs ranged about in jars of china, which would have made the fortune of a European bric-à-brac shop. By a Christian these jars were not, alas! to be bought for love or money.

No two houses were alike, some were tall and pink, others were squat and yellow, and both perhaps were neighboured by dwellings of a superior order, which stood back, not hidden, but sheltered by plantain-trees, and tall cocoa-nut palms, spreading their elegant fan-shaped leaves against a crimson background, for the fervid sun was setting. These houses had in general two tiers of wooden verandahs, with shutters. The ground-floor was partly open, and supported by pillars of wood, richly carved, and on the projecting beams and latticed frames there was many a quaint device. I was charmed

with these irregular old dwellings. A dead
wall, with the pyramidal summit of a Jaina
temple appearing above it, would vary the scene,
or a mosque, with broad dome and airy pinnacles,
and sometimes we came upon a Hindoo temple,
adorned with highly-coloured mythological subjects, with lights in its interior, which cast a
glow upon some hideous copper idol, or figure
of stone, daubed with red paint, and greasy
with libations of melted butter. Every step
was a surprise.

CHAPTER III.

Hindoo Women—Arabian Beauties—Rites of Betrothal—
Funeral Procession—English Chambermaids in India
—Flower-market—Jain Establishments for Superan-
nuated Animals—Drive to Malabar Point—A Brah-
man Village—The Esplanade—Island and Temples of
Elephanta—Description of one of the Temples—The
Three-faced God—Sculptured Figures—Rock Temples
—Curious Ants' Nest—Western Ghâts.

THE appearance of the Hindoo women was
very striking, with their tall forms, dignified gait, and classical drapery of dingy blue or
red, relieved by a bright bordering. Many of
them balanced baskets or brass vessels upon
their heads, their shapely arms straight down,
unless they bore infants, and then the wee
thing was placed astride on the mother's well-
developed hip. Older children, bronze or black,
played in the gutters, or swarmed about the
houses—wild creatures, innocent of clothes,
with flashing eyes and unkempt hair, adorned
with a variety of ornaments. The girls wore
necklaces, armlets, and anklets, and the boys

had silver waist-chains of beautiful workmanship. These ornaments are of considerable
value, the metal of which they are made being
very pure. They are, however, dangerous possessions. There is seldom a newspaper in
which there is not a notice or advertisement
respecting some child who has been inveigled
away, and either robbed or murdered.*

When we reached "the Stables," the Arab
beauties were trotted out to be admired. They
were gentle creatures, with small heads, delicate
ears, liquid eyes, and red nostrils, and appeared
to appreciate the caresses bestowed upon them.
As we returned, we were fortunate enough to
see a curious phase of Indian life. The month
and the conjunction of the planets being favourable, there were numbers of Hindoo marriages,

---

* The advertisements run as follows :—

"ROBBING A BOY OF AN ORNAMENT.—Curson Hurjee,
living at Nagdavee Street, stated that, whilst his son, aged
seven years, was playing opposite to his house on Thursday,
some Mahomedan enticed him away to Beebee-jan Street,
and took from him a silver waist-chain, valued at six
rupees."

"Baboo Butta reports that on Wednesday he went to
the Temple of Jeevun Lall, at Bhooleshwur, carrying his
child in his arms. When passing through a crowd at the
door of the temple, some person had cut off from the child's
person a gold ornament, called Ram Namee, valued at
twenty rupees. Inquiries are being made by the police."

or, to speak more correctly, betrothals. By the
rite of betrothal the connubial knot is tightly
tied, and all the necessary ceremonies and feasts
take place. Amongst the higher castes it is a
rule that a boy may be married at any time
after he has been invested with the sacred
thread, which must take place before he is eight
years of age, for before that time he is not considered to belong to the Hindoo religion, or to
be a member of his father's caste. The girl
must not be married before she is ten years old,
and her age must be less than that of her husband. The principal ceremonies are, the writing by astrologers of the names of the parties,
and the day and hour when the wedding is to
take place; the walking round a fire three times,
seven steps at each time; the tying together
the garments of the contracting parties; and the
Homa, or burnt sacrifice, after which the con-
tract is indissolvable. The girl is given away
by the father in his own house, where the bride
continues to reside for a few days, after which
she lives with her husband's family, at their
expense. It was most amusing to see the little
brides and bridegrooms on horseback, heading
gay processions of relations and friends, in
which silk umbrellas fringed with gold bore a
prominent part, the little people appearing

gaudier than butterflies in their spangled muslins and streaming ribbons. As for the horses, which I saw standing before some houses waiting for married couples, they were scarcely visible, being covered with velvet housings, gilded trappings, feathers, and wreaths of flowers. The short Indian twilight being over, the open chambers, the verandahs, the gardens, were brilliantly illuminated. We could see the guests, and hear the discordant music. Rockets shot up into the sky, and broke into balls of brilliant colours; crackers exploded in every corner, and Bengal lights tinged all around with their vivid hues. The natives have a passion for fireworks, without which no merry-making is complete.

In the midst of this festivity our carriage had to stop, in order to make way for a small procession of men, each of whom carried a blazing torch. The light danced over the face of a dead man, whom they were carrying along to the funeral pyre. As the bier passed, we caught the overpoweringly sweet odour of the Indian jessamine, which the Hindoos place in the hands of the dying, and wreath round the dead. I went to rest that night feverish with excitement; shadows of all that I had seen during the past six weeks floated before me, and then I fell into a deep sleep, for an airy chamber and a roomy bed are very delightful after a close cabin and a small berth.

There is surely no sensation more pleasant than that which attends the first awaking in a strange country. My slumbers were interrupted at an early hour by the vociferous singing of a bird. I at once concluded that the charming notes were those of the far-famed bul-bul, and jumped up in haste, in order to see what the bird was like; but, alas! the opening of the lattice put an end to the song, and the only feathered creature I could see was a handsome brown scavenger-hawk, which sailed off with a shrill cry. A man was slopping water in a primitive manner over a would-be green plot; further away lay the sleepy blue sea, and low woods, which sloped gently to the curving bay. Presently there entered a very black girl, swathed in dingy white muslin, bearing an earthenware pitcher of peculiar form. She was adorned with numerous ornaments, including a large filigree nose-ring, and several rings of a smaller description, set along the rim of each ear, a pretty silver necklace, and on her arms slender hoops of sparkling red and semi-transparent green glass, which, worn by a lady, might have passed for ruby and jade-stone. It is wonderful how these people contrive to pass rings so small over their knuckles. It would be impossible were their bones like those of Europeans, but, being half gristle, they are in some degree compressible.

The managers of the hotel had, at one time, a great wish to have English chambermaids, and, the story goes, that they induced a band of sixty young girls to come from England, but every one of them got married within a month of their landing, and the experiment was not repeated. G—— kindly took me to see the markets before the heat had tarnished the early beauty of the flowers and fruit. We got into one of the skeleton omnibuses, and found it a cool and clean conveyance. The little transit might have been the making of us, for on alighting we were presented with a couple of lottery tickets. We found the markets exquisitely clean and admirably arranged. The flower, fruit, and vegetable market is a circular building, lighted from above, which encloses a beautiful public garden.

Never had I seen such a luxurious profusion of beautiful flowers and fruits as was set forth upon the white marble slabs, which sloped up on each side of the broad promenade, which was thronged, not crowded, by endless streams of people, in strange costumes and gay apparel, ever passing into strange combinations, like the bits of coloured glass in a kaleidoscope. There were pyramids of flowers, not set forth in the European fashion, but picked with little stem and no leaves, and heaped up carelessly. There were lovely pale pink roses, and an endless variety of double jessamine flowers, pink and white, probably destined to be threaded together for the adornment of the temples. The tuberoses were almost too sweet. There were gorgeous hillocks of the double yellow marigold, to be woven into coronets for women, their intense colour being well calculated to set off the dark skins and shiny black hair which they were meant to adorn. Some of the smaller flowers and fragrant leaves, made into tiny sprigs, were intended to be thrown into the finger-glasses which figure at every Anglo-Indian's meal, the lemon-scented verbena being often employed for this purpose. Glowing fruits peeped forth from beds of cool green leaves. The more delicate sorts were placed in wicker baskets, artistically lined with pieces of the plantain leaf cut into shape. We bought one of these little boats, with its cargo of dull-hued lilac figs, luscious and small, with just one tear of liquid sugar upon each—the true *goutte d'or*.

Among the fruits with which I was familiar, were many species which I had never seen before; but to enumerate them would be tedious. The vegetables were of infinite variety, including gourds of the most grotesque forms, which Nature must have imagined in a mirthful hour. Some of them were intended for eating, but others would be carefully cleaned out, and the hard rinds converted into vessels for water, and other liquids. The capsicums and chillis were curious and pretty, some being large, shiny, and intensely green, while others were small and red and pointed, and made one hot to look at them. There were many varieties of the egg-plant, some of them white and smooth like ivory, others resembling balls of gold; and the long purple aubergines were very handsome. I could have spent hours with satisfaction in these markets, which were the finest I had ever seen; but time pressed, and we passed into the interior garden, a charming, cool, and verdant spot, in which there were numerous varieties of the palm tribe, all sorts of velvety, long-leaved plants, and trembling ferns of exquisite beauty. It was strange to see caneless clumps of the caladium of tender green, spotted with white and red, along with other plants, only at home to be seen in a hot-house, where one lingers for a

moment, in mortal dread of catching one's death
of cold on again breathing the raw air outside.
I should have liked to have explored the fish
market, which no doubt contained many curious
and strange varieties; but the sun was up, and
as we hesitated at the door of the market, we
perceived that its atmosphere was not as
odoriferous as that of the floral Paradise which
we had quitted.

I had a great wish to visit one of the Hindoo
—or, rather, Jain—establishments for super-
annuated animals. There was something very
pleasing in the idea of such a refuge for these
poor creatures. Alas! I found, on inquiry, that
the originally humane intention had degenerated
into a mere superstition, and that such institutions are now farmed out, and their inmates
much neglected. In the rural districts the
natives are, I believe, as a rule, kind to their
animals; but in large towns the bullocks and
horses are sadly maltreated. The society for the
protection of animals, lately established in Bombay, has, however, done a good deal, locally, to
amend their condition. The society has also
taken under its protection the snakes, and some
other small creatures, which are frightfully tormented by the conjurers. At breakfast I was
much laughed at respecting my Indian night-

ingale, which turned out to be a canary, whose cage my neighbour, an elderly gentleman, put out every morning on his balcony.

The prettiest drive about Bombay is to Malabar Point. We set off towards it as day declined, stopping *en route* to do some necessary shopping at an immense store called Treacher's, one of those tiresome labyrinths where one has to walk a quarter of a mile, and be put in the right path half a dozen times, in order to purchase a packet of pins or a skein of silk. There is a co-operative society in Bombay, but the managers and the shareholders do nothing but dispute : and as the prices are high, and the articles of inferior quality, it is probable that its existence will be short. Of the two roads that lead to the Point, we took the higher in going and returned by the shore. Not so very many years ago, Malabar Hill was an unwholesome jungle of palms, with a thick undergrowth of prickly bushes. It is now partially cleared, and has become a fashionable quarter of low, far-spreading white houses, which are surrounded by beautiful grounds, and shaded by the tall trees of the original jungle. I was well acquainted with the date-palm, but not so with its cocoa-nut rival, which, with its splendid fan-like leaves, is in many respects the finest of

the two. The thin and slightly-curved stem
of the latter is, however, a drawback upon its
merits. Massed together, they had a very fine
effect as they stood out dark against the red
sky.

It was curious to see the agility with which
the natives climbed the cylindrical stems, using
their flexible feet as a second pair of hands, and
sliding down with amazing rapidity. There is
a celebrated tank upon Malabar Hill, which
interested me much, as it was the first I had
seen of these ornamental sheets of water,
so intimately connected with the religious and
domestic life of the Hindoo people. It was
enclosed by walls with highly ornamental
balustrades, from which broad flights of steps
descended. It was shaded by tall peepul-trees
and far-spreading banyans with numerous roots,
under which rose groups of pagodas, and a
Brahman village, the little white houses of
which were inhabited by the priests and their
families. Every Brahman is a priest. It was
a very pretty scene. The Government house at
Malabar Point is a square building of imposing
size. G—— thought that I might like to visit
it, but to my mind a modern palace, with
nothing particular in its interior, presented few
attractions, and I was desirous of employing the

golden hours in driving round by the towers of silence, the fine temples, and in observing the general aspect of the country.

The Point was a savage-looking spot, swept by the burning wind. All vegetation had ceased, but the wet season was advanced, and possibly after the rains a change for the better might come over the spot which now appeared to be so desolate. The fort is long, narrow, and low, but its hidden strength is great. It has been altered indeed since the days of Captain Cook, who found it " a pretty well-seated but ill-fortified house." Four guns of brass were then the whole defence of the island. It has an ugly shore, piled up with splintered pieces of rock, which not even the eternal beating of the waves has rendered less angular. Even the black sea-weed refuses to cling to the hard ungenial basalt, and gets washed into crevices, where it petrifies. The celebrated Esplanade is a fine drive, commanding a glorious view over the rosy sea when the sun dips below the horizon. As we passed along it we saw plenty of handsome carriages, elegant toilettes, and well-mounted equestrians.

Our last day in Bombay was spent in visiting the island and rock-cut temples of Elephanta; and as G—— wished to show a little attention

to some of our fellow-passengers who still lingered on at the hotel, a party was made up,
and a steam-launch secured, which was well
supplied with light refreshments and iced
drinks. We set out with light hearts to enjoy
ourselves. The island of Elephanta is about
six miles from Bombay, and we sped gaily towards it over the crisp waves. Visitors had
formerly to be carried on shore if the tide was
low, but this is no longer necessary, as a long
jetty has been thrown out, formed of great
square blocks of concrete, which, in order to
humour the waves, have been placed half a foot
apart. Our transit over them was not pleasant,
for they were covered with fine green sea-weed,
which was very slippery. At high tide the islet
is but three miles in circumference, but at low
water the sea retreats so much that its area is
doubled. It is formed of a mighty volcanic
mountain, which has thrown up two lofty
craterous peaks. The excavations are in the
grip between them. The ascent would have
been toilsome had not the winding road been
cut into wide steps, now worn into hollows by
the feet of the pilgrims and the devotees who
at certain periods repair to the island in order
to worship at its famous shrines. In the Spring
of the year a great fair is held in the very
temple itself.

Cut through forest and jungle, nothing could be more romantic and beautiful than the scenery. Tall palms of different species all but met overhead. There were numbers of the fig tribe, glossy and green, and tall grapes and strange plants grew at their feet, dead and brown, but perfect in form. The stems of great creepers coiled snake-like round many a tree which they would ultimately strangle; others were knotted into the most intricate tangles, and their streaming tendrils swept down to the very ground. Some men of very wild appearance offered beetles for sale, but I did not purchase any, which I have always regretted, as they were very beautiful, looking like frosted gold. I was told that they would die in an hour, and, like Aladdin's glittering fruit, fade into a dull grey hue. The same men had also handfuls of the seed of the liquorice plant, scarlet berries with a black spot, which jewellers once used in their tiny scales, and which the natives are fond of stringing into necklaces.

At last we reached the plateau which was our destination. It was a sylvan scene, a green spot, in the midst of which stood the rude hut of a forest keeper. Some pretty white goats were playing about with their kids, and a group of magnificent trees spread a shade which was

very welcome after our hot walk. We had to
pay a fee in order to be free of the caves; the
money is so collected in order to prevent impo-
sition on the part of the guides. After certain
sums are deducted, the remainder is distributed
among the different charitable institutions in
Bombay. A couple of men were told off in
order to accompany us, and to see that we did
no mischief, which duty they fulfilled by lying
down in a corner, and going fast to sleep.

We suddenly came upon a high craggy face
of black rock, half concealed by bushes, and in
the dim obscurity caught sight of the front of
the mysterious temple, which the natives attri-
bute to the shadowy sons of Pandu. A curious
thrill shot through me as I bowed my head
under a streaming fringe of hanging plants, and
stood amidst the strange gods of this great
branch of the Aryan race, so far separated from
me by religion and country, and yet to whom I
was bound by a common ancestry. It is a spot
calculated to inspire awe. In its dark recesses
many a human sacrifice has doubtless been
offered up. The jagged roof is supported by
pillars, the shafts of which, though symmetrically
shaped, are rough-hewn, as if to contrast more
effectually with the finely-polished surface of the
black basalt above, which bulges out into beau-

tiful flutings, compressed in more than one place by fillets of large beads or sharp-cut leaves. The capitals represent cushions with tassels, on which rest the great beams cut from the ceiling. With the usual irregularity of Eastern art, the columns are placed at unequal distances, a circumstance which, strange to say, does not detract from the general harmony; indeed it is only upon examination that the fact is discovered.

The temple has two wings or side chapels, independent excavations, which stand back, and have no direct communication with it. It would require an abler pen than mine, and a far greater knowledge of the subject than I possess, to attempt any regular description of this curiously-wrought rock cave. I can only speak with authority of the effect its salient points produced upon my mind, in which profound interest, wonder, and a certain kind of admiration, struggled with some feeling akin to fear. I do not think that I could have borne to have been left alone in this twilight place, with the stony eyes of the assembled gods fixed upon me. I should have fancied that the thousand eyes of Indra regarded me with displeasure; that Vishnu's third organ of vision, which is to burst into fire and consume the world, had begun to kindle; that the hooded cobra twined about his arm was uncoiling, or that streams were trickling from the deity's wave-crested head-dress, the cradle of the three rivers which united form the sacred flood-tormented Ganges.

Fortunately I was not alone. I shook myself free from such nightmare fancies, and hastened to join my companions, who were assembled in full conclave before the Trimurti, a three-faced bust, which is infinitely solemn and dignified. The faces represent Brahma, the creator; Vishnu, the preserver; and Shiva, the destroyer. They are very grave, and seem to look at you sternly, as if offended that you do not bow down and adore them, as millions of our race have done before.

Every available part of the temple is sculptured in high relief with mythological figures, colossal in comparison with human beings, but, for aught I know, they may be miniature representations of the gods themselves. The scenes depicted are explained only by the wildest stories which can possibly be conceived. Both these and the distorted figures I at first felt to be distasteful, but this feeling partly wore away when I came to be better acquainted with their hidden meaning. The Sinya chapel, placed in the principal temple, is a large square erection, with four doorways, but the doors themselves are gone. There, on a raised platform of black basalt, worn by the feet of millions of worshippers, stands the cone, the emblem of this most ancient worship. Gigantic figures in high relief, two and two, guard every entrance, each attended by a hideous dwarf. These figures are exceedingly interesting, as they probably embody some ancient idea respecting the early Aryan warriors, the dwarfs, of course, representing the conquered aborigines. In one of the side chapels traces of paint remain—simple squares of red and white, set together in a board—and from underneath the chapel a spring of pure water still bubbles up, and forms a pool, which no doubt has for centuries been used as a bathing-place by devotees and pilgrims. After all, these excavations are not very old, competent judges believing them to have been executed between the eighth and tenth centuries of the Christian era.

Mr. Fergusson has made some remarks respecting vast caves in general, which are very much to the point.* Though so deeply inter-

* "Considerable misconception exists on the subject of cutting temples in the rock. Almost everyone who sees these temples is struck with the apparently prodigious

exted in these caves, they cast a shade upon my spirits, and aroused feelings of gloom and sadness which I was unable to define, and I was glad to step forth into the cheerful light of day, to see the bright sea glitter, and hear the twitter of birds and the hum of insects.

There are some smaller excavations scattered over the island, supposed to have been cells inhabited by hermits. With the exception of a few Government officers and their followers, no one now resides at Elephanta. It has been deserted in consequence of the extreme insalu-

---

amount of labour bestowed on their excavations. In reality, however, it is considerably less expensive to excavate a temple than to build one. Take, for instance, the Kylas (Ellora), the most wonderful of all this class. To excavate the area on which it stands would require the removal of about 100,000 cubic yards of rock ; but as the base of the temple is solid, and the superstructure massive, it occupies in round numbers one half of the excavated area, so that the question is simply this—whether it is easier to chip away 50,000 yards of rock, and shoot it to spoil (to borrow a railway term) down a hillside, or to quarry 50,000 cubic yards of stone, remove it probably a mile, at least, to the place where the temple is to be built, and then to raise and set it up. The excavating process would probably cost about one-tenth of the other. The sculpture and ornament would be the same in both instances, more especially in India, where buildings are always set up in block, and the carvings executed *in situ.*"—FERGUSSON'S *Hand-book of Architecture.*

brity of the rice-bearing swamps at the foot of the mountain. As we strolled along the jungle paths, a member of our party, a keen sportsman, made an arrangement with one of the guards to bring his gun next day. The sport promised consisted of hogs, hares, wild cats, snipe, and other animals. It was not the season for quail, but there are periods when they cover the shore.

Shortly after we visited the island, I saw in *The Times of India* that a fine tiger had been taken there—an unusual circumstance. It is supposed that the beast had swum over from the main land. There are many of these wild animals in the deep ravines of the Bhor Ghât. M. was fatigued, and reaching a pleasant spot, sat down under a tree, and fell asleep. I preferred to stray about in a scene which to me was new, strange, and delightful. In my wanderings I came upon a curious ants' nest, and I saw suspended many long bags, made of fibre, the work of the weaver bird. Under a leafless tree a quantity of large brown pods of tamarinds strowed the ground, and climbing a steep bit of rock, I sat down to enjoy their sharp refreshing flavour. The view from my lofty perch was charming. At my feet were numbers of waving trees; the sea was an intense blue, and on the opposite shore of Salsette the hills were covered with wood.

The head of the bay was closed by lofty mountains, range above range, and peak above peak. They were the great Western Ghâts, which we were to cross upon the morrow. The word ghât, in Indian parlance, means a mountain leading up to a plain above. It is also applied to the broad flights of stairs which ornament the tanks. The word is familiar to those who are acquainted with the secluded district of Cleveland, in the East Riding of Yorkshire. It there signifies a narrow passage between two houses. A small but interesting history of Cleveland has lately appeared, containing a glossary of the many Danish words embedded in the dialect of that country, and the word ghât is one of them.

The refreshing sea breeze fanned our cheeks as we wended our way down the Pilgrims' Steps. Two or three sailors who were loitering about presented us with some fruit, the size of a small apple, which they had gathered from off a palm-tree, from whence they hung in heavy clusters. It contained a clear white jelly, which, although a little mawkish and sticky, was not altogether unpleasant. I have never been able to make out the precise species of palm from which it was gathered, but suspect that the fruit was immature. Before re-embarking, we strolled along the sands, searching for shells, but all that we found were of a very ordinary sort.

In returning, the tide was with us, and we stood well out into the middle of the bay, which is very beautiful. The amphitheatre of mountains, the Eastern characteristics of the island we had just quitted, the smiling shore, with here and there a domed and pinnacled mosque, rosy red in the rays of the setting sun, made a delightful scene. Many islets were dotted about—Butcher's Isle, and Old Woman's Isle, and a third, with long rows of empty barracks, built at vast expense, and then deserted in consequence of their fatally unhealthy position. During their occupation, numbers of soldiers died of that most painful malady, the Guinea worm, which generally proceeds from drinking unwholesome water.

As we approached the harbour, the scene became most animated. Noble three-masted P. and O. steamers lay at anchor. A little apart from these were others, belonging to different companies, amongst which our own *Hindoo* cut no mean figure. There were stately sailing vessels and small craft innumerable, which were not huddled together in confusion, but lay at a friendly distance from one another. Every spar, every rope stood out against a background of fiery crimson—such a sunset, such vivid colouring as I had never pictured to myself as possible even in an Indian sunset. As the soft twilight stole on, the hue intensified—the world below the horizon might have been in flames. It was a magnificent conclusion to one of the most delightful days I ever spent.

CHAPTER IV.

THE time which G—— was able to spare for Bombay came to an end all too soon. We took leave of such of our *Hindoo* companions as still remained, and stepping into a flight of shigrams, set forth on our journey. Belgaum, which was our destination, is in the southern part of Máhratta. A few years ago the district in which it is situated formed part of the Madras Presidency, but was handed over to that of Bombay for some reason relating to the better distribution of troops. There were two routes open to us. The easiest would have been to have taken a coasting steamer to Vingorla, which would have placed us within sixty miles of our destination, but this not falling in with G——'s arrangements, we took the longer but far more interesting line which lay inland.

I was delighted at the prospect of journeying for three hundred and thirty miles through a country so new and strange. We were aided as far as Poonah (a hundred and nineteen miles) by the Great Indian Peninsular Railway, the accommodation on which is first-rate. We had previously engaged a saloon carriage, to which was attached a dressing-room, with water laid on—a great luxury. This again led into an airy compartment, set apart for ladies, of which we also took possession, being the only first-class passengers. The fares on this line are naturally high, for its formation was a stupendous undertaking—one of the greatest triumphs of railway engineering in the world.

Leaving the town, we passed through the Portuguese suburb, in the midst of which stands a handsome Roman Catholic church, to which large schools are attached, and on through the district where the dyers dwell. It was covered with shallow cuttings, filled to the brim with deep rich colours—blue, and red, and saffron,

and stretched out in all directions were
the long cotton saris, in which the Indian
women drape their elastic forms. There is
very little variety to be found in the Indian
dyes, the natives being unsuccessful in their
attempts to produce solid mixed tints ; with
one exception—a mixture of blue and green,
which is very harmonious, and much used by
sportsmen in the jungle. The process of print-
ing is executed in a curiously primitive manner, the patterns principally consisting of dots
and lines. Greater success is attained in
dyeing silks, the hues of which are lasting as
well as brilliant. At the desire of the English
Government the forest commissioners have
lately had a meeting upon the subject, experi-
ments under the direction of good chemists
have been made, and it is expected that great
improvements in this kind of manufactures will
be introduced.

For some time we sped along a swampy rice-
growing country, passing extensive salt-works,
the dirty hillocks and shallow pans, as usual, an
ugly sight ; but we caught charming glimpses of
the sea at the head of the bay, with Elephanta, and
the other islands, shadowy and uncertain in the
beams of the hot sun. Reaching a large junction,
we turned abruptly to the south, and steadily

progressed towards the Ghâts, the masses of mountain which lay between us and the Deccan, the level plains which were to be our abiding place. These mountains are formed of various sorts of trap, very hard and highly crystallized. At the stations glittering specimens were exposed for sale. At Nassel we plunged into a narrow ravine, where the rough rocks nearly met overhead, and began to ascend. The most considerable railway incline in Europe is that on the Sömmering pass, between Vienna and Trieste; but its proportions are on a far smaller scale than those of the Bhor Ghât, which ascends eighteen hundred and thirty-one feet, and is nearly sixteen miles in length; in parts the latter is wonderfully precipitate, the gradient being one in twelve; the average is one in forty-eight.

The noonday heat was overpowering (in Bombay, March is the hottest month in the year), and caused G—— and M. to withdraw into the lattice-closed ladies' saloon; but I was too much excited by the novelty of my position to follow their example. No good view was to be obtained without kneeling upon the seat and putting my head out of the window; the eaves sheltered my head from the fierce rays of the sun, but the heated air struck upon my face like blasts from an oven.

The scenery was glorious. The lofty mountains and the deep ravines—Paubul, an abrupt rock, with a flat top, two thousand five hundred feet high, and the immense shoulder of the Bhor Ghât still loftier—always threatened to bar our progress which ever way we turned. (Bhor is the Máhratta word for the juguba tree, which grows plentifully upon this mountain—hence the name.) Fort-crowned Moteran is a prominent object, presenting to the north a perpendicular face of small black rock, which rises two thousand feet above the narrow plain that separates it from the sea.

On a plateau near the top, which slopes to the brink of a frightful precipice, there is a sanitarium for sick soldiers, and a collection of cottages, to which the Europeans who live in Bombay, thirsting for cool breezes, thankfully resort in the hot season. The coloured view of this place, with its formal gravel paths, and stiff gardens, in which nothing appears to grow, reminded me of a sea-side advertisement at an English railway-station. As we mounted, the view became superb, embracing the "peaks familiar with forgotten years," the piled-up mountains of the Western Ghâts, the far, dim plains of the Concan, and the lovely harbour of Bombay, its indigo waters flecked by innumerable white-sailed ships, reduced by distance to the size of sea-gulls.

The Máhratta mountains are of most peculiar shape, resembling, with occasional exceptions, gigantic cones, from which ages of monsoons have swept the tops, leaving exposed the skeleton summits, perpendicular walls of basaltic rock, lofty plateaus, natural strongholds, which the war-like chiefs converted into impregnable fortresses. On many of these plateaus there are abundant springs of fine water, and when such is not the case, the hard nature of the rock is admirably adapted for reservoirs. Our ascent was, at first, very gradual. We crossed a lofty embankment, entered a narrow rock-hewn passage, and on through a dark tunnel, to emerge upon a lengthy viaduct. As we advanced, the iron road became more difficult for the panting engine to climb. I rejoiced over its laboured pace, for every minute developed the majesty of the prospect. We swept up the mighty Bhor Ghât, curving in and out of its bulging sides, catching sight of airy tracks far above our level, stretches of the road which we were about to traverse. *Terra firma* seemed to vanish; we appeared to be sailing past the mountain side, with a deep, deep valley beneath. We were, in fact, gliding along a bench of rock wide enough, but no more, to receive the iron way. It was frightful, utter annihilation, if a wheel should break, a chain become uncoupled, or a train warped by the burning sun. The character of the scenery was quite new to me. Here Nature was on so vast a scale. Broad as were the valleys, the effect was lost in their profound depth, where a deep green line of jungle marked the home of the tiger and of the still fiercer panther. And then the colouring of the tangled vegetation, which, though dead, had suffered no decay. Changed to a tint of burning gold, it still clothed the mountain side, save where the polished surface of the huge masses of black rock were so smooth that nothing could cling to them. This Indian landscape was, beyond everything, solemn and grand. One vast promontory lives in my memory. It stood boldly forth, rooted for all time in the horse-shoe valley beneath, a fit position for the blazing beacons which guided the fierce Máhratta marauders on their midnight march when steam power lay an embryo in the womb of time.

The station at the top of the incline is called the reversing station. There was a short delay, which we employed in looking back upon the

mountains we had traversed ; and in endeavouring to trace the iron road we had passed along,
we obtained occasional glimpses of narrow cuttings from the rock, mere threads they looked,
banks formed upon arches, or upon lofty piers
built into the mountain sides. No wonder that
this gigantic undertaking cost a fabulous sum.

Leaving the station, we doubled back again.
The two lines proceeding from a common source,
one mounting, the other descending, have a
curious effect, and make a striking photograph.
As we slowly journeyed we obtained a fine
view over the Concan, a vast stretch of country,
varying in width from twenty-five to fifty
miles, which here spreads between the ghâts
and the sea, but runs far south, and along the
coast of Malabar. In this space different
languages are spoken, and Hindoo geographers
divide it into seven parts. It would not be
India, did not some old-world fable seek
to account for the existence of these great
plains. One of the Paorans (a collection of
mythological stories regarded as sacred) re-
counts how, Puresham having extirpated the
Kshittrees and oppressive Rajahs from a certain
country, conferred the conquered territory on
the Brahmans, but they ungratefully refused
their benefactors permission to reside amongst

them, so Puresham, in search of a home, bent his bow, and let fly an arrow from the top of the great western mountains, at which the ocean was intimidated, and receding before the arrow to the point at which it fell, left dry the extensive tract of country now known by the name of the Concan and the Malabar coast.

The country at our feet appeared to be cultivated. The fields now sterile were, for the purpose of irrigation, divided by banks of earth into squares. There were tanks of shimmering water fringed with trees, under which were groups of white temples, with conical roofs, and noble trees were dotted about, principally teak, the wood of which is even harder and more enduring than that of oak. Then, though all small objects became indistinct in the sultry atmosphere, we could still trace the blue line of hills which bordered the coast.

Before us were many strange funnel-shaped hills, and basaltic rocks of remarkable form. They represented castles and obelisks, gigantic figures and grotesque faces. One rock is known by the name of the Duke's Nose; but our pace had quickened, and before we were disenchanted they were gone. Shortly before reaching Lanowlee M. pointed across the valley to some trees clinging round a jutting rock, with a dark spot in the centre, the entrance to the far-famed Cave of Karli. A tantalizing vision. She had ridden up the slippery path which leads to it, a narrow ledge cut from the rock, with nothing to protect it from a steep precipice. Karli is considered to be the finest chaitya cave in India. It is supposed to date from the second century before the Christian era, and is in excellent preservation; the curious teak wood ribbed roof, and the screen, being, without doubt, as ancient as the excavation.*

It was at Karli that Captain Stewart, who

---

* The geographical distribution of the caves is somewhat singular, more than nine-tenths of those now known being found within the Bombay Presidency . . . . . I was at one time inclined to connect this remarkable distribution with the comparative proximity of this side of India to the rock-cutting Egyptians and Ethiopians, but the coincidence can be more simply accounted for by the existence of rocks, in both countries, perfectly adapted to such works. The whole cave district of India is composed of horizontal strata of amygdaloid and other cognate trap formations, generally speaking of very considerable thickness and great uniformity of texture, and possessing besides the advantage of their edges being generally exposed in perfectly perpendicular cliffs. So that no rock in any part of the world could either be more suited for the purpose, or more favourably situated than these formations are. In the rarest possible instances are there any flaws or faults to disturb the uniformity of the design.—FERGUSSON's *Hand-book of Architecture.*

had taken possession of the Bhor Ghât in the previous November (1779), was killed by a cannonball. He was mentioned in the despatches as " a most gallant and judicious officer, and possessed of the true military spirit !" To this day his name is familiar in the Máhratta country by the appellation of the Stewart Phakray, a circumstance which marks the strong impression made by his conduct.*

We took advantage of an hour's delay at Lanowlee, to give the children some refreshment. There is a messman at this station, but those who prefer it can bring their own provisions ; and unless things are borrowed, no fee is expected. India is not the land of fees. Lanowlee, with its green slopes, grey boulder stones, and tangled woods, is a charming spot. The scattered bungalows, encircled by wide verandahs, were almost hidden away under the high-pitched tiled roofs, which, sweeping down, sheltered them alike from sunshine and storm. They were covered with beautiful creepers, and their white pillars were festooned with sprays of every colour, crimson predominating. It is a place of popular resort during the hot weather. M. had spent part of the previous

---

* Grant Duff's History of the Máhrattas.

season there, and was delighted with the beauty
of the surrounding country, and the abundance
of wild flowers.

We now entered upon a comparatively flat
country, with fields and hedges of prickly pear.
We had reached one of the Deccan plains (the
Deccan consists of a series of table-lands), and
many a green thing served to remind us of the
elevation we had attained. We breathed again.
The hills retired, and formed a fine background
to the open country.

Some time before reaching Poonah, we came
upon a barren, sun-scorched plain, but a green
oasis in M.'s memory, having been the scene
of the large camp of exercise held during the
previous year; and, in spite of the order that
neither women nor silver spoons should be admitted into its precincts, her husband, being
Provost-Marshal, she got smuggled in. She
had a large tent, connected with G——'s by a
canvas passage, and this was so delightfully
encumbered by piles of fruit, presents of almonds, pumalos, oranges, plantains, more fruits
than I can name, and little boxes containing
extra delicate productions, that she could
scarcely stir. She ate as many of them as she
possibly could; and, G—— having no time to
eat, the residue was given to the troopers.

G 2

There was no end of the delights—the noblest
elephants and stateliest camels were brought
up for her to paint; and most charming studies
she made of the picturesque creatures and their
wild attendants. Her ears were tickled by the
moanings of the chiefs who wanted places
allotted to them, at the forthcoming review, for
numerous carriages which they did not possess;
and, above all, at the said review she had the
felicity of being close to Indore's great prince,
Holkar, with his cotton robe, heavy face, and
splendid jewels, mounted upon a horse, streaked
with red, and got up with a lilac tail.*

Kenkee, with its famous memories, a heath
with a few scattered houses and long lines of

---

* Holkar, though by no means the richest, or owner of
the largest territories amongst the native princes, is one of
the most independent.—"Throughout the length and
breadth of his Highness the Maharajah's possessions no private individual has anything like permanent, hereditary, or
alienable rights in land. Registered proprietorship is un-
heard of in this part of India. Every cultivator is a tenant
at will of his Highness. The population of Holkar's territories is roughly estimated at 600,000 souls, and the area
at 8,318 square miles. The revenue of the state from all
sources is about thirty lakhs of rupees, and the expenditure
twenty-two lakhs." (A lakh is £10,000.) " Holkar maintains a military establishment of 2,050 irregular cavalry,
and 500 artillerymen, with twenty-four field guns equipped."
—*Times of India Calendar*, 1876.—The Holkar family are
Sudras of the shepherd tribe, and rose to eminence at the
end of the seventeenth century.

cavalry barracks, had for us a personal interest. G—— was born there, and, we will hope, christened in the prim little brick church which presents such a remarkable contrast to the fine group of Jain temples in its neighbourhood.

After the heat and excitement of the day, it was very refreshing to sit in the wide verandah of the Napier Hotel, look over the pretty flower garden, and up at the quiet stars. The heat next morning was considerable. The thermometer in our sitting-room standing at ninety-eight degrees, it was impossible to venture out of doors. The great drawback to Indian travel are the many hours of enforced inactivity, when one is obliged to sit chafing within doors, until the sun is down, and only the short twilight remains in which to see the surrounding objects of interest. Had I been able to manage for myself, I should have been up with the lark (there are plenty of larks in India), and have explored half the wonders of the place before breakfast. As it was, I sat down in a half-closed room, with a fan in one hand, and Grant Duff's "History of the Máhrattas," in the other (I was too old a traveller to be unprovided with books), and improved the shining hours by making out what I could respecting these old marauding villains.

I boldly skipped the pages, until I came to the mention of Sevaji, the great national hero, the founder of the Máhratta kingdom. Born in 1627, he came of a long line of princes, and was brought up near Poonah. Poonah, however, did not become a place of much importance until a later power, that of the Peishwa, arose. (Peishwa is a Persian name for a certain Government officer.) They were a Brahman race from the Deccan, hereditary Prime Ministers to the rajahs of Sattara. Gradually rising to power, they became supreme chiefs of the Máhratta nation, and in the year 1750 they made Poonah their capital.

At the *table-d'hôte* luncheon I fell in with several friends. It was a sociable meal; dogs walked about at their ease, and small birds flew over us, perching upon the sides of the dishes when removed from the table, and helping themselves to the viands with the utmost coolness. The afternoon was enlivened by the arrival of itinerant merchants, who laid their goods open for inspection in the verandah. One of them, a handsome dark man, with a red turban, had some excellent toys—animals made of strong grey linen, the features being stitched in with coloured thread. We bought an elephant, with magnificent trappings of scarlet cloth, and a spirited horse, with flowing mane and tail; the former, under the name of Miss Emmeline, is still dear to the hearts of the youthful part of the family.

Another man had scarfs and slippers, and many sorts of embroidery, as well as fancy baskets made of Kusha grass. They looked as if they had been made by the weaver-bird, and spangled with the wings of its insect victims. These baskets are peculiar to the Poonah district. A third travelling merchant had trays full of jewelry, some bracelets and brooches worked in a manner which was quite new to me, in which delicate arabesques of gold were fused into green and blue enamel. These ornaments were strikingly pretty, but very expensive. There were also some fine Mocha stones (so called from having been first polished at Mocha), in which floated exquisite little branches of red and green sea-weed. The precious stones, set in rings and small *parures*, were expensive, and not pretty.

The sun was a great glowing ball, sinking beneath the horizon, when we drove down to enjoy the freshness of evening in the public gardens. The band had ceased to play, and the gay world were flocking away. Underneath the heavy-leaved trees was the vacant band-stand, surrounded by large plots of shrubs and flowers ; but most of the smaller plants were in pots, and although they were well arranged, to my unaccustomed eyes the effect was unsatisfactory, the absence of turf being a great drawback. Nothing could be more delightful than the situation of these gardens, placed upon a high cliff, along the brink of which ran a broad terrace, with stone balustrades and seats, which overhung the wide, swift river Múlá, with its bridge of many arches, and the bund, or embankment, by which it is protected. Low hills, clothed with wood, sank into the water on the opposite side of the stream. It was a scene of peaceful beauty, which our weary eyes thoroughly enjoyed. It suddenly became quite dark. There are no "violet Summers' eves" in India, and we had some difficulty in threading our way to the carriage. There was a bright light upon a near hill-side, which we took to be a burning cottage, but it proceeded from a pile of wood, which at certain times is kindled, in order to light the descent to the mouth of a cave in which there lives a very holy ascetic. This was not the only blaze on the surrounding heights ; flickering flames ran along the ground. It was the season for firing the thick scrub, in order to get rid of the dried vegetation before the rains. There being no moon, we saw the full effect of the red forks of flame which shot up, casting a lurid glow around. It was a curious sight; but until G—— remembered that it was the evening of a great Hindoo festival, we were puzzled to account for a stationary line of brilliant light which streaked the side of a conical hill at no great distance. It was the celebrated place of pilgrimage, the mount and temples of Parvati, which were thus illuminated. Later in the evening we sat upon the house-top, and watched the clustered lamps which marked out the steep flights of steps leading to the shrines; and when we went to bed they were still shining in all their beauty.

The following day was a busy one. There arrived five bullock carts, which were to convey our baggage (in Indian parlance, kit) to Belgaum. They were to travel at night, and catch us up on the third and fifth day of our passage. The bullocks were handsome creatures, with calm eyes, creamy white coats, hanging dewlaps, and great crescent-shaped horns tipped with ornamental brass work. I was sorry for the poor patient beasts, who had to bear so heavy a yoke, and be driven with a line passed through the nostril. The dogs (the great twin brothers), and Dick's goats, shared a vehicle which had a cover to it. Spread out ready to be packed was the *batterie de cuisine*, which G—— had bought in Bombay. It consisted of imposing-looking vessels of solid copper, with rough-hewn exteriors. I especially admired some which were very bulky, with sloping shoulders and broad rims. One pot was such a monster that I was puzzled as to its probable use. Three rounds of beef could have been boiled in it without jostling one another. "What on earth is that for?" I demanded, pointing to it. "That," said M., in her decisive way— "that is my oven." Calmly surveying the scene from the roof, where he was perched, was a large, glossy brown scavenger-hawk, who at intervals gave forth a shrill, quivering, mournful cry. This evening, to my great satisfaction, we set out on our drive before the sun was down.

I was disappointed with the European part of Poonah, having expected to see a handsome town—a small Bombay—instead of which nothing was to be seen but small bungalows, widely separated, and surrounded by ragged shrubberies and dried-up gardens. After the rains, they would probably look very different. The native town, which keeps strictly to itself, was nearly two miles from our starting-point.

Fifty years ago it was the very Paradise of priests. A writer of that day speaks of having seen eighty thousand Brahmaus assembled there at one time.

We drove to the fort, which stands in the centre of the town. The entrance is exceedingly fine, consisting of a lofty, towering archway, surmounted by a small iron balcony, from whence the Peishwas used to review their troops, and on certain occasions exhibit themselves in all their splendour to the people. The arch is set in a broad frame, which is frescoed over with lotus leaves and blossoms upon a cream-coloured ground, the colours well preserved. On each side is a massive round tower, pierced with numerous embrasures for guns of small calibre. The iron doors which closed the archway were barbarously magnificent, and told of days long since numbered with the past. In parts they bristled with deep rows of sharp spikes, more than a foot in length, so placed in order to prevent the elephants from battering them in. We were admitted into the interior by a door cut through the superior one; it was so small that we had to double ourselves up in order to pass through it. The fort is now a mere shell, but the lofty walls are perfect, and enclose a considerable space of ground. The only chambers which remain are those above the gateway. These small-windowed rooms were in 1773 the scene of a tragic event—the murder of Náráyan Ráo. He was only eighteen, and had been but nine months Peishwa. The unfortunate youth had confined his uncle in an apartment in the palace. The uncle had been able to bribe two of his guards to seize the young Peishwa, and thus bring about his own release; but his vindictive wife secretly changed the word from seize to kill. (If Eastern women are celebrated, it is always for evil, and never for good.) The assassins stabbed the young Peishwa, killing at the same time a faithful servant, who had thrown himself upon his body. A terrace runs along the old gateway, to which a still more mournful interest attaches. It was the favourite walk of another young Peishwa, Mahádeo Ráo, who, at the close of the last century, threw himself down from it, dying two days after from the injuries he received. It happened during one of the great national Máhratta festivals, which was being conducted with unusual splendour. The young Peishwa had received his great chiefs, and the ambassadors of foreign countries; he had shown himself to his troops, who had passed before him thousands strong; but the restraints imposed upon him by his tyrannical minister, the celebrated Náná Farnavis, had so wounded his pride that he destroyed himself. Such stories have little interest for those who have not visited the spot, but they are full of significance with regard to the manners of the period in which such horrors could take place with impunity. There is not one of these Eastern strongholds that has not been drenched in blood.

We crossed the great enclosure, solitary now save for the presence of a few soldiers at drill, and half-a-dozen white-robed individuals, who were amusing themselves in an inoffensive manner by accompanying us to the castle gardens, which are still kept up in a lazy Oriental fashion. There were the trees under which the Peishwas had sat and hatched dark plots, the tanks in which they had disported themselves, and the wells from which they had drunk, now green with beautiful black-stemmed giant maidenhair, some sprigs of which we gathered to send home. As we were leaving the fort, our Hindoo followers, who had lingered behind, came up, and gracefully presented each of us with a little prim nosegay of roses and pinks, for which attention G—— thanked them in their own language, and they continued to salaam until we were out of sight. Close to the fort is a narrow street, in which, under the Peishwas, offenders were executed by being trampled to death by elephants, an admirable mode of disposing of an enemy, as it combined vengeance with amusement. One of the Holkar family was put to death in this cruel manner whilst the last of the Peishwas sat at his window and gloated over the agonies of his victim; but that very same year his brother, Rão Holkar, was splendidly revenged by winning the battle of Poonah.

The town is full of curious old houses, the exterior galleries of which have shutters and frames for lattices, finely carved; and there we saw Saracenic arches, of horse-shoe form. These were supported by wooden pillars richly carved with figures and foliage. These old houses were once the residences of great ministers and court favourites. We alighted, and stepped into the court of that which had belonged to Nánã Farnavis. It was a mouldy place, with broken fountains and dry tanks; the rooms were small and dismal, and the narrow passages quite dark. A large house was pointed out to us as having been, at the end of the last century, the dwelling of a most extraordinary character—a woman, Spanish by birth, but

an English subject, being the wife of a Mr.
James Hall, a respectable barrister in Madras,
from whom she was separated. She sought her
fortune in the military service of the native
princes. Her active career was, however, cut
short, in consequence of her having caused the
death, by beating, of a thievish Brahman who
was attached to her household. For this grave
offence, which would have entailed capital
punishment had she been a native, she was for
many years confined in a hill fort near Poonah.
The military name assumed by this heroine was
Jamel Serdar (Elegant Lord, or Elegant Commander). Her dress at Poonah was of a very
manlike stamp, although still not entirely mas-
culine. In Mogul style, she wore a flowing
robe and loose trousers; an enormous sabre and
a plumed helmet graced the well-formed person
of this daring Amazon. "I have heard,"
says Mr. Moor, " that she was offered the command of the battalion of women that the Nizam
Ally Khan raised for the interior duties of the
Mahl, or ladies' apartments, or what we call the
Seraglio. The battalion consisted of five or
six hundred women, regularly dressed and
disciplined, commanded by officers of their own
sex. Armed with light fusees, they mounted
guard regularly over the ladies' apartments, and

the vicinity of them, and are described as, on the whole, a very well set-up corps. It actually took the field when the Nizam waged the disgraceful war of 1793 against the Poonah Government."

The streets of Poonah are very striking to strangers; the exteriors of many of the houses are brilliantly painted with figures of gods and goddesses. Idols squatted under the peepul-trees. The very streets were named after mythological personages, and an endless stream of strange-looking people flowed up and down. The whole population of the place appeared to have turned out to breathe at ease once more after the sultry day. In the outskirts of the town stands a large Jaina temple, enclosed by walls, on which a whole pantheon of deities were disporting themselves. No Christian is allowed to enter its sacred precincts, but a door happened to be ajar, and as there was no one to interfere with us, we gazed unchecked into the sacred pile. It was profusely painted in rich dark colours, and bore no little resemblance to a Tartar building. Colonnades lined the oblong court, and there was a tank shaded by a banyan-tree. Poonah is the head-quarters of the once numerous Jain sect. I believe that years ago Lady Falkland visited the interior of this temple, and gives a description of it in a book called " Chow-Chow ;" but I have not been able to meet with it.

I was early on the terrace roof next morning, being anxious to obtain a good view of Singhar, before the air became dense with heat. It is one of the most renowned fortresses in all Máhratta. It is situated upon a conical hill, which appears to be perfectly isolated, but is, in fact, joined, by a narrow neck, to the great Schyadri Ghâts. It stands four thousand one hundred and sixty-two feet above the level of the sea. Its craggy triangular plateau, high walls, and strong towers, were so clearly defined against the pale green sky that I could scarcely believe that " The Lions' Den " was eleven miles away. It is, indeed, even in decay, a magnificent stronghold. In olden times, safe in its lonely strength and terrible precipices, no one thought of being surprised in it. Surprised, however, it was by one of Sevaji's heroic generals, on a starless night, the ninth night of the dark half of the moon, in the month of October. Three hundred Máhrattas escaladed its steepest point, and silently entered the fort. A desperate conflict ensued. " Har ! Har ! Maha Déo !" was the cry of the invaders. Not a man of the garrison submitted, and daylight found five hundred gallant fellows dead or dying, several hundreds having chosen the almost desperate alternative of venturing over the rock, and many were dashed to pieces in the attempt. The leader of the assault, Sevaji's favourite general, was killed, and upon hearing of the misfortune, his master is said to have exclaimed, "Alas! alas! the den is taken, but the lion is slain! We have gained a fort, but I have lost Tanaji Malusre!" Upon this occasion each private soldier was rewarded by the gift of a solid silver bangle.

CHAPTER V.

Travelling Arrangements in India—The Southern Cross—
The Travellers' Bungalow—Fakirs—Noble Banyan
Tree—Fishing in India—The Singadari—Orthography
of Indian Proper Names—Climate of Western India—
Ascent of the Kamski Ghât—The Magellanic Clouds
—Crossing the Koo-i-nor—Arrival at Sattara—Ruins
of the Fort—Labyrinths and Dungeons—Palace of the
Rajah.

IT was nearly five o'clock when we started on
our journey. I was all impatience to be
off, to see two hundred and twenty miles of
Indian country, with its strange people, native
towns, rural villages, and temples. To me
every bush by the roadside was a source of interest, because it grew in a quarter of the
world which my mind had been accustomed to
dwell upon as a far-away mystery. Our mode
of progression was by no means romantic. We
rolled along in a couple of very comfortable
britskas, drawn by horses, or tattoos (the
native pony), as the case might be. The three
grown-up people, and Mr. Bustle, occupied one

interior, the nurses and children filled the other; and on the box of each carriage a man-servant sat by the side of the driver, one being the cook, a very important person in Indian travel. In addition, each carriage was provided with a scantily-clad individual, who, smothered in dust, perched as he could upon the piles of bags and boxes strapped on behind. But appearances are deceitful, for with the exception of G——, who held the money-bags, he was out-and-out the most important personage of the party—he was the steersman. The coachman, whom I have mis-named the driver, held the reins, but the guard directed the horses whenever there was a difficulty. If we were likely to go over the side of the road, which on the level was frequently banked up, to get into a ditch, or to meet a cart, or if the Deccan ponies gibbed or ran away, an amusement to which they were equally addicted, this person was, or ought to be, at their heads in a moment. About every second port (a port being in general seven miles) the guard was changed. Some of these men were vigilant, others were sleepy, and once we had an unfortunate who was afflicted with leprosy, which was not pleasant, as he sat upon the luggage.

We were soon out of English Poonah, and

passing under the sacred hill of Parvati. The white temples upon its summit were flushed with rose colour, the ruined palace was bathed in light, and the glass still remaining in the horse-shoe window, from whence the last of the Peishwas beheld the total rout of his large army by a comparatively small English force, flashed in the rays of the setting sun. Even stern, black Singhar had caught the glow, and was dyed in glorious purple light. Our road lay across a tolerably fertile plain, bounded by the great ghât we were about to cross. It was nearly dark when we began to ascend. Our doors would fly open, and had to be secured by ropes; the wheels were very ricketty, and nothing would induce the candles to burn. Dick roared, so the hurricane-lamp was lit, and hung in the second carriage. There was no moon, but the night was clear and light. The road, which was excellent, was perpetually winding round sharp spurs of rock; and although every really dangerous part was protected by a substantial two feet wall, still, when one looked over it, and glanced down, far down, into the deep black gorges, the sight was enough to make one shudder. Many a camp-fire blazed upon the plain of Poonah, shining out at first large and brilliant, but waning as we mounted

higher and higher, until at last they appeared
as mere specks of red light, which finally vanished.   Near the top of the ghât we passed
through a long tunnel, with rows of lamps along
each side.   The ribbed brickwork with which
it was lined was admirable, and, as far as we
could judge, appeared to be the very perfection
of masonry.   We had climbed to another level
of the Deccan, and had no descent to encounter.

The horses were changed in the most leisurely
fashion.   The pauses were not unpleasant, as
we generally walked about the while, and
watched many a novel scene.   Rows of patient
horses stood in long open sheds.   Dim lights
flitted to and fro, glimmering upon big turbaned and ebony men; and when the harness-
ing really began, a great bundle of some dried
thorn was cast down and kindled.   Instead of
blazing up, it gave forth a glowing light, beautiful as a fire-work.   The rest of our night's
work lay under vaulted avenues of large-limbed
trees, with heavy foliage, which showered down
sweet blossoms upon our heads.   We came to
no harm, although they were mango flowers,
which play a great part in Hindoo mythology.
The mango flower is sacred to the God Káma,
the Indian Cupid.   He is supposed to be armed
with a bow of sugar cane, the string of which

consists of bees, and he bears five arrows, each tipped with the blossom of a flower, which pierce the heart through the five senses. His favourite weapon is that pointed by the mango flower. The beautiful double white jessamine, used at religious ceremonies, wreathes itself round this favoured tree, and is called "The Bride of the Mango." Here and there a giant limb had paid the debt of Nature, and through the space left open by its fall the extreme grandeur of the moonless sky became visible. The stars were wonderfully large and luminous, and shone with a calm, steady light. In the latitude in which we were now travelling, the twinkling effect observable in Europe is seldom seen.

We were a silent party, each thinking his own thoughts; and as I gazed upon that grandest of constellations, the Southern Cross, I for the first time realised that I was in the East. My somewhat solemn reverie terminated abruptly, when we turned down a narrow lane, and drew up before the travellers' bungalow, with the exciting reflection—what was to become of us if it was full? But, by a happy chance, three rooms were vacant; and our arrangements being quickly made, the supper we had brought with us was soon spread and demolished, and thankfully we sought repose upon the broad sofas, which, though not furnished with bedding, were capable of being made very comfortable.

I was awake with the birds, which were twittering away at a great rate. G—— had promised me a walk, in which we were to see a fine banyan-tree, populated by monkeys. In the verandah we paused for a moment to take a preliminary cup of tea, and look at the landscape before us, which was very pretty, with green hedges and fields, and far-stretching mango woods, lit up with such light-tinted blossoms as those whose influence we had escaped the previous night. The branching trees concealed the broad river which flowed at their feet, but not the bright brown line of hill which extended further away. We wended our way through the single long street of the little town, which we considered just too large to be called a village. G—— pronounced it to be exceptionally clean. To my unaccustomed eye there was much in its aspect that was strange and picturesque. Groups of dark people were squatted in the open huts, for they were little more, with possibly a dark chamber in their rear. Strange little altars, ornamented with rough patterns in red and yellow, were scattered about. There was a lofty tree, a sacred peepul-tree, with a wide circular ring of masonry around it, and a large, rough, red-smeared stone, with a wreath of flowers twined round it. Strange men—Fakirs—with plaited petticoats, and great fans of palm leaves, were loitering about, and no doubt extracting money from the pockets of the poor. To me all was new and interesting.

We took a country path, which brought us to the banyan, a noble tree, with a deeply-indented bole—in fact, a collection of boles grown together in all directions; brown tendrils were hanging down, anxious to root themselves, and spring forth in independent beauty. The leaf of this tree is large, a fine deep green, and very glossy; and the shade it casts is profound. The brightest sunbeam cannot penetrate through the dense foliage. But where were the monkeys?—we looked in vain, but not one was visible. It was no unusual disappointment—in other countries, at Gibraltar, in the glen of the Chiffa, and in Kabylia, I had been promised a similar spectacle, but with the same result. We pursued our way along the broken ground, which rose a few feet above the river Néra, a broad, swift, and by no means muddy stream, which caused G—— to sigh as the fish rose to the surface and spread circles in the water.*

---

* I believe the following remarks as to fishing in India

Half a mile brought us to a pretty range of
rock, green with many an unknown plant and
flowering shrub. A lively little stream came
tumbling over the boulder stones. It might have
been a Yorkshire beck; but looking down upon
it, instead of a spired church, there stood a
Hindoo temple, with a pyramidal roof, which
we climbed up to explore. It was a rude,
square edifice, lighted from the doorless entrance. A conical stone, " the Singa," occupied a
low platform in the centre. An intelligent-

---

to be true :—" If one only knows where to look for it, there
is certainly as good fishing to be got in India as in any
other country in the world. We once knew a brave old
gentleman in Northern India—who, by the way, used to
fish from an elephant—that pronounced India to be *the*
great fishing country—not altogether without reason, we
think. A writer in the *Field*, of October 9, 1869, speaks
of catching seven hundred and one pounds in five days with
the rod, in the Punjab; and in one day he landed three
hundred and thirty-eight pounds. The river was the
Punah, an affluent of the Jhilam, that rises in the Pir-Pan-
jal. This river, which is about a hundred and twenty
miles in length, is about the breadth of the Tweed at Cold-
stream; but the pools are deeper and the current more rapid.
The Mahsir, or Indian salmon, is the fish that affords the
best sport in this, as in every other river of India. It is a
grand carp that attains a weight of seventy pounds and
upwards, and affords more play to the angler, and as dainty
a dish to the gourmet, as the Spey or Ness salmon. The
Mahsir is often fished with a fly."—*Times of India Hand-
book of Hindustan, p.* 108.

looking young man, who, with the simple curiosity characteristic of Eastern manners, had followed us, said that it was not a real Singa —I suppose that meant a Singa not properly consecrated—adding, "that he, being a Mahomedan, thought it very strange that men should worship a stone." I ventured to remark, through G——, that some few did but regard it as a symbol, upon which he shook his head and fell back.

The Singadari are a distinct and very large sect of people, who are exceedingly stern and opinionated. They will not eat what has been cooked by a Brahman, and differ in their religious tenets, denying the doctrine of Metempsychosis, rejecting caste, and leaving in abeyance some domestic observances which are rigidly practised by other Hindoos. Professor Wilson believes the Singa to be the most ancient object of worship adopted in India, subsequently to the ritual of the Vedas, which was chiefly, if not wholly, addressed to the elements, and particularly fine. The Singadari do not in general burn their dead. They prefer burying them, and that in a sitting posture. A man of this sect is at once recognised by the silver box he carries at his side, containing the emblem of his faith, if not by a little silver relic-box, hung to a necklace of beads or berries. The very poor wear a stone wrapped up in a bit of cloth, suspended from the neck by a string.

On a ledge of rock close to the temple were ranged three colossal horses' heads, fairly carved in wood, and painted in glowing colours, the meaning of which I eagerly demanded. G—— was puzzled, and referred to our self-constituted guide, who informed us that they were ornaments, the prows of old barges which had glided for many a day up and down the placid river at our feet. The Néra is a charming stream, smooth and clear for many months of the year, but during the Monsoon it swells into a devastating muddy torrent. The short green herbage was stained with dark spots, which told the sad tale that it was the burning Ghât, the plateau from whence the charred bones of many "a rude forefather of the hamlet" had been cast into the purifying waters below. A few tombs were dotted about, mere steps of stone, with a pillar in the centre, memorials of those whose bodies had suffered cremation there, tributes from the living, which must soon lose their significance, for upon such stones no name is ever recorded.

Having nothing particular to do during the

heat of the day, I investigated the travellers bungalow. Small things interested me greatly, for they were now imbued with all the charm of novelty. It was a low bungalow, consisting of a ground-floor placed upon a raised platform, encircled by a wide verandah, completely shaded by the overhanging eaves and lattice work, in and out of which twined creeping plants. I was charmed to find a small self-sown sensitive plant, which I experimented upon to my heart's content. The interior of the bungalow consisted of three long rooms, scantily furnished, a table, a few chairs, a wide cane sofa, to serve as a bed, and, perhaps, some rough shelves, suspended from the white-washed wall, and a skeleton frame, intended to receive the metal basin, which the traveller is expected to supply, as well as a looking-glass, should he consider such an article necessary. To each chamber was attached a bath-room, lighted in a Saracenic fashion, open spaces being filled in by tubular tiles split in half, and placed in rows one above the other, forming a very effective pattern. If the road be much frequented, a messman is attached to the bungalow, whose duty it is to provide a simple meal if demanded, as also to lend linen and *couverts*, as our French friends would say. It sometimes happens, however, that no

messman is at hand, and that nothing edible
can be procured, in which case the wary traveller generally takes care to be provided
beforehand with tinned provisions, biscuits, and
liquor, as a stock to draw upon. Water is an
extra charge. Chambers cannot be occupied as
a matter of right for more than three days, after
which time the accommodation can be claimed
by other people. On leaving, each person pays
a shilling for the accommodation he has received
during twenty-four hours' halt. These bungalows
are generally placed at a little distance from a
town, and are now in much greater request
than formerly, the extravagant hospitality of
olden days having much declined. They are
surrounded by a couple of acres of ground, on
which the offices are placed. In India, the
kitchen is invariably some distance from the
house, as the odour of cooking would be intol-
erable in so hot a climate, and meals are in
consequence served upon hot-water plates.

Nothing to the stranger is more puzzling than
the orthography of Indian proper names, which
are too often rendered according to fancy on
maps, in books, at the post-office, and by the
friend whose aid you seek in a dilemma. At
our first halting-place I experienced my first
difficulty, in consequence of being unable to

determine whether it was called Sherwan, or Sherwell, or Sirwull, or any other similar variation that inquirers chose to put upon the sound with which their demands for information were answered. Some of the most accurate maps give the names of towns twice over, printed one above the other. This incongruity will, however, in time be remedied, for it has occasioned so much confusion in Government offices, that a book is about to be issued, and forwarded to all officials, giving the names of places according to a uniform rule—a measure which will be productive of great comfort to those who, like myself, find Hindustani words, of every kind and class, a perpetual stumbling-block.

I was sitting in the verandah, when a boy came up, carrying a little copper-coloured child, with great eyes, and a wild expression of countenance—altogether, such an uncanny-looking thing that I stretched out my hand to touch it, to see if it really was a baby. Away flew the boy on the instant to what he considered a safe distance, when he turned at bay, ready for another start if he found himself pursued. I mentioned the circumstance to M., who replied, "Of course he ran away, for in his opinion your touch would have polluted the

child.   Don't you know that the first rising in
the Mutiny was occasioned by a clergyman who
put his hand upon the head of a little Hindoo
child?"—a fact of which I very humbly professed my ignorance.   I was much rejoiced when
long shadows began to fall, and I saw signs
of packing, a task which was soon accomplished,
for it is one at which Hindoo servants are very
expert.

Like the camel driver in the song, "we had
many a mile to go,"—forty, I believe, before we
should be entitled to the supper and beds which
awaited us at Sattara, and we consequently set
off on our journey earlier than usual.   The
evening was beautiful, and we looked forward
with confidence to the continuance of such delightful weather—a confidence which is one of
the most pleasant features in the climate of
India.   One knows with certainty that for
months together, for so many hours of the day,
the wind will blow from east to west over the
heated plain, followed by the blessed change
which is produced by a cool breeze setting in
from the Indian Ocean.   In making so compre-
hensive an observation, I am aware that I am
falling into a somewhat loose manner of speaking, for there are as many different climates,
customs, and races in the 1,287,483 square

miles of its vast territory as in the whole of
Europe. The term, as used by me, refers to
Western India, the only part of the Peninsula
with which I have at present a personal acquaintance.

Before reaching that shelf of the Deccan in
which Sattara is situated, we had to ascend the
Kamski Ghât, which is exceedingly steep. We
changed horses at the foot of the pass, and
unfortunately got tattoos, which were addicted to jibbing. Although at first the ascent
was easy, unless backwards, the brutes again
and again refused to go forward, and more
than once came to a perfect standstill. G——
and the other men, along with volunteers collected on the road, had, after each pause, to
start the vehicle by main force. If at last the
ponies moved in the right direction, well and
good, G—— vaulted into the carriage and on
we went. If they did not, or there was a considerable drop on one side, M. had to scramble
out over the closed door, with her carriage cloak
in her hand, whilst I followed with Bustle
under my arm. I saw with satisfaction that,
however badly the horses behaved, they were
never flogged. Their only punishment was that
of being scolded in torrents of the harshest
Máhratta. The brutes at last gave up all idea

of the stable they had quitted, and then, beginning to turn their minds to the stable that was to come, went on, not, however, without continuing to indulge in some ebullitions of temper. As the road grew steeper and steeper, their pranks became dangerous, and we agreed that it would be best to get out and walk to the top of the ghât. The black gulfs below were profoundly deep, and the mountain spurs were rugged and abrupt; while our road was but a blasted path cut out of the crags. The night was very dark, and as the crescent moon had vanished long ago, we saw that beautiful appearance, the Magellanic Clouds, to great advantage; and the Milky Way—"the Great River," as the Arabs call it—was singularly bright. Still there was not sufficient light to make the road we traversed visible, and one of our men—Moideen (the Light of Religion)—alas! a perfect scamp—was obliged to guide us with the hurricane lamp. As we marched along in single file, the effect of our gigantic shadows thrown upon the smooth surface of the rock was exceedingly droll—M. and I, with our pointed hats, resembling nothing so much as a couple of witches on their way to a Sabbath meeting; G—— a burly giant; Bustle a bulldog on stilts; and the Light of Religion a stick

with a turban stuck upon it. If any poor super-
stitious Hindoo caught sight of the shadowy
procession without hearing our voices, he must
have been sadly frightened. When we reached
the post-house at the top of the mountain, we
were quite tired, and continued to be for some
time very anxious. We looked into the black
night, and neither saw nor heard anything of
the second carriage, concealed as it was by the
abrupt turns in the road, until it was close upon
us. We were thankful that we had no descent
to encounter.

One more trial awaited us, as we had to cross
the Koo-i-nor, close to its junction with the
sacred Krishna. During the rains the Koo-i-
nor is an impetuous roaring torrent, the terror
of the mail-cart. In dry weather it retreats into
its deep bed, leaving its broken cliffs and muddy
strand exposed. Bridge after bridge has been
built and washed away, consequently it has
either to be forded or crossed in a ferry-boat.
The easiest time for crossing it is when the
passage is made at full flood, the water then
rising level with the steep banks. The most
difficult is when the river is neither high nor
low, for then there is no secure landing for the
carriages ferried across the stream. G——
grew anxious as we approached the steep, tor-

tuous declivity, especially as it was very dark; and when the light we carried for a moment pierced the clouds of dust we raised, it disclosed a cliff with a crumbling brink, a precipitous descent, with no protection whatever. I believe that we owed our safety to the rush the horses made into the river, which they gained with a splash and a thud. M. grasped her cloak, I hugged my dog, and with the hands which were at liberty we clung to the vehicle, fully prepared for a ducking. The carriages rocked and bumped, but there were numbers of men at hand ready to steady them. The plunging of the struggling tattoos, the dancing lights, the momentary glimpses of the rushing river, the noise and shouting of the men, made it a scene of some variety, and of indescribable confusion. Not the least part of the difficulty lay in the steep gully the panting horses had to climb when the opposite side was reached. Half dragged by them, half pushed along through the pulverized mud, we did at last reach the level road. After we had arranged the carriage, we walked about to compose ourselves. The delay was tedious, but unavoidable, for an important package had slipped from its ropes, and was missing. At last, however, it was found, half buried in the dust of the opposite bank, and once more it was in our power to proceed. Having seated ourselves, the horn was blown, and the horses started, but, alas! mistook their direction, and wheeling round, made a rush down the steep track by which we had mounted. Their heads were seized, they were steadied for a moment, and once more we were compelled to lay hold of our precious possessions, and jump out. How the carriage was turned without being upset, I cannot say, but our unfortunate cook had his foot a good deal crushed. It was two o'clock in the morning before we reached our destination. I shall ever remember the river which flows from those mountains of light, the Koo-i-nor Hills.

When I awoke in the morning, I could scarcely believe that I was in Sattara. Sattara —I loved to caress the musical name, which sounded like that of an old friend, for there had M.'s year of Indian life been spent. In my faraway home hung a view of it, taken upon the spot. Many a time had I gazed at it with a yearning feeling, and now the reality was before my eyes. There, not a mile away, was the isolated mountain, with its craggy sides, ancient walls, and perpendicular precipices. It made me shudder to look at the narrow, tortuous ledge up which she had so often ridden her much-prized thorough-bred Deccan pony, laughingly declaring that his legs were much safer than her own. The grim battlements, even in clear early light, could scarcely be distinguished from the rock itself; still I could discern three out of the seven round towers from which the fort derives its poetical designation.

Sattara is a corruption of Sath-Istara—that is, the Seven Stars, or Pleiades. No fortress in all Máhratta has been more connected with the historical events of many centuries, and its Rajahs were among the most powerful of the Deccan princes. An ancient copper-plate, with an inscription, shows that it was founded in the year 1192. In due time it fell under the dominion of the Mahomedan kings, who reigned at Bejipur; but in 1673, after a protracted siege, it was captured by the great Sevaji, and afterwards, with its town, became the capital of the Máhratta Government. Six years afterwards, it was besieged by the Monguls, two thousand of whom perished by the inopportune explosion of one of their own mines. How the rocky mountain must have trembled! For hundreds of years was this spot dyed in blood, and over the perpendicular scarp, which I saw cutting the blue sky with so sharp an edge, thousands of victims had been hurled. Now the Seven Stars are ruined, the English having effected in an hour what neither time nor the enemy could accomplish. Its fate has been that of many a mountain eyrie. Its defences were blown into fragments by gunpowder—no unnecessary proceeding after the Mutiny, it being judged that, in case of another rising, the existence of these strongholds might be exceedingly dangerous.

M. and her husband, along with a friend, once spent a week in the fortress, choosing for their abode in it a very long room, probably the old banqueting-hall, which had been spared. Down the middle of this apartment ran a long line of pillars, connected with one another by light arches, made of hard dark wood, and beautifully carved. They brought up to it camp furniture, and partitioning off a room at each end, enjoyed themselves exceedingly. M. spent great part of her time in sketching, drawing the gateway, with the two fish, the emblem of nobility, carved above it, and the ruined temples. (There were originally sixteen of them, eleven of which were dedicated to Shiva, whose worship was that of a stern religion, and five to the cruel Bávane.) Only one of the number remains perfect, with a gilded image of the bloodthirsty divinity in a squatting posture. Nor did M. neglect the old tanks, and the fern-covered wells. Under the fort labyrinths of narrow ways lead to the dungeons—dark holes hewn from the hard-hearted black rock. What sufferings must have been endured in the bowels of this hill, outwardly so sunny and so free! There are also secret passages, by which access to the open country is obtained. These were constructed to afford means of escape in times of peril.

One of the legends attached to the place, although very horrible, is thought not unlikely to be true. It is said that when the fort was built a youth and a maiden were buried alive under the principal entrance. A circumstance which may not be improbable, when we remember that in many parts of India a belief in the efficacy of human sacrifice still lingers, and that this horrible practice is still perpetrated among the wild hill tribes, who have never yet been conquered by the Aryan race. The Mahrs, the supposed aborigines of the country, who still exist in the town of Sattara, at certain seasons of the year ascend to the fort in their gala dresses, and in a very cruel manner (too cruel to relate) sacrifice a buffalo in front of the temple.*

---

* Many of the Hindoo temples are small. It is considered sufficient if they are large enough to contain the idol, the officiating priest, and the sacrificial instruments.

The fort commands a beautiful view over a fertile plain, completely surrounded by hills of every varying form, swelling into mountains towards the west. Among the blue plateaus and peaks the lofty Ambali is a prominent object, a hill which, according to Hindoo mythology, was a pebble which slipped from a mountain that Hanuman (the monkey god) was carrying to help in making a bridge from India to Ceylon, in Rama's war with the monster-headed king of the island.

CHAPTER VI.

IN consequence of its mountainous ring we
found Sattara so hot that it was impossible
to venture out until the evening breeze set in,
when we took chairs and sat under the coolest
verandah. Numbers of scavenger eaglets were
swooping about, to the terror of the clucking
hens, who, the moment these birds appeared,
collected their broods and hid themselves.

Meanwhile, M. was surrounded by old servants, some of whom had come to make their
salaams, others in the hope of re-entering her
service. One of them, an old man, she declared
that she had never seen so amply clad. In

order to present himself he had borrowed a
cumlie, a narrow woollen blanket, sewed together, and put over the head, in which he was
wrapped up, in spite of the ninety-two degrees of
heat. M. had employed him in the capacity
of carrier. She had a partiality for strawberries,
a luxury not to be procured nearer than Mahá-
baleshwar, which, by the hill paths, was thirty
miles off. There and back, twice every week,
did the "old man" trot (he was probably under
forty), returning with baskets of rosy fruit,
and considered himself well paid in receiving ten
shillings a month, that is two and sixpence for
every journey of one hundred and twenty miles.
After a little conversation, it was agreed that he
should return to the service of his old mistress,
not as strawberry-carrier, but to look after the
dogs and poultry. But before he could leave
Sattara, his affairs had to be arranged, as he
was in debt, owing no less than seven shillings.
He accordingly received a small sum of money
in advance, with which he trotted off to Belgaum
at once with a beaming countenance. The
transaction took place in the Máhratta language,
which I thought sounded very harsh.

Late in the afternoon G——, who had been
occupied with his inspection all the morning,
returned with a carriage, and took me to see the

old palace. We drove through a wide street, in which endless numbers of respectable-looking people were taking the air, for by this time the sea-breeze had set in. The men were habited either in white, or partially enveloped in the duthi, or waist-cloth—a long piece of yellow-white cotton (the produce of a shrub which attains the height of some six feet), which is wound round the body, passed between the legs, and tucked in, in some mysterious fashion. The palace has, externally, only its size to recommend it, but it stands advantageously on a large open space, which had no doubt many a time been filled with Sevaji's fierce mountaineers. A few of the Rajah's soldiers were loitering under the colonnades. Near the entrance door was a large iron cage, which contained a panther, which G—— pronounced to be a remarkably fine animal. As we approached its cage, the animal's fierce eyes lit up with an angry glow, and it darted out its claw, hoping to catch G——, who stood unpleasantly near. This greatly enraged Bustle, and it was fortunate that I held him in a strong string, for our small champion made a rush towards the beast, and was all anxiety to attack it. The natives who were loitering around were much amused, and absolutely laughed.

We were received by a venerable-looking old gentleman, who spoke English perfectly. He at once conducted us into the vast audience-hall, which occupied the centre of the building. It was very lofty, supported on each side by finely-carved wooden pillars, forming colonnades. The side walls were pierced by lofty arches, now partially closed by lattice-work; outside these now ran narrow tanks, with water-works so arranged that on festive occasions one tall feathery jet would shoot up in the centre of each. Numberless lustres of various sizes, wrapped up in red cotton bags, were suspended from the ceiling of the hall. The effect when they were brilliantly lit up must have been very fine. The end of the saloon was occupied by a large square erection—the shrine in which the family deity was placed. All great Hindoo families have their familiar god or goddess, to whom they offer sacrifice, and look for protection. The frame of the temple was made of wood, the interior being hidden by hangings of the richest brocaded satin. The old man drew aside the curtains, and facing us, raised in a sitting posture upon a throne, we beheld a large cross-legged figure in silver—Sevaji's own Bhavani, appropriate goddess for the ruthless chief of a cruel age. She was represented with eight arms. Her oblique eyes seemed to regard us with sinister expression. She wore a nose-ring, necklaces, bracelets, and anklets, and had a conical head-dress. Her altar was dressed with green velvet, magnificently embroidered in gold.

In this sanctuary lay Sevaji's sword, which he called Bhavani, after his tutelar goddess, a weapon which is now an object of worship. Strewn about the daïs were the sacrificial vessels and instruments, consisting of dishes, lamps, cups, bowls, animals bearing upon their backs the lotus flower (probably for incense), and other articles, the use of which I could not divine. These various objects were in silver, beautifully chased, and probably very old, for in places the patterns were worn away. Parallel with the banqueting hall were long courts, surrounded by two-storied buildings, which had once been the ladies' apartments. The latticed window-sills of horse-shoe form, the balconies, the projecting beams, were of dark wood, finely carved with figures and foliage. These rooms looked down on the hall, which on grand occasions must have presented a charming *coup d'œil*. We lingered about for some time waiting to see the relics, and were invited to sit down upon a comfortable sofa, our conductor taking a chair.

There was a great commotion at this end of the hall. Men were running about with curtains, and carpets, and wooden frames. A play in the Máhratta tongue was about to take place. Suddenly three or four dignified-looking gentlemen made their appearance. Our guide arose, we bowed, and the Hindoos, salaaming with gravity and grace, passed on, and squatted down in a corner. They were relatives of the late Rani, and of the present occupant of the palace, whose position is still under the consideration of the English Government. The Rajah of Sattara, who died in 1848, having no son, immediately before his death adopted a boy, a usual mode of proceeding under such circumstances. Lord Dalhousie, however, struck Sattara out of the list of native states, bestowing liberal pensions on the Rajah's widow and adopted son.

At last the honoured relics made their appearance. The sword is a fine Fèrrara blade, four feet in length, with a spike upon the hilt to thrust with. The hilt will only admit a very small hand. It is a matter of surprise that so small a man as Sevaji is said to have been could have wielded such a weapon with the remarkable skill which has passed into a proverb. His precise stature is not known, but his weight is a matter of history, one of his popular acts having been that he was weighed against gold, and his weight was found to be equal to that of sixteen thousand pagodas (a gold coin so called from its being marked with a pagoda), which is equal to ten stone, the whole amount being distributed among Brahmans. The next object of interest was his quilted coat of peach-coloured satin, made to pass the knees, and which contained very fine chain armour; this was matched by a cap made with flaps, in order to protect the head. The united weight of the cap and coat was something amazing. This suit is said to have been specially made in anticipation of an approaching interview with his deadly enemy, Afzool Khan, but it was probably the ordinary array in which he went forth to the combat. The Máhratta troops always wore quilted vests, an excellent protection against sabre cuts, which we read of both in Egyptian and Grecian warfare.

Last of all we were shown the wagnuks, or tigers' claws, with which the western hero is said to have torn open the stomach of the envoy whom he went forth in amity to meet. The story to which these relics bear silent witness, is worth relating, in order to show by what treacherous means the Indian princes of the seventeenth century gained the undying applause of their fierce countrymen. We therefore extract the following passage from Grant Duff's "History of the Máhrattas "—

"The Mahomedan Afzool Khan was the ambassador of the Bijipur king, who ardently desired the destruction of the powerful Sevaji. He, however, diplomatically masked his hatred. His enemy pursued a like line of conduct, and it was arranged that an interview should take place between the envoy and the Máhratta prince. Sevaji prepared a place for the meeting at the foot of the renowed fortress of Pertabgurh. He cut down the jungle and cleared a road for the Khan's approach; but every other avenue to the spot was carefully closed. Fifteen hundred of Afzool Khan's troops accompanied him to within a few hundred yards of Pertabgurh, where, for fear of alarming Sevaji, they were desired to halt. Afzool Khan, draped in a thin muslin garment, armed only with his sword, and attended by a single armed follower, advanced in his palanquin to an open bungalow prepared for the occasion. Sevaji had made preparations for his purpose, not as if conscious that he meditated a criminal and treacherous deed, but as if resolved on some meritorious and desperate action. Having performed his ablutions with much earnestness, he laid his head at his mother's feet and besought her blessing. He then arose, put on a steel chain cap, and chain armour under his turban and cotton gown, concealed a crooked dagger, or beechwa (the beechwa, or scorpion, named from its resemblance to that reptile) in his right sleeve, and on the fingers of his right hand he fixed a wagnuk, a treacherous weapon, well-known to the Máhrattas. Thus accoutred, he slowly descended from the fort. The Khan had arrived at the place of meeting before him, and was expressing his impatience at the delay, when Sevaji was seen advancing, apparently unarmed, and, like the Khan, attended by only one armed follower. Sevaji, in view of Afzool Khan, frequently stopped, which was represented to Afzool as the effect of alarm, a supposition very likely to be admitted from his diminutive size.

" Afzool Khan advanced two or three paces to meet Sevaji, and when they were introduced, the treacheous Máhratta, while they were performing the customary embrace, struck the wagnuk into the bowels of Afzool Khan, who, quickly disengaging himself, clapped his hand on his sword, exclaiming 'Treachery and murder;' but Sevaji instantly followed up the assault with his dagger. The Khan had drawn his sword, and made a cut at Sevaji, but the concealed armour was proof against the blow. . . . A general scuffle ensued, the bearers had lifted the wounded Khan into his palanquin, when some followers of Sevaji's came up, cut off the head of the dying man, and carried it to Pertabgurh."

The wagnuk, or tiger's claw, is a small instrument of steel, made to fit on the four fingers. It has three crooked blades, which are easily concealed in a half-closed hand.

Along with the other relics were produced two of these weapons, one of which was furnished with four claws, while the other had but three. Before leaving the palace, I was allowed to make a hasty sketch of these terrible instruments. The story, with which they are connected, has been gathered into the folk lore of the Máhratta people, is chanted at many a feast, and taught to little children as soon as they can lisp. The use of the wagnuk in warfare has long since passed away, but it still figures in the amusements of some of the princes of the day.

Monsieur Roussellet, who visited the coast of Baroda in 1864 (during the reign of the lately deceased Gackwar's brother, and who has since published a magnificently illuminated volume of Indian travel), became still more famous after he was invited to attend

at an entertainment called the Naki-ka-
kausti, the combat with claws. The combatants, entirely nude, and adorned with
crowns and garlands, tore one another with
claws of horn; but "formerly," we are as-
sured by the French gentleman, "the claws
were made of steel, when the death of one of
the combatants was unavoidable." The steel
claws, however, have been suppressed, and
those of horn, which have replaced them, are
fitted into a kind of handle, which is fastened
to the closed fist of the right hand by means of
thongs. The combatants, intoxicated with
bang, rushed upon one another in a state of
fury outstripping all bounds, and with such
force that their necks and bodies were soon
covered with blood.

The Gaekwar was accustomed to stare at
this deadly struggle in a condition of such wild
excitement that he could scarcely restrain himself from imitating the movements of the combatants. The unfortunate one whose destiny it
was to bite the dust, was borne away, sometimes in a dying state, while the conqueror,
with the skin of his forehead hanging down
in shreds, would prostrate himself before the
Gaekwar, to receive from him a necklace of
pearls, and a richly embroidered dress.

Instead of returning through the town, we struck off into a quiet country road, passing close to a low stone building, which reminded me of one of our Kentish martello towers. It was the Parsee "Tower of Silence"—one of those abodes of the dead which no one, with the exception of the guardian, is allowed to enter, unless it happen to be empty. The reply, however, of a Parsee, when questioned upon the subject, throws some light upon their mode of proceeding :

"Our Prophet Zoroaster," he said, "who lived six thousand years ago, taught us to regard the elements as symbols of the Deity. Earth, fire, water," he said, "ought never, under any circumstances, to be defiled by contact with putrefying flesh. Naked," he added, "we came into the world, and naked we ought to leave it. But the decaying particles of our bodies should be dissipated as rapidly as possible, and in such a way that neither Mother Earth nor the beings she supports should be contaminated in the slightest degree. In fact, our prophet was the greatest of health officers, and following his sanitary laws we build our towers on the tops of the hills, above all human habitations. We spare no expense in constructing them of the hardest materials; and we expose our putres-

cent bodies in open stone receptacles, resting on
fourteen feet of solid granite, not necessarily to
be consumed by vultures, but to be dissipated
in the speediest possible manner, without the
possibility of polluting the earth or contaminat-
ing a single living being dwelling thereon. God
indeed sends the vultures, and, as a matter of
fact, these birds do their work much more ex-
peditiously than millions of insects would do if
our bodies were committed to the ground. In
a sanitary point of view nothing can be more
perfect than our plan. Even the rain water
which washes our skeletons is conducted by
channels into purifying charcoal. Here in these
fine towers rest the bones of all the Parsees that
have lived in Bombay for the last two hundred
years. We form a united body in life, and we
are united in death."

It is a pity that the great law-giver did not
promulgate a few more sanitary rules, for the
Parsees are in some respects the dirtiest people
in Bombay. Without exception they throw
every sort of refuse into the street before
their dwellings. It is an extraordinary fact
mentioned, but not explained, by Mr. Moor,
that "an expiring Parsee requires the presence of a dog in furtherance of his departing
soul."

The bodies are placed upon iron gratings, which slope downwards, so that eventually the remains fall into a pipe, and from thence into a pit beneath. Some people asserted that an upper grating protects the body from the assaults of birds, but such is clearly not the case. In the official report of the Bombay health officers, it is stated that it is disgusting to see the vultures swooping upon their prey, and carrying away pieces of flesh and bones. The vulture which haunts these spots is of a peculiar species, and it is said that the early Parsees actually imported them on account of the rapidity with which they accomplished their horrid task.

On the following day we had a treat, as we went to Máhuli, a celebrated spot of great beauty, where the rivers Krishna and the Yena unite. In India the junction of two rivers is always holy, and in this instance it is particularly so, for the Krishna is a very sacred stream—the most considerable of the five declared by the Brahmans to be sacred, which flow from the site of the temple of Múhá Déo, in the Mahabaleshwar hills, the fruitful birthplace of many rivers. The Lady Krishna, as she is called— for the imaginative Hindoo, with his love of symbolising, considers all rivers to be male or female—is regarded as the Deity Krishna, in the female form, and as such is worshipped during a course of eight hundred miles, finally emptying herself by herself into the Bay of Bengal. The basin of the Krishna is computed to be 94,500 squa re miles.

Our road lay under a shady avenue of pee-pul-trees. Religion in this country is so intimately bound up with the domestic habits of this people, that they worship not only Nature, in trees, flowers, and streams, but also the most ordinary objects. If no idol is at hand, the Hindoo will make a god of his earthen pitcher, which the Englishman looks upon merely as a useful vessel, while his Eastern brother regards it as the source from which he draws the spring of life, the type of his creator.

An endless throng of people flowed along in their gala dresses, so rich and various that I could scarcely believe that the scene which danced before my eyes was real. It was the 6th of March, a day on which, in this year, occurred a great festival in honour of Shiva, for these annual commemorations vary a little in time, as they depend upon the state of the moon. The story runs that on a certain night a mighty hunter took shelter in a bel-tree (a species of fig). To amuse himself he plucked branches and threw them by chance down upon a Linga stone, which so gratified Shiva that he immediately carried the hunter up to Kailás, his celestial abode.

The ceremonies had commenced on the previous night. The devotees fast during twenty-four hours, and pray in the temples with a Brahman, who pours water on the Lingham, the emblem of Shiva, which he also decorates with flowers. He then reads over the thousand names of the god, and at each name the votaries cast bel leaves upon the Lingham. The men were chiefly in white, and different castes wore turbans of different dimensions and material, some of them indeed being enormous. It requires considerable skill to coil this kind of head-dress into the proper shape. The rich Hindoo had stripes of silver or gold woven into his fine muslin. Those amongst the crowd who were worshippers of Shiva—and they greatly preponderated—had their peculiar sectarial mark—the terrible eye and the perpendicular lines painted in white upon their foreheads.*

---

* The Hindoo religion is split into two sects (which are again subdivided), the worshippers of Shiva, and the worshippers of Vishnu, who differ greatly from one another. It is supposed that the former is the most ancient; and many believe it to be mixed up with the superstitions of the conquered aboriginal tribes.

Many of the women were good-looking, or would have been so, had they not been disfigured by that most grotesque of ornaments—the nose-ring. They had smooth, dark, but not black skins, shiny with cocoa-nut oil, fine eyes, broad, but not ugly features, and a wealth of jetty hair, well greased, and ornamented with coronets of yellow flowers. They wore vests, sometimes of crimson, but so short as scarcely to cover the bust, and to leave the finely-rounded arm bare ; their only other garment being the national savi, a piece of cotton, a yard and a half in width, and eight or nine in length. Where this covering begins or ends I know not, it is so artfully wound round the waist, and passed between the legs, hips, and shoulders, sometimes also forming a scarf for the head. The intense though dusky hues of these savis, which are bordered with some colour affording the utmost contrast, are well calculated to set the native women off to advantage. If she is tall and shapely, the dress is decidedly elegant ; but woe be to her if she is fat, which, however, is fortunately seldom the case. When this costume is seen for the first time, the exposure of the leg above the calf, and part of the side, has a curious effect ; but, as I have before remarked, the dark skin is in itself a covering.

The Mahomedan women, of whom only the very poor appear upon the street, also wear the savi, but in such a manner as to reach the ankle. I was surprised to see even these unveiled women, as the faces of the same class in Turkey or Algeria would have been concealed. Up to a certain standing the Hindoo female has all the liberty of a European, but that point passed, she is more carefully secluded in the Zenana than the Turkish woman in the Harem.

The people of Western India are noted for their love of gold and silver ornaments, possessing nose-rings, and toe-rings, and ear-rings in abundance, sometimes half-a-dozen of the latter being stuck round the rim of each ear. Then they have necklaces, armlets, bracelets, and anklets, and sometimes handsome silver bands round the waist. Their workmanship is good, and the metal pure, but there is no variety in the designs, some of which, however, are curious. I never wearied of looking at the mothers, with their infants astride upon the hip, on which the little black things, all eyes, ride in the utmost security, in an attitude equally picturesque and graceful. The older children ran along innocent of clothes, which they do not wear until they are six or seven years of age, but they also were bedizened with silver.

On this occasion there was a fair at Máhuli, and all those who were returning from it were bringing home their purchases. The women and girls balanced upon their heads a brass vessel, called a loto, which has bulging sides, a narrow neck, and a very broad rim. It is not only used by the Indian women for holding water, but also as a market basket. They must be rather expensive at first, but they are handed down in families, and in the long run cost less than earthenware vessels would, considering the fragility of pottery. It was strange to see the children hugging brightly-painted idols to their bosoms instead of dolls, while many carried little shrines and altars instead of baby houses. Nor were they without their miniature lotos, which would very likely serve for the smoking incense with which they would fumigate their toy-god. The ever-shifting scene was bewildering. Had I possessed as many eyes as Indra, I could have employed them all.

The Ascetics, or Saints, with their wildly-rolling eyes, long tangled locks, and every bone in their wretched bodies visible, were horrible objects. It was formerly their pleasure to appear entirely naked, but government obliges them now to put on some clothing, which is probably regarded as a penance. Even these creatures were less objectionable than those whose sleek, well-nourished bodies were streaked with lime, or grey with funeral ashes, which they stick on with the juice of the banyan-tree. I felt quite angry at seeing beautiful garlands of fresh flowers round the bull necks of these degraded beings, and sincerely did I pity the emaciated horses which some of them bestrode. As a class, these men are horribly vicious, and are in possession of large sums of money, which they often bury, thus explaining how it is that treasure is so often found concealed in this country. Some fine elephants, with trappings of scarlet and gold, came along with stately step, carrying Hindoos, who were the petty chiefs of the neighbourhood, and possibly their wives, in the latticed howdahs, which were carefully closed. The well-to-do Bunneah class rode their tattoos with an air of great importance, each man attended by a servant on each side, and an umbrella-bearer in the rear. If very rich, the beast on which he rode would surely be spotted or piebald, animals so marked being very dear to the native heart.

On reaching our destination, we paused to take breath under a noble banyan-tree, but no repose of mind was to be obtained under its shade. It was a self-contained little world.

Suspended from its branches were hundreds of black objects, exactly resembling large shrivelled up kid gloves—flying foxes, huge bats, who had hooked themselves up to rest after a night of thieving and shrieking; and there were swarms of white-faced monkeys, whose antics were most amusing. Throughout India the Sattara monkeys are renowned for their size and wisdom. They flew from branch to branch, seemingly regardless of the little ones, who clung round their necks. All at once they caught sight of us, and recognising us to be strangers, began to grin, and chatter, and hiss. When their anger was a little expended, they clasped their arms round their babies, and swinging themselves from bough to bough, sought for a place of greater safety at the top of the tree. These monkeys, being sacred animals, and under the protection of the Brahmans, are never molested. I could have watched them for hours instead of minutes, their movements were so animated and amusing,

Near the tree, raised on a high platform, stood a pile of buildings, which I in my ignorance took to be a cluster of temples; but the apparently separate parts, each with its stepped roof, formed one harmonious whole. It was a Jaina temple, with the peculiar architecture of which I afterwards became better acquainted. Long bands of white woollen were stretched from one part to another. We were allowed to stand and look into the open hall, which was supported by curiously-carved pillars. We saw that it contained a throne, on which squatted a Buddha-like figure, with folded legs. It was surrounded by lights, wreathed with flowers; the air was heavy with incense, and the divinity looked down with a hideous leer upon the devotees who were performing their puji (worship), bowing their heads to the earth, and then, standing upright, raising the closed palms of their hands above their heads.

The scene from the high bank above the river was beautiful as well as striking. The sharp spit of land which seemed to oppose the union of the Lady Krishna with the Yena was the holiest of ground. Upon it was erected a large open shrine, with a Lingham in the centre (more than one sect appeared to celebrate this festival). It was adorned with ropes of flowers, and heaps of blossoms brought by the votaries were piled around it. They also performed their puji, and threw small coins into the dishes held by the officiating priests. On each side of the broad clear stream formed by the united rivers were groups of temples. One sacred building

which stood alone is said to have been founded
in the sixteenth century by a banker at Sattara,
a lucky man, who chanced to discover a large
cavity filled with treasure. In three places fine
broad flights of steps, like our mountain friends,
called ghâts, and for the same reason, descended
to the water. In some parts of India these
ghâts are built with great architectural magnificence, and even here the monotony of the
wide stairs was broken by handsome balustrades.
A little above the level of the water was an
irregular piece of ground, the burning ghât, or
place of cremation, dotted over with pyramidal
tombs, memorials of the rich whose bones had
been collected upon the spot, and thrown into
the sacred waters beneath ; and, awful thought,
on this spot hundreds of women had suffered
suttee. Half imbedded in the sand lay the
sculptured form of some colossal animal, probably a bull, but worn past all knowledge by
hundreds of monsoons.

The previous year the Rani of Sattara, scarcely
a middle-aged woman, had succumbed to her
love for cherry-brandy, and G—— was present
at her funeral procession and cremation, which
occurred here by torch-light. The dead woman
was seated in an open palanquin, and the lurid
glare played upon her face, and lit up the jewels

with which the corpse was magnificently adorned. In front walked her adopted son, clad in
yellow garments. The funeral pyre consisted
of sandal and other sweet-smelling woods,
with costly gums and precious essences, the
whole saturated with fine oil. Her costly
robes and precious ornaments were removed, she was gently laid upon the pyramid,
and her son, with averted head, fired the com-
bustible mass, from which soon shot forth flames
that concealed the corpse from the gaze of
the bystanders. The pyre was watched for
many hours, after which the Brahmans collected
the bones into a silver dish, and, with prayers,
they were committed to the holy keeping of the
sacred Krishna.

By the side of the road there stood, on wheels,
a wooden erection of considerable dimensions.
It rose in shelves, which were supported by
slender, carved pillars. We were not invited to
inspect the gaudy paintings with which it was
covered, for it was a car of Juggernath, and the
designs depicted on such vehicles are often
exceedingly impure. Interesting as were the
scenes around, we were not sorry to leave them
behind. The sun was hot, the colours and
movements of the ever-shifting crowd dazzled
the eyes, and the incessant beating of the cy-

lindrical drum, the clang of the cymbals, and the squeaks and groans of some instrument sounding like a bagpipe, made us feel as if some accompanyist were beating time upon our heads. The musicians who play upon these instruments are a race apart, supposed to be descended from some of the aboriginal tribes. They have played their part in history, and sometimes these bands have had lands and forests allotted to them, which has brought about local wars. They were ill-favoured black men, with features rather of the Negro than the Hindoo type.

As we were returning home, G—— pointed out a large pile of rough brickwork, an unfinished temple, on which a fabulous sum of money had been spent by the late Rani. It was erected to the memory of a favourite white elephant, drowned in fording the Krishna during the rains. White elephants are highly prized in India, not on account of anything beautiful in their appearance, but simply because they are rare. The absence of the colouring matter in the skin and eye produces this albino species. A spurious sort of white elephant is produced by the constant grooming of the skin with pumice stone.*

---

* The Burmese believe that such animals are transmigrating Buddhas, and revere them accordingly. An amusing

The people of Sattara are a primitive race, and have retained more of the manners and customs of their ancestors than the inhabitants of any other part of the Indian peninsula. They have a rich folk-lore of old border songs and stories, which they chant and sing in minor keys at their festivals, as they did in the war-like times which have passed away. Although the task would not be without difficulty, it is a pity that no attempt is made to collect these relics of ancient poetry. It could, however, only be done by some one not only conversant with the old Máhratta language, but also popular enough with the people to gain their con-

account of one of these sacred animals is given by Mr. Frank Vincent, in his amusing book, " The Land of the White Elephant." "One of the proudest titles," he says, "of the King of Ava is, ' Lord of the White Elephant.' The Mandalay animal I found to be a male of medium size, with white eyes, and a forehead and ears spotted white, appearing as if they had been rubbed with pumice stone or sand-paper, but the remainder of the body was as black as coal. He was a vicious brute, chained by the fore-legs in the centre of a shed, and surrounded by the adjuncts of royalty, gold and white cloth umbrellas, an embroidered canopy, and some bundles of spears in the corner of the room. The attendants told me that a young one, captured in the most eastern part of British Burmah, near Taunghoo, had recently died, after a short residence in the capital, and that the king had been out of sorts ever since. The animal was suckled by twelve women.

fidence. The elements of secretiveness and suspicion, which appear to be inherent in the Hindoo character, have been cultivated for ages by these mountaineers, who have ever opposed force by cunning. Their lives have always depended upon their vigilance, and to this day no stranger, should he ask the most trivial question, would receive a simple, straightforward, truthful answer.

CHAPTER VII.

SHORTLY after leaving Sattara, we had a
charming view of the Seven-Starred Fort,
and of the fortifications which crown some of
the adjacent hills. The country was wild and
pretty, and, according to M., delightful for
riding. Not a group of the many trees which
dotted the green downs, not a swelling hill
which gave variety to the landscape, with which
she was unacquainted. Our drive would have
been delightful, had it not been for the careless-
ness of our driver, who many a time drove us
dangerously near the edge of the road, from
whence there was a deep descent. On one occasion we felt sure that an awkward upset was

inevitable.   The front wheel was fairly over the brink, and we had just time to jump out, when, being lightened of our weight, the struggling horses were able to pull the carriage across the road.   The other carriage not coming up quickly, we were anxious as to its safety ; but our anxiety was soon relieved by its appearance.   Then we had to ford an awkward river, the bridge over which had been swept away during the last monsoon.   The night was as dark as pitch, but a hundred torches threw their fitful light upon the dangerous stream, where numbers of men were at work upon a new bridge, cheering their labours by singing in chorus.   They were a wild set of people. We were thankful when we got safely across, and were again on our way.   Camp fires blazed at intervals in sheltered spots near the road. Great waggons were drawn up in semi-circles, and peaceful bullocks jingled their bells as they munched their hay, whilst their drovers stretched themselves near the flames, baking rough cakes, or watching the grain simmering for their evening meal.   These tranquil scenes, these quiet peeps into native life, were very pleasant.

Before reaching Koohad, which we did not do until the small hours, we were disturbed by the prospect of crossing another river ; but happily we had no trouble this time, as it was spanned by a magnificent bridge of many arches. The morning's light shone upon a plain covered with tombs. Fine domes arose at a little distance, and in their midst was a building, which looked like a fortification. This was delightful, for, having a clear two hours before me, I obtained leave from G——, and set off along with Bustle upon an exploring expedition. I found myself in a vast cemetery, in which there were acres and acres of crumbling monuments. In one spot I thought that I recognized the Hebrew character upon the sloping stones peculiar to Jewish places of interment. Further on a large raised platform, enclosed by a breast-high wall, arrested my attention. I climbed a handsome flight of steps, which led to the open entrance. The tombs within were large, but no inscription, no carving, told their tale. As they rose in steps, however, I took them to be Hindoo memorials. These special burial-grounds were but spots compared with the vast extent of ground, containing thousands of Mahomedan graves, which spread around, a very city of the dead. These graves bore no resemblance to the turbaned monuments of the Turkish Moslem. Still less was their resemblance to the few rough stones,

misplaced by the jackals, with the bit of splintered rock at the head, which marks the grave
of the Arab. Here, over the rich man's dust,
rose the patterned dome and the fretted
minaret, one of which in particular struck me
as being exceedingly beautiful. It consisted of
four lofty pointed arches forming a square, and
set upon an estrade, and it was crowned by
a low dome, half hidden by tufts of the Indian
fig and the trembling mimosa. There were
three monuments in the interior—plain and
rude structures. It is strange to see so much
richness of architecture lavished upon these
dwellings of the dead, when their immediate
coverings are often appallingly barbarous, the
white plaster above being often moulded into a
ghostly resemblance of the form beneath. This
cemetery was evidently the occasional resort of
living Hindoos, for here and there, marked by
stones, were circles, in the centre of which rude
shrines, formed of slanting slabs, sheltered a
shapeless red-daubed stone, before which the
poor idolater had made his meal of grain or
cocoa-nut, after offering the first portion to his
god. The nearer I got to the building, which
I was determined to reach, the more was I
puzzled by its appearance.

As I threaded my way round groves, and

avoided great bushes of prickly pear and strange thorny shrubs, two beautiful white doves kept flitting across my path. The natives of India, both Mussulman and Hindoo, believe that the souls of the recent dead thus dog the footsteps of the living, and take due cognizance of human affairs. That such a superstition exists in China we know from the pictured story upon the Wedgwood plate ; and the Russians affirm that for three weeks the soul of a deceased relation hovers about the house, in order to satisfy himself that he is sufficiently mourned by those from whom he is now separated by an impassable gulf. A very unpleasant idea! A white vulture next came swooping from above, perhaps with the idea that Bustle would make a delicate morsel. The doggie, being intent upon his own affairs, did not seem to perceive the bird of prey. He started a fine hare, pursued it until I thought that he would be lost, and when puss suddenly disappeared into a hole, he stood transfixed, with a look of comical surprise.

At last I reached the object of my curiosity, but was still unable to form any conjecture as to its probable use. The building consisted of a lofty brick wall, with a funnel-shaped tower at each end. I reckoned its length to be about two hundred feet, and it was two or three feet thick, while there was a narrow path along the top. Passing through a small aperture right in the centre of the wall, I faced round, and found myself before a highly ornamental screen. The only projection was in the centre, where an imposing flight of stone steps led up to a platform, at the back of which, let into the wall, was a fine-pointed arch of stone, a kind of niche, which was walled up to a certain height, in order to form a shelf or seat. Eight high-pointed stone arches, four on each side of the steps which were formed in the wall, ornamented the base of the building, and a row of miniature arches, connected together above them, ran the whole length of the screen. The edifice was beautifully finished by patterned edging. The brickwork was worthy of the best period of Rome, and the pale grey stone let into the time-subdued red wall had a charming effect. It was certainly a very fine piece of architecture.

I afterwards learned that this building was called an Idgar, and that it was used for certain Mahomedan services, divided into smaller and greater Ids. G—— told me that insignificant erections of this sort were common in India, but that he had never met with so fine a speci-

men as this which I described to him. These
Idgars must, I think, be peculiar to the East.
I had never met with anything resembling them
either in Turkey or in Northern Africa. The
existence here of one of peculiar merit, and the
vast size of the cemetery in which it stood, were
explained when I came to know, alas! too late,
what an important part Karhad had played in
the early Mahomedan dynasty, which ended in
the middle of the twelfth century. My attention, indeed, was attracted by two tall towers
which rose above the houses of the town,
scarcely a mile away, and I feel a blush of
shame at having betrayed my ignorance by
asking if they belonged to some sort of manu-
factory. My excuse must be that in spite of
the antiquity of these towers, which had existed
for at least eight hundred years, they did indeed bear a striking resemblance to the chim-
neys of a cotton mill.

There is nothing striking in the scenery
between Karhad and Kolhopur, but the country
is well cultivated. We saw many villages half
hidden in foliage—the huts, indeed, were
scarcely visible, so comfortably were they
covered by their steep-pitched roofs. There
were fine trees by the road side, principally
mango and Indian fig. The Government is

very strict respecting these avenues, which afford so delightful a shade to the traveller. No man, even on his own ground, may cut timber within a certain distance of the highway.

Our progress was very enjoyable until we came to a good-sized river, which had to be forded, and the passage of which was accomplished amidst the usual tremors, noise, and confusion. In consequence of the delay we did not reach our destination until two in the morning, and as we were to spend two days at Kolhopur, and expected visitors who were sure to come early, we had to rise betimes, in order to get one of our two rooms ready for their reception. The weather was very hot, and as soon as the last caller had departed, we were glad to rest until the evening breeze sprang up. We then set off to see the sights of the town.

Kolhopur is a large native state, which is at present under the management of the English, as the Rajah is quite a boy. He is entitled to a salute of nineteen guns, the status of a native prince being indicated by the number of guns in his salute, ranging from nine to twenty-one. Kolhopur boasts of possessing in its government school one of the handsomest modern buildings to be found in all India. It is built of fine grey stone, in the Saracenic style, and fully deserves its high reputation for architectural beauty as well as learning. We were conducted over it by two grave-looking elderly men, said to be famous scholars, and employed in the establishment as teachers of Sanskrit. A knot of pupils followed in our wake—intelligent-looking young men, who spoke English with facility, but did not always understand the questions put to them. They were handsome boys, probably Brahmans, judging from their pale brown complexions. Their costume was of spotless white, and they bore upon their foreheads the dreadful eye, in red or yellow, placed between two perpendicular lines, which denoted the sect to which they belonged.

The centre of the building is occupied by a spacious lecture-hall, with an open roof of teak wood; a balustraded gallery, splendidly carved in arabesques, runs round the interior. From this gallery sculptured doors of equal beauty open upon various apartments. At the end of the hall there stood a marble bust of the late Rajah, who died in Florence at the early age of twenty-three. Many people may remember the interesting accounts which appeared in the English papers of the period respecting the curious ceremonies which accompanied the erection of the costly funeral pyre by the banks of the Arno, on which the rite of cremation was performed. This prince was a highly enlightened man, and a great loss to his people. The bust, which gave one the impression of being a likeness, was good in an artistic point of view. It was both modelled and worked by a native of Kolhopur. We questioned the pupils as to the abilities of the young Rajah, and asked if he was acquainted with Sanskrit. They looked grave, shook their heads, and when pressed, said, " No, only with a little English—nothing else." We afterwards heard that the young gentleman was a very naughty boy indeed, and exceedingly sly, giving his English tutor a world of trouble ; but as he is only about twelve years old, he has time to amend his ways. He is educated along with another young prince, the Rajah of Sawant-Wadi.

We were ushered into a fine library and reading-room, and I was amused at seeing Dr. Oswald's works placed next to " Vanity Fair," and speculated as to what the Hindoo boys would make of Becky Sharp. The education in these government schools, it is scarcely necessary to remark, is purely secular. Still attended by our suite, we were taken up to an adjoining roof, which formed part of the palace, from which we looked down upon the quadrangular court and surrounding pile of buildings. The space enclosed was of considerable extent, and is used for reviews, and sports of various sorts. It was a queer old place, rudely painted in stripes of many colours, in which red predominated, and was undergoing the reparation which it sorely needed. The mother and widow of the late Rajah live in a low bungalow, erected upon the flat roof of the vast audience-hall. It was painted blue and white, and had an air of homely comfort; the lattice-work around was covered with creepers, and the terraces set with shrubs and pretty flowers in pots. Closo at hand, in a dark chamber with an open door, there reposed two immense kettle-drums, which are used on festive occasions.

We were next invited to ascend a winding staircase leading to a small platform, which commanded an extensive view both over the town and the surrounding country. The narrow streets teemed with white-clad men, duskily robed women, having glittering lotos on their heads, and naked children; the wooden houses looked poor and dark. Kolhopur is a walled town, with five gates, which are closed at night, and guarded by day. The one by which we had entered was surmounted by a lofty Saracenic arch. Away from these busy haunts were several large houses, surrounded by stately groves of mango, and tamarind, and palm-trees. They, like the palace, were profusely decorated in bright colours ; but by far the most interesting spot in the whole place lay at our feet. It was a Jaina temple, covered in by three separate graduated roofs, one of which was surmounted by a spire, indicating the cell of the idol. The building was enclosed by colonnades of pillars, and the whole was carefully hidden from the public gaze by a high wall. In the far distance spread the shimmering waters of the tank, or lake, on the banks of which were groups of white temples, shaded by sacred trees. We drove there afterwards, and did not find that we were rewarded for our pains.

Kolhopur is situated upon bare, undulating downs—pretty, it may be, when the rains have renewed their carpet of green, but looking utterly desolate in their present dried-up condition. Returning home, we passed the newly-made Badminton ground and Government gardens. They were pretty and shady, advantage having been taken of a group of noble old trees; and the soil evidently suited the double-pink and red geraniums which grew in

rich clumps. We were not able to examine the
other flowers, having to hurry to the bungalow
in order to dress for a dinner-party.

Our next day's start was later than usual.
G—— had his Arabs up to try for the first
time. M. accompanied him, but being no heroine, I declined to join the expedition. About
half an hour before we left, a heavily-laden carriage drew up. The top was piled high with
bassinets and cribs, and bedding and baths;
and the inside was a very hive, out of which
poured innumerable small children. I think
that their number must have been made up of
twins or triplets. A scene of utter confusion
ensued—the outgoing baby roared, the incom-
ing baby screamed, the nurses and ayahs got
into a muddle with their bottles and baskets,
and all talked at once at the top of their
voices. Great was the excitement, and in the
very midst of it another large vehicle came
bowling up, with a solitary individual—a host
in himself, a red-nosed, irate colonel. When
told that he was too late to obtain shelter, his
wrath was amusing. "It was the third time,"
he said, "that he had found this very bungalow
full, and the authorities should hear of it." The
bystanders laughed, the warrior shot withering
glances from under his shaggy brows, bowled

away, and was lost to sight in a vast cloud of dust. The calm which ensued when we were once off was perfectly delightful.

Kolhopur is a large military station, but the people condemned to live there are, during the hot season, sincerely to be pitied. Provisions, too, are scarce. Mutton is not to be got; the beef is very indifferent; and it is impossible to procure a tolerable supply of vegetables. As we passed along, all the bushes and small trees were shrouded in dust, and were either dead or appeared to be so. There were, however, some signs of future growth, as people were busy planting out slips of sugar-cane, but only in places which could be irrigated. The evening was very fine, and when night came on it was still so clear that we could see with great distinctness far-distant objects. The crescent moon, too young to obscure the calm, steady light of the stars, soon sank behind a low line of hill, and we lay back, enjoying the scene in silence.

While we were enjoying the cool sea breeze which had succeeded the cruel heat of the day, we fell over suddenly on one side, with an alarming bump. My dog was in my lap. As we did not know what was about to happen, G—— jumped out, and we scrambled after him. Our wheel was off, and it was four miles to any station. The second carriage immediately came up, and its contents being disgorged, we all sat down in a string by the side of the road. Two passing peasants were hailed, and all the men set actively to work to repair the mischief, the box of the wheel having gone wrong. The light of the improvised torches cast their glare upon red turbans, dark faces, glittering eyes, and teeth of dazzling whiteness. How a Dutch artist of old would have delighted to paint such a scene. We strayed about until we were tired, and the children were sent to their slumbers. It was a pretty spot, close by a great banyan-tree, which cast a deep black shadow in the distance; low hills were clearly cut against a greenish background, and on a plot of grass away from the road a huge boulder-stone was set upright upon a pivot, perhaps so placed by hands which had been dust for centuries. We did not dare to sit near the tree, for fear of snakes, so we nestled down by the boulder, and watched the progress and decline of a fire in the distance, which we imagined to be that of a bungalow burning. At first the flames shot up vigorously, but at last they died down, leaving behind an ardent glow and a bright spot, the brilliancy of which gradually declined, till it disappeared altogether.   Then the post, who came galloping by, stopped for a moment to give advice, but offered no assistance, and tore away into darkness.   We then turned our eyes to the sky, and gazed at Orion, and the ever-glorious Southern Cross, which stood erect before us.

We were soon again *en route*. Nipani, the next place to which we came, is a town of some historical interest, as for centuries its powerful chiefs had waged constant and fierce war with their neighbours, their principal feud being with the Rajahs of Kolhopur and the chiefs of Belgaum, and in 1796 matters were going so badly with the reigning Desay, or Nipanikar, that Major-General Campbell was ordered by General Wellesley to march to his relief. In consequence of this timely assistance, the Nipanikar for a time co-operated with the English, but still continued at enmity with his Kolhopur neighbour, whom in 1808 he totally defeated, taking five thousand men, and all his cannon, colours, and elephants, the Rajah himself being sorely wounded.   But the struggle continued, and after a time was found to be so troublesome to other states, that the Peishwa, then supreme in power, not only insisted upon peace, but arranged a marriage between the Desay of Nipani and one of the Kolhopur princesses. The marriage was celebrated at Kolhopur, but a considerable gloom was cast over the festivities by the sudden departure of the Nipani chief, who, suspecting treachery, decamped in the night, along with his bride. Time went on. The Nipanikar outwardly supported the English, but it was known that he meditated treachery.

Strange stories of the Desay's cruelty, originating, no doubt, in the fear he inspired, are still current in the neighbourhood. On one occasion he is said to have amused himself by making several young and beautiful women stand side by side on a narrow balcony without parapet, overhanging one of the deep reservoirs of the palace. Passing along inside the line of trembling women, he would suddenly thrust one of them headlong into the water below, in which he would watch her drowning struggles, and gloat over her dying agonies.

In 1831 the Nipanikar endeavoured to impose a supposititious child on Government as his heir, but the fraud was discovered. It came to light that one of his wives, Táy-Báy, had been taken to a house in Nipani, on the pretence that she was about to bear a child. A widow who expected soon to be delivered was conveyed to the same abode. When the child, a boy, was born, he was placed in Táy-Báy's arms, and given out to be her offspring. The widow was murdered, and information was given by the owner of the house in which the affair took place, but he soon after died with suspicious suddenness. His story was confirmed by the discovery of the widow's body. Government, in consideration of the Nipani chief's age, and of the services he had rendered to the British army in 1800 and 1803, did not accede to the recommendation of the political agent immediately to confiscate his saringam, or territories, but determined to punish the Desay by declaring that the estates were to lapse after his death, and that no son of his body or of his adoption would be recognized as heir to the saringam, though he would be allowed to inherit the chief's personal property. General Munro writes thus respecting him :

"He is too wary, and has still too many possessions, acquired almost entirely from his connection with the British Government, to run any risk of losing them. He is, besides, not ignorant that he is detested by the inhabitants of jaghirs (villages and the lands attached to them), for his opposition and wanton cruelty. During the late campaign I received invitations from most of the villages to take possession of them."

At last the Desay became so unmanageable that General Munro determined to march on Nipani, intending to lay siege to the fort, unless the Desay agreed without reservation to the terms he proposed. This compelled the Nipanikar to submit, which he did immediately on the arrival of the army before Nipani. He had from the beginning of his career pursued a system of throwing into prison all the rich inhabitants, not only of his own districts, but of every district in which he obtained temporary authority, with a view of extorting money from them, and of seizing and keeping in confinement the women the most remarkable for their beauty. Many of these unfortunate people had been in prison ten or twelve years, and many had died every year from the cruel treatment to which they were exposed. When General Munro was near Nipani, he heard only of a few prisoners, whom he ordered to be released, but when he marched from the place he learned that about three hundred remained in confinement. He wrote to the Desay, commanding him to release them, and many were set at liberty, but by no means all. The General therefore directed that some of the villages on the south bank of the Krishna should not be restored until all the victims of the Desay's tyranny were released.

The Nipani Desay had for some time past been failing in health. He was very infirm, and subject to fits, under which, for a time, he completely lost his reason. On June 28th, 1839, he died, having previously adoped Morar Ráo, the son of his half-brother, as heir to his private estates. No sooner was he dead than his six widows began to quarrel over the property. The eldest had the custody of the heir, and the five others kept up continued complaints against her. She died at the end of 1840, and the management of the property was entrusted to the rest of the widows. Two of the remaining ladies induced the boy's father to seize his son, adopted by the late Desay, and with the aid of the Arabs, whom to the number of five hundred the Nipanikar had kept in his service, to take possession of the fort and set the authorities at defiance. The aid of the military had to be called in, and the fort, being attacked on September 20th, 1841, surrendered on the following day, and was afterwards dismantled at the expense of the young heir, who had to pay also the whole cost of the expedition. This story of crime and intrigue, abstracted from the records of the Bombay Government, I have been induced to give, in spite of its length, as illustrative of the state of Máhratta family life even in this century. Not a castle-crowned hill in all the Deccan but could tell of similar atrocities.

The travellers' bungalow at Nipani stands in the shade of the ancient fort. There were masses of ruined battlements, scattered into wild confusion by gunpowder, not fifty yards from my chamber window. I was not long before I threaded my way amongst them, peeped down into the deep ditch, and climbed the fragment of a bastion still *in situ*. Its grass-grown summit was strong even in decay. From my lofty perch I commanded a complete view of the crumbling walls, to which Nipani once owed its troublesome strength. Acres and acres of ground, once covered by buildings, were now abandoned to a few straggling herds of cattle, who were trying to keep life in them by munching the sun-scorched herbage.

I was pondering upon the past, and Bustle was intent upon a tit-mouse, when M. and G—— came forth and beckoned to me. There were but two buildings in the whole *enceinte*— the Travellers' Rest and a great square pile of brick in the distance, the wicked Desay's ruined palace. It had not at all the appearance of an Eastern building, but more resembled Hampton Court, seen from a distant reach of old Father

Thames, than anything else. Not being able to pursue a straight path towards it, we had to search for gaps in the green walls of prickly pears, formidable barriers, from which I bore away a six weeks' remembrance in the shape of a fine sharp thorn. These plants were covered with flame-coloured fruit about the size of eggs, the sweet, mawkish substance of which was so well armed by nature against the hand of the wayfarer that it needed no other protection. In Spain, and probably in India, this fruit is made into little cakes, stained in every variety of colour, and pressed into elegant shapes. beautiful to look at, but dust and ashes in the mouth.

Passing under a lofty archway, we entered the palace, and as we rambled over the building we saw sufficient indications to lead us to the conclusion that it had never been completely finished. The great beams of teak and other wooden fittings were finely carved, and some vacant places suggested the idea that some of them had been removed. There were vast, echoing corridors, and on each side, hollowed out of the thick walls, were cells, unprotected by the doors which had once secured them. These recesses were scarcely four feet in width, and no adult could have stood upright in them.

Miserable must have been the lot of the poor cramped victims of the Nipani's cruelty who were imprisoned in them. The Desay had evidently had a fondness for tanks, there being two in front of the palace, two in the centre court, and two in a cloistered court beyond. They were very ornamental, still full of water, and surrounded by broad copings of sculptured stone. One, which was overhung by a balcony, we supposed to be that into which the wretched old man was wont to hurl the victims of his capricious cruelty.

We had to be careful in mounting the narrow corkscrew stone steps which led to the upper story; nor were the wide passages altogether safe, though they appeared to have been strongly built, the dislocation of the stones and the wide cracks which we observed being probably the effect of earthquakes. The rooms to which these stairs led were long, low, narrow, and dark, but semi-obscurity is a luxury in the East. The unplastered walls had once been concealed by rich hangings; and there were numberless hooks for suspending lamps and lanterns. What scenes may have taken place in these chambers when the old chief's wicked will ran riot.

At the end of one corridor there was a large

window, which commanded an extensive view over the town and the flat country beyond, and from it we overlooked a seventh tank, which was evidently the one used by the people, being very large—quite a lake, in fact. In the middle of it rose a small square island of red rock, which had been shaped by art. It was perfectly square, with a deep cutting on one side. It was probably the site of some ancient temple, and the spot from which the place derives its name, Nipani, in Máhratta means " the Town of the Water."

Recrossing the sandy plain, we came upon that most melancholy sight, the solitary grave of an Englishman in a distant foreign land—a spot over which I always feel inclined to linger, as if my sympathy could avail the dead. This tomb was raised to the memory of a certain " George Sandford, Overseer P. W. Department. Aged 31."

We had, alas! but one more night to pass before the end of this journey, which to me had been delightful. How I did enjoy opening my eyes each morning upon a new scene, and roving about whilst the dew still glistened! We were to sleep at Soutguttee, and in order to reach it, had to cross a short but steep ghât, the abrupt sides of which were shaggy with jungle. The plain beyond was mapped out into fields, divided from one another by low banks, which at a later period would be irrigated. The dark earth exposed had a gloomy appearance, but I was told that, after the rains, this district would be luxuriantly green, covered, as it would be, with rich crops of sugar-cane, tobacco, the castor-oil plant, maize, many other sorts of grain, and yellow blossoming cotton. It is the black earth which makes Baroda so exceedingly fertile; but there is not much of this precious soil in the district of Belgaum.

We had to rise before daybreak, but by the time my small personal arrangements were made, there was a glimmer of light. Having half an hour at my disposition, M. advised me to take a walk by a path through the woods, which led to a very remarkable banyan-tree, under which *the* Duke of Wellington is said to have camped. The roots, which had shot down and sprung up again in stems, had become united with the parent-tree, and formed a corrugated wall, which I measured with my pocket-handkerchief, and found to be thirteen yards in length. I ran, in order to get a peep at another banyan-tree, which is still more curious. The weeping roots had formed a hundred independent stems, which clustered round their parent stem, and mingled their leaves with its foliage. A regiment might have bivouacked beneath the shade of this magnificent tree. It is neither safe nor pleasant to loiter under these trees, which afford famous cover for flying foxes, snakes, and monkeys, which find shelter beneath them in legions. The scene recalled to my memory those famous lines by Milton, from the ninth book of " Paradise Lost "—

> " The fig-tree, not that kind for fruit renown'd,
>   But such as at this day to Indians known,
>   In Malabar or Deccan spreads her arms,
>   Branching so broad and long, that in the ground
>   The bended twigs take root, and daughters grow
>   About the mother-tree, a pillar'd shade
>   High over-arch'd, and echoing walls between ;
>   There oft the Indian herdsman, shunning heat,
>   Shelters in cool, and tends his pasturing herds
>   At loop-holes cut through thickest shade ; those leaves
>   They gathered, broad as Amazonian targe ;
>   And with what skill they had, together sew'd,
>   To gird their waist."

Soutguttee is a delightful place, situated on the slopes of a narrow valley, watered by the Gatpanba, the same river which, rushing over the high black precipices at Gokak, forms the famous falls. At Soutguttee it is a fine clear stream, winding along a rocky bed, and forming deep pools, in which the alligator loves to dwell. The river furnishes fine sport to the fisherman, and the jungle on its banks abounds in big as well as little game. No wonder that this spot is in great request in hot weather. People from Belgaum bring thither their tents, and pitch them under the lofty trees. It has one drawback, however—that there is a good deal of fever about the place, and the adjacent villages of the district, which belong to a native chief, are unhealthy.

We had now to mount a steep but short ghât, our last, our way being through very thick jungle. M. bade me remark the number of leafless climbing plants, which she told me were superb after the rains. We traced the old palanquin road which passed over the steepest part of the hill, paved, and so narrow that no wheeled carriage could have used it. At last we began to descend. At our feet lay a great plain, embraced by long low hills—fells, we should have called them in the north of England, overtopped towards the west by great ghâts, and they again by the peaks of a mountain chain, bounded by the Portuguese territory, which slopes down to the coast of Malabar. We passed a village with an ancient domed mosque and tanks, and a craggy hill, with a ruined castle on its summit; and then M.

pointed to a long dark line of wall, broken here and there by a bulging battlemented tower, over which waved a mass of rich green foliage.

The fort of Belgaum loomed larger and larger out of the hot atmosphere as we gradually approached it. We crossed a deep *fosse* in which the water shimmered, passed under a low gateway, flanked by bastions, curved between red battlemented walls, plunged into the darkness of the vaulted main guard, dimly visible by a light which was suspended over the head of a many-limbed divinity under a shrine, and emerging near an extensive ruin, with painted arches, passed a little green on which stood a domed and minaretted tomb, turned suddenly under shady trees, drew up under a pillared portico, and I was welcomed to our Indian home.

CHAPTER VIII.

Belgaum—Records and Traditions of the Fort—Stormed
by Mohammed Shah—Mahmoud Gavan—Ismael Khan
Shah—Khoossan Toork—Sevaji—Changes of Name and
Fortune—Besieged by a Force under General Monro
—Garrison at the Time of the Mutiny—Execution of
the Chief of Nargund—Description of the Fort—The
English Church—The Station Library—Favourite
Spots—Architecture of the Jaina Temples.

IN Máhratta, although there are many forts
which play a more important part in history than that of Belgaum, still its crumbling
walls, ancient sites, and picturesque ruins tell of
an eventful story, which is not without interest.
Placed upon no lofty plateau, and defending no
mountain pass, but situated in an obscure part
of Western India, it owed its former celebrity to
the fact of its being a border fortress, situated
amidst territories which were constantly at war
with one another, and frequently changing
masters. It derived not a little of its strength
from the deep jungle by which it was until
lately surrounded. The natives still consider

Belgaum to be in the jungle, and within twenty years bison have been shot close to the ramparts.

Tradition declares that the fort was founded by a certain Jaina King called Jaza Rajah, who built a large mud fort, surrounded by a ditch, on the site of the existing fortifications, and the existence within the *enceinte* of three Jaina temples of great beauty and interest tends to favour the idea.   There is, however, no positive record as to the foundation of the existing fort, but we learn, from an inscription on copper, the date of which is 1294, in which many names are recorded, and which was found in the *fosse*, that at one period a certain family, who were Jains, held, for seven generations, the hereditary chieftainship of Belgaum.

After this period we have more information regarding the history of this place, for the district is remarkably rich in inscriptions in the Canerese character, beautifully cut in relief, upon large slabs of a compact black basalt, which takes a beautiful polish, and resists the influence of the weather. Many petty wars, and events of local interest, are recorded upon these stones, but nothing of general interest until the year 1472, when it is stated that Belgaum fort was besieged by Mohammed Shah,

the Mohamedan King of the Deccan. It must at
that time have been a place of strength, as it is
mentioned in history as being protected by
strong towers and lofty walls, guarded by a
deep wet ditch, and by a pass near to it, the
only approach to which was fortified by re-
doubts. When Mohammed Shah set himself
down to subdue it, he commanded the fire
workers, as they valued their own safety, to
effect a particular breach in fourteen days, and
ordered his soldiers to throw quantities of wood
and earth into the ditch. The enemy in the night,
however, always removed them, upon which he
placed his guns in another position, but only
finally succeeded, by mining, in forming three
breaches. The troops of Birkana Ray, Rajah of
the fortress, advanced gallantly to defend the
place, and nearly two thousand of the king's
troops fell in the attempt to storm. The besieged had nearly repaired the works with wood
and stones when the Shah, advancing to the
assault, drove the enemy before him, and gained
the ramparts. When opposition had ceased,
the King entered the citadel, and gave thanks
to God for the success of his arms. One of his
first acts was to expel the image of Dymávavera,
the tutelar goddess of the fort, but the sorrow-

N 2

ing Hindoos were allowed to place it in a little temple outside the walls, which still exists.*

The history of Belgaum remained intimately connected with that of Bijipur until the decline of the Mussulman power in Western India, when it relapsed into the hands of the Hindoo princes. The king bestowed Belgaum and its dependencies upon Mahmoud Gavan, a very distinguished general, of royal blood, being connected with the Shah of Persia. His career was one of curious vicissitudes. He first served in the Deccan, to which he came in the year 1461, and where he was successful in many campaigns, rendering his royal master great services, for which he was made Governor of Bijipur, was given a seat in the Council of Regency, and was appointed a guardian of the young prince, Nizam Shah. He also rose to the dignity of Vizier, and distinguished himself at the siege of Goa, but was finally murdered by Mohammed Shah in 1481. He was very famous for his learning, justice, and munificence, and left

---

* Once in every twelve years a great festival is held in honour of Dymávavera, when buffaloes, sheep, and goats are sacrificed to her. The slaughter takes place on a platform outside the little pyramidal building erected to her. The jubilee took place shortly after M.'s arrival in Belgaum.

behind him a library of three thousand volumes, principally in the Persian language.

In the same year the Mussulman king again visited Belgaum, probably for the purpose of resuming his full authority over it. He inspected the city and examined the fortifications. Thirty years of petty warfare ensued, and then the golden age of the old fort commenced.

Ismael Khan Shah began his reign at Bijipur in the year 1511, when he was a minor, and the attempt at usurpation made by his guardian was the means of bringing conspicuously forward Khoossan Toork, a Persian, who, as he took part in the deliverance of the young king, was honoured with the title of Azad Khan, and the Government of Belgaum was conferred upon him. He was far the greatest man who ever reigned over it; and even to this day his name is a household word among the people, who love and revere his memory. It is to his wise measures that the town has ever owed, and still continues to owe, its comparative immunity from cholera. He altered and repaired the walls of the fortress, every inscription on which is in the Persian character. He also erected a grand palace, which, with its offices and stables, covered a large space of ground. There are existing records of the magnificence which he maintained. His household servants—Georgians, Circassians, Abyssinians, and Hindoos—amounted to two hundred and fifty. He had sixty large elephants, and one hundred and fifty of a smaller size. In his stables were four hundred and fifty Arabian horses, exclusive of those of mixed breed foaled in India. Two thousand seven hundred pounds of rice were every day prepared for his household, in addition to fifty sheep, and one hundred fowls. It was he who first introduced the fashion of wearing the waistband of cloth of gold, and the dagger, a custom which has since been adopted by persons of rank in this country. He also attempted to ride elephants with bridles instead of managing them with the goad; but as these animals are rather unsteady, in consequence of the sudden vicious starts to which they are frequently prone, this mode of guiding them was, according to the old chronicle, not found to answer.

Years flew by, during which Azad Khan was constantly at war, and proved himself a most successful general, acquiring great riches, in the form of gold, jewels, and elephants. On one occasion, it is related that, after a battle, the King of Bijipur presented him with five large and six small elephants; and at another time,

when he had taken a large quantity of baggage
and twenty elephants, the king gave him all
these animals but one, which he reserved for
himself, and called Alla Baksh (the Gift of God).
Towards the end of his life, when very ill, he
succeeded in frustrating the design of a neighbouring chief, Nizam Shah, who had a great
wish to possess himself of Belgaum, with which
design he entrusted a large sum of money to a
Brahman, who was directed to employ it in
corrupting the soldiers of the garrison, in the
hope that they would deliver the fort into his
hands, in case of Azad's death. The Brahman
had nearly succeeded in his commission, when
the plot was discovered, and the chief agent in
it, in spite of his high caste, was put to death,
along with seventy of the soldiers whom he
had bribed. Old age having rendered Azad too
weak to contend with a deep-seated malady, he
prepared to meet death, and in lines (of
which the following is a translation), he en-
treated the King of Bijipur to honour him with
a farewell visit. "Come like the morning
breeze to the bower of friendship, Come like
the graceful cypress to the garden."

Ibraham assented to the request, and on his
arrival finding his old friend had breathed his
last, he administered consolation to his family

by attaching all the late Khan's estates and treasures. The fine old chief died in the year 1549, having held Belgaum during thirty-three prosperous years. He left a name not only dear to his people, but celebrated in the history of the period; and we have heard that his standard, on which was embroidered an angry lion, was bestowed as a great honour upon Kishwar Khan.

In the year 1557, the treacherous King of Bijipur lay on his death-bed. He had, on religious grounds, quarrelled with both of his sons, the eldest of whom, his heir, was under surveillance in Miraj, whilst the youngest was in confinement at Belgaum, under the charge of Kishwar Khan, the governor, where, upon the accession of his brother, he was still kept prisoner. Though treated with kindness and generosity, he determined to rebel, and having persuaded the governor and the garrison to assist him, he took possession of the fort, and raised the standard of rebellion, upon which a renowned general, Elias Khan, was sent with five thousand men to besiege the place. Great confusion followed, and in order completely to quell the insurrection, a further force of twenty thousand horse and thirty thousand foot, was sent against Belgaum, under Ein-ul-Mulk, who, treacherously pretending to be the friend of the young prince, persuaded him to take the field, with those who were willing to espouse his cause, and march upon Bijipur. The unfortunate Ismael fell into the trap laid for him, and was taken prisoner and executed. Nor did it fare better with the double traitor, Ein-ul-Mulk, who was also put to death, his head being sent to Bijipur, where, for a certain time, it was exposed upon a pole in front of the palace, and afterwards blown from a great gun.

The next important prisoners confined in the fort were the Portuguese ambassador and his suite. About this time, in consequence of a change of territory, Belgaum ceased to be a frontier fort, and no particular mention of it appears until 1673, when the renowned Sevaji, with his famous light cavalry, swept down and sacked both town and fort. At the fall of Bijipur, in 1688, the fort reverted to the Máhrattas, and was in the possession of Aurangzib, second son of the powerful Prince A'Zam, at which period it acquired the name A'Zamnagar. After the lapse of some years the name was changed to Mustáfabad, after a Kiledar who thoroughly repaired and strengthened the ramparts; and this appellation it still retains.

One year after the battle of Kirhee, the English, under General Munro, marched against it. He encamped near Sharpur, on the morning of March 11th, 1818, with a comparatively insignificant force of native soldiers, and three troops of His Majesty's twenty-second Light Dragoons, a force so weak that it tended to confirm the garrison, and the inhabitants of Belgaum and Sharpur (who had a high opinion of the strength of the fort), in the belief that it could not be taken.

The English were unable to obtain accurate intelligence as to the state of the ditch, which was the great defence of the place, otherwise the attack would not have been made from the points selected. On the fifteenth, the fort was invested, but nothing particular occurred until the twentieth, when the force marched to the north of the fort, and encamped about two miles and a half from it. On the twenty-second, the first battery opened on the defences, and on the following day the pioneers broke ground, and began opening trenches. On the thirty-first, the magazine belonging to one of the batteries, in which there was a considerable amount of ammunition, blew up. The garrison took immediate advantage of this misfortune, and making a sally, succeeded in passing over the battery, but were immediately repulsed. During the following days such steady progress was made by the English that on or about April 9th, the Kiledar (acting governor) sent out a flag of truce to propose terms, but General Munro did not accept them. Next day all the batteries kept up a heavy fire on the fort, and the breach, though not exactly practicable, began to have a more favourable appearance, in consequence of which the Kiledar found himself under the necessity of accepting the condition offered by General Munro, which was that he should give up possession of the gateway, the garrison being allowed to march out with their arms and private property. This they did on the following day, to the number of one thousand six hundred, having lost seventy men. The loss of the besieging army amounted to twenty-three killed and wounded. By the capture of the fort, General Munro obtained possession of thirty-six guns of large calibre, sixty smaller guns, and numerous wall pieces, besides stores of every sort.*

I never read the record from which this ac-

---

* The two breaches effected by the English were near the main guard, and are plainly visible, the masonry which fills the gaps being still ungnawed by time.

count is abstracted without mentally fighting the battle of the fort, and wishing for the success of its brave garrison. The fall of Belgaum completed the conquest of the Peishwa's territory south of the Krishna. The breaking out of the Mutiny found Belgaum garrisoned by two native regiments, a battery of European artillery, and the depôt of an English regiment, withdrawn to serve in Persia. The native troops were believed to be ripe for revolt ; all the European women and children were brought into the fort, and the small English garrison had good reason to take every measure to provide for their safety. The walls, which had been somewhat neglected, were put in a state of defence, the breaches were repaired, and the artillery were quartered in the fort. It was thought necessary to make an example of certain emissaries of the rebels, who were taken in the act of corrupting the native soldiers, and they were blown from guns. People have told me that they stopped their ears in order to deaden the horrible sound. Fortunately, no actual outbreak took place here.

The year of the Mutiny is remembered with horror by the natives in Belgaum, on account of the execution of the Brahman chief of Nargund, who was put to death for the cruel murder of Mr. Manson, the deputy collector. Mr. Manson had been sent to negotiate with him, but having no escort, his palanquin was attacked by order of the chief; his bearers ran away, and the unfortunate young gentleman was cut and hacked to pieces. The chief of Nargund was ignominiously hanged upon an elevated spot, which still bears the name of the Brahman's Hill. I have met with many people who still cherish the memory of Mr. Manson, who was much beloved.

The fort of Belgaum is situated in the midst of an extensive undulating plain. As it now stands, it forms an irregular oval, enclosed by a deep ditch, still full of water, which is cut out of a softish red stone, which hardens on being exposed to the air. The exterior of the fort is surrounded by a fine broad esplanade; the *revêtement* rises about thirty-two feet above the bottom of the ditch. The interior is level, and extends about a thousand yards in length, by eight hundred in breadth. The original entrance was made between two magnificent battlemented bastions, which still exist, although the gate, which once opened upon a bridge, has been walled up. The present main gate, which is a solid pile of building, is considered to be a fine specimen of Indian architecture. There is an open guard-chamber, with a groined roof, which has once been ornamented by pendents, and the exterior is elaborately decorated with grotesque representations of animals and birds (rather curious ornaments for a Mahomedan building, but a Brahman architect is said to have been employed). The effect has been somewhat destroyed by time, and the frequent application of various coats of colour; but the ostriches still run races, cats with open mouths still conduct water from the roof, and one elephant has been drinking for centuries out of the same bottle. The little niches scattered about, intended to receive lights, and slippers, and water-bottles, are very graceful. The shrine of the many-armed Durga, the goddess of castles and of war, is an excrescence placed in a corner by the Hindoos when they regained the fortress. "Let not," say the most ancient laws of Manu, "foes hurt a king who has taken refuge in his Durgar." The exterior of this curious shrine is covered with richly-coloured mythological figures. Some of the unpopular gods, like the pictured celebrities of other nations, have had their faces scratched out, and their noses destroyed.

Passing under a lofty unguarded archway, we reach the outworks, and then come to a fine gateway, with solid iron-plated doors, which have once been thickly studded with iron spikes, like those at Poonah, and with the same intention. Under the arch is an inscription in relief, sculptured in Persian characters, to the following effect: " Jakub Ali Khan, who is a joy to the heart, by whose benevolence the world is prosperous, built the wall of the fort from its base as strong as the barrier of Sicardis." From every point of view these gates and outworks present a most picturesque appearance. The fine red colour of the battlements, the peeps obtained down into the deep ditch, where the still water lies in shade, and, like a black mirror, reflects the walls it protects, and the tall palms which fringe its outer bank, the mysterious light which gleams through the fretwork in the doors enclosing the cruel goddess, all tend to give this spot a romantic charm which I have rarely found equalled. It is most beautiful by moonlight, but when fantastic shadows are thrown around, it looks a weird place, where one almost expects to see the tall forms of long-dead warriors.

On the western side of the fort there is a more modern egress, a substantial archway, which is gained by a descending road, and a sharp turn leads to a narrow causeway which bridges the *fosse*. It is guarded only by low loops of thick chain, attached to ricketty old cannon, and I confess that in crossing it I have often sat behind the fresh young Arabs with a beating heart and closed eyes, thankful when the sound of their hoofs on the hard road told me that the dangerous spot was passed. The walls of the fort are crowned by lofty scalloped battlements, standing clear of one another, and pierced with long loop-holes, just so wide as to have admitted the muzzles of the old jaugals (literally teazers), which now lie rusting in the arsenal.

The Station library was a charming retreat. The books, which numbered nearly four thousand, were arranged in cases which lined the walls of the long low room, and reached up to a ceiling which was supported by great time-honoured beams of rough-hewn teak wood. In olden days this house had been the residence of the Kiledar. In its deep, shady verandah, set with plants, it was twilight at noonday, but it was a pleasant place, where one could just see to read. It commanded a charming peep, between the boles of the peepul-trees, of the ruined gateway where the Naubat played, and through the deep, dark archway, to an ever-blooming garden, where, fanned by the gentle breeze, the rich-hued blossoms, ever combining, looked like the changing colours in a kaleidoscope. Outside the arsenal the great guns and pyramids of ball, as seen from our garden, were picturesque objects. There was little to invite attention in the interior of the building. Some two years ago it contained a curious collection of old native weapons, but they had been carried off to Woolwich, or some other place. Shreds of silk dangling disconsolately from bare poles were all that remained of colours which had fluttered over many a battle-field, and the piles of rusty jangals lay in obscure corners—all else was fresh, trim, and ready. Some of the long corridors were paved with sections of petrified palm work, the rings of which were so perfect that with a little pains one might have deciphered their age, and told which side of the tree had received the warm rays of the rising sun. Though last, not least, I must make mention of our little snug Gothic church. Its cockney aspect presented a striking contrast to the crumbling antiquities around, but the interior was pretty and airy. There were a few memorial tablets upon the walls, but none of general interest, excepting that which recorded the sad death of Mr. Manson. The edifice stood upon a small maidan, which G—— hired for the benefit of his cattle, it being very desirable to graze it down; for the long grass served as cover for cobras, which more than once were seen fighting by the assembling congregation.

Completely shut out from the exterior world, there could not, to my mind, exist a more delightful and romantic spot than that enclosed by the old red walls. The grassy ramparts, which are banked up until the rounded battlements alone are visible, make a charming walk which commands a panoramic view of the surrounding country, of the undulating plain, with its woods, cultivated fields, green pastures, and little villages, sheltered by lofty mango-trees, the distant mountains, the jungly hills, the rolling downs, ever-changing, peaceful in the sunshine, purple and threatening in the storm. Not even water was wanting to enhance the charms of the landscape. The tank, in reality a lake of some extent, lay glittering within a stone's throw of the main gate. Banked up on one side by a lofty wall with a stone coping, it was otherwise at liberty to lie at rest, calm and blue, or to swell out into a turbid inland sea, specked with unfamiliar islands. At morn and eve the tank was a busy scene. I had favourite nooks from which I often watched the great herds of cattle which were brought up to water. The buffaloes delighted in their early bath, and waded about with just their noses out of the refreshing element. They are docile creatures, obedient to their owner's call, not half so difficult to manage as the fierce little untameable cows. Serene-looking bullocks drank, and gazed about them, and drank again. Some pet animal was readily distinguished by its brass collar, garland of flowers, or necklace of cowrie shells, put on to ensure good luck. Occasionally a great black elephant came slowly down, and dabbled its "lotus feet" in the water, whilst it was scrubbed by its driver. One of these sagacious creatures had a curious trick of bending its ears forward with its trunk, in order that the skin behind might come in for its share of the washing. Camels came striding down in long file, they alone looking discontented, for not even the cool morning's draught could please these peevish creatures.

Another favourite resting-place was the top of the flag-staff, or Chevalier battery, a stronghold built by Azad Khan, within the walls, but towering far above them. From its summit the flag with the angry lion had floated for many a year. It was a delightful spot at the hour of sunset, when the western sky was flooded with amber or rosy red, and the mala was heard from the minaret of the musjid in the Durga camp, in which the old Khan's bones repose, calling the faithful to prayer. While the cattle slowly crossed the plain to their rest, and the short twilight deepened, ghostly bands of white-robed people would glide along, and disappear beneath the deep shade of the mango-trees. Occasionally a procession might be seen return-ing from some ceremony, the shrill notes of the musicians toned down by distance, and red-robed women, bearing fire in their brass vessels, on their way to some time-honoured temple. How beautiful must this plain have been when covered up to the very foot of the distant hills with a waving sea of green, a jungle of palms, and bananas, and bamboos! Many a time have I lingered, until suddenly it was dark, and I had to descend and cross the pathless grass, in mental fear of the snakes. There is a tradition that three hundred and sixty Jaina temples were pulled down, in order to supply materials for building the present walls of the fort.

This part of the Deccan was once the head-quarters of that curious sect whose habit it was to build their temples, which are not very large, near together. There is no doubt that almost all of the immense blocks of stone which have carving upon them, and which are built into the walls irregularly, and without design to adorn, are of Jaina origin. Their style of ornamentation is very peculiar, and cannot, when one once becomes familiar with it, be mistaken. There are long narrow stones, strips of friezes or cornices, with stiff-pointed lotus-flowers cut upon them (the stiff-cut lotus of Indian art does not mean to imitate Nature; it is merely used as a symbol of the power of those kings who ruled over countries where the lotus grew) ; and others upon which musicians, playing upon such instruments as are still in use, pipe to dancing women with distorted bodies and light drapery. They are covered with bracelets and bangles, and long rows of beads hang from their necks ; these bands are generally grouped between pillars, such as now serve for gate-posts at almost every bungalow in the fort. Some of the carved divinities are seated in rows, with animals at their feet; some are well-proportioned, and cut in high relief; others are rude, and rendered almost undecipherable by time. Long after I imagined myself to be acquainted with every piece of sculpture around, I came upon bits which were new to me—stones which had been hidden away by tall balsams, or bushes of the many-hued lantana (wild sage). One magnificent stream of the black-stemmed giant maidenhair fern died down and disclosed the figure of an elephant, with a chain round the body, which was in the act of treading a man to death, representing, it may be, some act of vengeance which had taken place near this very spot. From many a corner the hooded head of a cobra, once worshipped, peeped through the long grasses. Another curious study was furnished by the monumental stones, which are supposed to have been erected to the memory of warriors slain in battle. They are divided into three or more compartments. The lowest part of one, which is in the fort, represents a fight, in which a soldier is attacked by armed men and slain. In the next compartment nymphs are bearing him on high, whilst above he is seen worshipping the Linga. Upon a second stone the hero is represented curvetting along upon his steed, with his sword-bearer in advance. The middle one pictures the deceased man rising with extended arms, whilst the fore-finger of a gigantic hand points to the skies. In the third compartment there is a bust of the warrior, by the side of which a kneeling figure worships the Linga. Numbers of these memorials (all relating to war) lie scattered about the whole district, and it is a pity that they are not removed to some place of safety, and that no endeavour is made to collect any legends attached to them. In all probability the stories they picture have been gathered into the chants and songs of the people.

It would be tedious to dwell upon the sculptured objects which ornament the ancient walls rising up in every compound, cropping out of the loose stone walls which surround them, and peeping from the very ditches—gods and pirates, dancing women and shrined ascetics, beautiful tracery and grotesque animals, jostling one another in strange confusion. Doubtless our feet have passed over many a hidden treasure. The fort of Belgaum is indeed a glorious place for those who love old stones.

CHAPTER IX.

Sect of the Jains—Their Opinions—Jaina Saints—Architecture of the Jain Temples—Sena Rajah—Legends—Decoration of the Hall—Ornaments in Sculpture—Shrines—Spacious Dome—Dedication Plate—The Sacred Cell—The Second Temple—English Indifference to the Antiquities of the Country—The Musjid Safa—Concealed Treasure—Curious Relic—Memorials of the Past.

BEFORE attempting to describe the peculiar style of the Jaina temples, it may not be amiss to say a few words respecting the religious opinions of the sect by whom they were built, which at one time bade fair to strangle Brahmanism, and to become dominant throughout India. The followers of Jainism, which seems to have risen upon the ruins of Buddhism, were probably seceders from that religion, which had become corrupt; and it is not unlikely that their desire was to return to some older faith upon which Buddhism itself was founded.[*]

---

* It is curious to remark in Eastern religions how frequently the grotesque borders on the sublime. According

The Jains deny the divine origin of Sakya Sinha (Buddha), whom, however, they deified after death, believing him to have been a most holy man, whose mission it was, not to found a new religion, but to reform the abuses which had crept into one already existing.

The Jains are equally sceptical with regard to Brahmanism, for they deny the divine origin of the Vedas. They abhor the Homa, or burnt sacrifice, so dear to the other Hindoos, alleging that everything thus consumed contains animal life, for which they have the most exaggerated respect.* The Jain priest walks about with a

to the Singhalese belief, their great teacher, Buddha, died of eating pork. " Buddha, with a large company of disciples, came to Kusinagara, in Gorakpur, and encamped in the mango garden of one Chunda, a smith. The worthy smith meant to be hospitable, and served up pork. It was too much for the worn-out frame of the hoary sage. Diarrhœa ensued, he travelled a short distance, with frequent stoppages, but at last being unable to proceed, a temporary couch was provided for him in a shadowy grove. A message of comfort was sent to the poor smith, the princes of Malwa were summoned, and having made them a long speech, he ceased to exist."

* The orthodox Hindoo has also a great horror of taking animal life. " He is taught that God inhabits even an insect ; but it is no great crime if he should permit his cow to die of hunger ; and he beats it without mercy. It is enough that he does not really deprive it of life, for the indwelling Brumhu feels no shock but that of death. For

cloak over his mouth, lest he should swallow small insects, and carries a broom, in order to eject them from the spot on which he chooses to sit. Another tenet which distinguishes them from the rest of the Hindoos, is the worship which they pay to a certain number of Jinas, or deified teachers, who they imagine have, by constant deeds of mortification and self-inflicted torment, attained a station superior to that of the gods. "The Jains enumerate by name the twenty-four of the past age, the twenty-four of the present, and the twenty-four of the age to come." A Jaina saint is called Lord of the World, Omniscient, God of Gods—all sorts of transcendent names are bestowed upon him. He has certain superhuman attributes—beauty of form, fragrance of body, the white colour of his blood, the curling of his whiskers, the non-increase of the beard and nails, his exemption from all natural impurity, from hunger and thirst, from infirmity and decay, and so on through a long list.

The back of his head is surrounded by a halo of light, brighter than the disk of the sun, and for an immense space around him. Where-

---

killing a few small insects an orthodox Hindoo must repeat an incantation while squeezing his nose with his fingers."

ever he moved there is neither sickness nor enmity, death nor war. The Jain reformers in the early stage of their history were austere in their lives, and practised, as well as inculcated, self-denial. Their zeal was great, and their rejection of the Brahmanical system of caste drew multitudes after them. The countless temples scattered throughout the land bear silent witness to the power they attained, and their peculiar ideas are wrought upon the stones of many an ancient building which knows them no more. Jainism itself became in time corrupt, and the more attractive creed of the wily Brahman ultimately prevailed. The sect now numbers but a few hundred thousand disciples, who are chiefly to be found in the west of India.

The Jains have an extensive and independent literature of their own, but do not profess to have any inspired writings. They are among the very few Orientals who have adopted any sort of armorial bearings. With regard to their architecture, it must be borne in mind that neither they nor the other Hindoos have any form which is not derived from that of the Buddhists. The oldest remains in the fort are the three Jaina temples, which are very curious and beautiful. Many a time have I pictured to myself the sacred ceremonies which must have attended the foundation of these temples of an ancient creed. In a very ancient Hindoo treatise upon architecture, of which only fragments remain, very specific directions are given as to the manner of preparing the ground for the erection of a temple. "It is to be ploughed—the form, material, size, and construction of the plough are prescribed, even the oxen that are to drag it are selected with due reference to their age, shape of horns, &c. The maimed, the weak, the meagre, the toothless, or the lame, must be rejected, while those with a white spot on their legs and foreheads, with eyes resembling the petals of the lotus, are to be preferred. They are to be decorated with fillets and other ornaments, their horns and hoofs with gold and silver rings. The architect, clad in fresh vestments, and adorned with chaplets of flowers, having ascertained the auspicious moment for the duty, draws the first furrow with due religious ceremonies. The ground is sown with sesamum seeds, pulse, and kidney beans, incantations are repeated, and oxen and ploughs are presented to the spiritual teacher. When the crops are matured they are grazed by cows for one or two nights, and thus purified, the ground is ready for the future temple."

The mode, it is remarked, for ascertaining the cardinal points is striking and correct, and in principle the same as that adopted by Europeans, when they wish to ascertain a meridian line.*

On a copper-plate found near one of the temples was engraved the name and titles of the Rajah who erected it, as well as some particulars relating to his family. Some of the most interesting sentences run as follows:

"I adore Svarti and Siva Buddha, the preserver and supporter of the Jaina religion, who has brought under his rule the Devatas, the Cow Kamdheuna, has conquered the three passions, the soul of his disciples, whose breast is vast comprehension . . . . Great among all kings, who, conquering all princes, established his throne firmly; such was Sena Rajah. His son was Kartaviry, the great, the powerful, the possessor of all virtues, the renowned. His spouse was the beautiful Padmalla-Devi, ornamented with virtues. Her son was called Lakshmi-Bhee-Pati, he was to his father and mother a——" Here follow the names of many

---

* "The Land of the Veda," by the Rev. PETER PERCIVAL.

gods and warriors—"superior even to these, of higher merit. His wife, Chandala-Devi, had two sons of valour and liberality. Into the mind of this Rajah it entered to perform what would make him renowned among those of this world. In full enjoyment of his kingdom, when residing at Venegrama" (Belgaum), "in peace and happiness, he caused to be erected a temple, in which were installed I're Santnatha Deva, and the protectors of the eight priests;" for the maintenance of whom, and the expenses of their annual festival, offerings are appointed to be made.

Jaina temples are built according to a general plan, which is seldom varied. There is a square hall, or naos, generally open at the sides, an inner sala, or chamber, an oblong ante-chamber and a small square cell, in which the idol sits enthroned. When perfect, it is believed that every one of these erections was enclosed by an oblong court, with pillared colonnades, set with long rows of shrines, in which were standing Jains, or squatted Buddha-like figures. With the exception of the colonnades, one of the temples in the fort is quite perfect, and is considered to be a fine specimen of its kind of architecture. A few observations respecting its decorations, as illustrating the religious notions of the sect, if not very interesting to the general reader, may be tolerated for their bearing on the subject of which we treat.

A flight of steps leads up to the hall, which is partially enclosed by a long but strong balustrade, and roofed in by an expansive dome of great beauty. Circle after circle of concave lotus-flowers reach to its centre, from which hangs a magnificent pendant of four decreasing layers of lotus-flowers and leaves, a foot apart from one another, and terminated by one large blossom. The weight of such an ornament could only be supported in a dome so built that the pressure is horizontal instead of perpendicular. Externally, this dome is covered in by a high pyramidal stepped roof, the front of each step being sculptured with the sharp-cut lotus-pattern. The weight of this double roof must be prodigious, though it is apparently borne by an insignificant number of pillars of no great size; but relief is obtained from a characteristic employment of dwarf pillars, set upon the balustrades by a system of bracketing. Some of the pillars are made of compact black basalt, highly magnetic, finely polished, and unusual in form; others are of the description generally employed by the Jains, of which there are hundreds scattered about Belgaum and its immediate neighbourhood, tall shafts of stone, with four equal sides, ornamentally carved. Posts are cut into sharp rings of unequal size, separated by a cable pattern, and occasionally these circles are divided by a wedge-shape piece of the original surface, pointed upwards. Sometimes a smooth block of stone is left, and so delicately engraved with rich arabesques that the patterns almost appear to have been taken from needlework, the embroidered strips of stone being finished off by looped fringes of hearts and heads. Sometimes the loops are trebled, and have tassels in the centre. These designs are very elegant.

The roof of the Sala is flat, except in the very centre, where it is raised by a curious process. In the middle of the chamber four pillars, some five feet apart, support architraves and narrow cornices, leaving a square space, which has been diminished by two layers of overtopping corner-stones, until it could have been covered by a single flag. Should this have been the case, the room must have been in total darkness when the door giving upon the hall was closed. From immediately under the aperture something has evidently been removed, as the earth is exposed. Perhaps some inferior god occupied the spot, and received the passing homage of the devotees, as they passed round it on their way to the cell. It was not judged respectful to approach the idol in a straight line.

The hall is decorated with superb and characteristic sculpture. I have noticed the beauty of the dome, but not that of the octagonal cornice on which it rests. In each division, carved in high relief, are five shrines, with stepped roofs, in every one of which squats a cross-legged, Buddha-like figure,* while between each shrine, and under a canopy, stands an upright naked man. These figures evidently represent the seventy-two deified Jains of the past, the present, and the future. In each angle of the octagon is a bracket, on which is placed the figure of a divinity, probably " the protectors of the eight points " referred to in the dedication plate. Round the spring of the dome eight great beasts, with chains round their stout bodies, jut forth ; their faces have been smashed away by the Mahomedan Iconoclasts. They are most likely but the ornamented ends of supports necessary to the structure. All the doorways, and many other parts of the temple, are minutely and beautifully carved with grotesque gods and mythical animals, which peep

---

* The figure of Buddha himself is generally represented with fingers and toes of equal length.

over the flowers, and sport in the foliage of sacred plants.

The sculpture in the Sala is evidently of an inferior order, and is chiefly remarkable for the frequent introduction of the hooded cobra, life-size, which forms the brackets, and twines round the tops of the pillars. In this room there are four large unornamented niches, and two square recesses, which can be closed by sliding stones, in which very likely the sacred vessels were kept.

The oblong vestibule is perfectly plain. Both it and the cell are in darkness. Not only is a light necessary for investigation, but for safety, as real cobras have been seen gliding about in the corners. In my frequent visits I was always armed with a candle and a stick.

The once sacred cell is very curious. The image is gone, but there stands the throne on which its cold limbs once rested. (It was probably a cross-legged, Buddha-like figure.) The platform, which is oblong, cut into angles, and ornamented by zigzag mouldings, is placed upon two elephants, the eyes of which, made of some semi-transparent stone, still glitter, although they have looked only upon darkness for centuries. At the back is the tasseled cushion which the Jains have always placed behind their idols. Although formed of black basalt, it has a look of wrinkled softness, as if the god had been sufficiently human to bend his back and seek occasional repose. On each side sprang up the stem of a tree, which diapered the wall with strange flowers, sharp-pointed leaves set into circles, from the midst of which depended long bunches of weeds. It was some time before I discovered that this tracery was populated by bands of sculptured monkeys, not an inch in length; and in one place appeared a mysterious arm and hand, beating a drum. It was very strange. The screen was stained by the smoke of incense; and though smoke be fleeting, its traces are eminently suggestive. The cell has a steep-stepped roof, which, according to the universal plan, must have been surmounted by a spire. It contains a chamber, but as it can now only be reached by means of a long ladder, I never explored it, nor did I ever meet with anyone who had made the ascent. I believe that some way to it exists in the thickness of the wall. I never visited this temple without making some new and interesting discovery.

Of the second temple, an enclosed hall, with flights of steps which lead up to a narrow portico, alone remain. The exterior is much ornamented with rows of dancing figures, musicians, and sharp-cut flowers. Mr. Burgess considers this remnant to be a remarkably fine specimen of Jain architecture ; and I congratulate myself in having been instrumental in prolonging its existence. The treacherous roots of two fig-trees of considerable growth, which had fixed themselves firmly upon the roof, had already overturned at least a ton of beautifully sculptured stones, when, in consequence of a piteous appeal to the proper authorities, they were removed. The neglected state of this building is one of a thousand instances of English indifference respecting the antiquities of a country which we occupy—indeed, it owes its very existence to the unromantic fact that it is used as a Government store-house for beer-barrels.

The third temple, judging from the size of the hall, which alone remains, and the splendid sculpture with which it is adorned, must have been the most important of the three. The vicissitudes of its latter days are curious. Some years ago the part that at present remains was built into a bungalow. What a cool and magnificent centre apartment must it have made with its lofty dome and wide portals ; but this phase of its existence was a short one.

Belgaum ceased to be a division, and the general and his staff no longer inhabited the fort. The anxious year of the Mutiny wrought other changes, and the house, with all its charms, its unrivalled hall, its extensive garden, the pride of the place, and its stately avenue of palms, was deserted, to be turned by Government into a patchery, or quarters for married soldiers. The old Jaina remains are shunned by the soldiers' wives, as they do not like their gloomy obscurity even by day. Its grim black carving would look weird indeed by the glimmer of a single lamp. The women even imagine the bedrooms above, which circle round the dome, to be haunted, and refuse to sleep in them. I am not quite sure that the place would be agreeable to many by moonlight, for I share Madame de Staël's ideas with regard to ghosts : " Je n'y crois pas, mais je les crains."

In the arsenal stands the Musjid Safa, the fine mosque, which was the old Khan's gift to the fort he loved so well. A Persian inscription, finely cut in relief, is placed above the great door. " In the time of Adil Azam, son of Adzil Khan, a man of high rank, who bore the palm of excellence from all the world, of good counsel, the aim of merit, the defender of the faith, who utterly uprooted the unbeliever from the country of the Deccan ; Azid Khan, the best of upright men, built this house of God, and good fortune, and with much labour. By the grace of God we call it 'the pure mosque,' (Musjid Safa) ; and the lustre of the religion of the Prophet grew greater." It is a fine building, with stately minarets. Daylight is admitted to the interior by means of openings cut in the form of intricate geometrical patterns, pierced in thin slabs of stone. In front of the edifice is a tank, in the middle of which stands a ruined fountain. Affixed to the eastern wall of the mosque is a small square platform, which was used by the Khan for the gymnastic exercises, in which he excelled. It is said that he could jump upon it weighted with shoes made of lead and iron, which are still preserved in the building, along with his quilted sabre-proof vest. His sword was stolen from the temple by a soldier just before the Mutiny.

Up to the time of the Mutiny, the Musjid was open for worship, but the Mahomedans availed themselves of its shelter, in order to plot treason against the English, and for years since that time it has remained closed. The murderous designs of the plotters were discovered. There are, or ought to be, three keys to the great padlock which secures the entrance. One of them was delivered over to the safe keeping of some English official, who lost it, another to the head Mola in the town of Belgaum, and the third was committed to the care of the head priest in Kolhápur.

One day, however, we were informed by a friend that an application, on the part of the Mussulman population, had passed through his office, praying that they might be allowed to resume a periodical custom, which had been suspended, an occasion on which the head Mola, key in hand, mounted upon a camel, and heading a procession, had been wont to enter the mosque, and repeat a certain form of prayer. Permission was granted, and everyone near the arsenal was on the tip-toe of expectation—even the old Scotch superintendent of the stores was thrown into a state of excitement. " 'Deed, ma'am," he said, "all the years that I have been here I have never been inside the mosque, and I would like to see the Khan's golden chair." A golden chair, that was a new and delightful feature in the cave. We kept the orderlies upon the look-out, and with heated faces they ran to and fro, bearing the latest news. " The brigadier in person was coming; the procession was to enter the fort at six o'clock precisely; a native company with colours had arrived." We stood in the garden ready to start. Bullock-carts came hurrying up, laden with men in resplendent turbans of red and gold, and gold and green ; and crowds of white-robed pedestrians, with bags full of flowers under their arms, began to assemble round the Musjid. The clock struck six, and the sound was followed by intense excitement. Then there was a long pause. Was it possible that the people were silently melting away? Improbable as it appeared, it was too true. There could be no ceremony now—the second key was lost. We afterwards heard considerable indignation expressed at the idea of allowing the false Mahomedans ever again to set foot in the mosque ; but that was by people who remembered with a shudder the anxiety of that period, when the troops were known to be wavering.

The natives have a tradition, to which they give full credit, respecting a secret passage, which, they affirm, leads from under the Musjid to the Dhers' (a very low caste) well, a mile and a half away. Why it should be supposed to terminate at that particular spot, I know not ; but there is no doubt that some concealed way does exist between the fort and the open country.

The people have also a firm belief in the existence of a concealed treasure, which they suppose to be buried near the building, but do not concern themselves much respecting it, as they imagine it to be guarded by gnomes, or malignant spirits, who would cruelly kill anyone who attempted to take possession of it. There is no doubt that a considerable quantity of jewels, gold, and silver, was either smuggled away or buried in the fort, when it was surrendered to the English. Sums of money have more than once been granted by Government for the institution of a search, but as yet nothing has been found. The quantity of money concealed in the earth by the Indian people was one reason why gold was withdrawn from the currency. When a jewel robbery occurs, the police immediately repair to the dwellings of suspected parties, and water the floors of the houses and grounds about them, a sure way, in this climate, of ascertaining if the soil has been recently disturbed.

I must mention a most curious relic which lies within the arsenal. It is a block with three legs, exactly resembling an ordinary butcher's block. It is cut in one piece out of hard iron-stone, and its weight must be prodigious. On one of the legs there is an appearance which seems to indicate that it terminated in a claw. In the centre of the block there is a round hole, large enough to allow the head of a goat to pass through it. Solid as is the substance, it is much corrugated by time, for it has every appearance of being wonderfully old. Some people suppose it to have been a sacrificial table, used by the aboriginal tribes who inhabited the deep jungles, which, until an almost recent period, covered this part of the Deccan.

One of the most interesting ruins of the Mahomedan period existing in the fort is a ruined gateway of great size, under which passed the road that led from the main gate to the palace. The fine pointed archway, with battlemented top, is flanked by wings set with smaller arches. On its summit the naubat, a large kettle-drum, was struck at stated hours, and on it salutes were played. Not less time-hallowed and suggestive of the period, is a beautiful tomb, with dome and minarets, which, shaded by lofty trees, stands on a little maidan, or green, close to our domain. Elegant little memorial stones, wrought with verses from the Koran, in Persian characters, are scattered around it. Would that I could have painted some of the picturesque figures which I have seen grouped about this spot. One scene is particularly impressed upon my memory. The sky was intensely blue, all around was bathed in such glorious sunshine

as brings happiness with it. I looked up from
my book. A large black elephant, munching
its sugar-cane breakfast, stood in relief against
the tender grey walls of the mosque tomb. Its
driver, a wild-looking being, with streaming
locks, was leaning upon his goad, whilst overhead a golden nikure, one mass of flame-
coloured flowers, relieved with feathery foliage
of leaden green, threw out its horizontal limbs,
and formed a right royal canopy. Sometimes a
pilgrim from over the sea, with staff in hand,
long rows of beads which had been blessed at
Mecca, and flowing beard of orange tinge, would
steal into the shade, mutter a short prayer over
the bones of the saint whose fame had reached
his ears, and pass on his restless way. In mo-
ments of idle reverie, I used to think what a
Paradise I could make of the old fort, if it were
my own property, and suddenly wake up to
the conviction that the improver's hand would
but destroy what, in its present state of partial
decay and neglect, is ideally perfect.

CHAPTER X.

WE had in the fort a great variety of fine timber-trees and beautiful shrubs. Some of them, which were rare in this part of the Deccan, had been brought to the little oasis, and assiduously cultivated in its golden age. In India the ramifications of certain vegetable families appear to be interminable. It is only possible to notice a few of the most prominent specimens. Having plenty of time at my disposal, I amused myself with preparing a collection of leaves and flowers for a sister at home. Had I commenced with a fair knowledge of botany, I should have derived much more pleasure from the pursuit; but even learning a few of their properties, and the native legends attaching to them, was entertaining.

Trees are worshipped by the Hindoos, as the forms of particular gods. They receive divine honours, and are set apart with the same ceremonies as are common at the setting up of the gods. Any individual who consecrates a tree says, " Oh ! Vishnu," or " Shiva, grant that for planting this tree I may continue as many years in Heaven as this tree shall remain growing in the earth. Grant that as I have set apart this tree to afford shade to my fellow-creatures, so after death I may not be scorched by excessive heat when I journey to Yama, the region of death." There are six trees which are particularly sacred, and are never cut down or burnt by devout Hindoos—namely, ficus Indica, mimusops elengi, terminalia citrina, philanthus emblica, melia azodaracta, ogle marmelos ; most of which bear odoriferous flowers.

The most sacred of them all is the banyan (*ficus Indica*), of which we had a noble specimen. Its furrowed bole was composed of many stems, welded together ages ago ; and its top formed a vault of verdure. This tree appeared to have long lost its tendency to throw down aerial roots, which had most likely been cut away, possibly by the conquering Mussulmans, for no Hindoo would thus have maimed the tree. The banyan attains great length of days, one being pointed out near the Nerbuddha, under the shade of which Alexander is said to have slept. It may be so, for according to some botanists these, and other patriarchs of the forests, are but aggregates of buds annually succeeding on the stem, which represents a living soil. Savants even go so far as to say that in the wilds of Africa there are trees which are five thousand years old. The wood is very astringent, and much used in Hindoo medicine ; and its soothing juice is said to be good for the toothache. It is also made into bird-lime. Nor must we forget that, according to Milton, this was the fig which grew in Paradise, the leaves of which were also taken to clothe our first parents. We had also the child-bearing fig (also *ficus Indica*) the aerial roots of which were less decided and not so numerous as those of the banyan. The women worship it, and eat the berries with which its tender branches are studded, as round as marbles, and as red as coral.

Set down amongst the scattered foundations of some building which probably they had been instrumental in destroying, were a row of peepul-trees (*ficus religiosa*), the roots of which are very destructive, if once they attain a footing in the chinks of masonry. It is an exceedingly sacred tree, and is to be found fenced round by a platform in every Hindoo village. Women especially venerate it, because they believe that Vishnu was born under its shade. Beneath it they perform the ceremonies succeeding childbirth ; and they use its sticky juice for smoothing their hair. It attains a great height, but the foliage is quivering, and not effective. Though the leaf is pretty in its bright green youth, it soon assumes a dull tint. It is heart-shaped, and the mid rib is prolonged into a softish spike, which extends a couple of inches. The wood yields caoutchouc. In Ceylon it is called the bo-tree. Sir Emmerson Tennant mentions one which, on documentary evidence, he believes to have been planted two hundred and twenty-eight years before Christ. The Buddhists adore this tree, as they believe that their great teacher, Sakiya, was reclining under it when he underwent his apotheosis. The most aspiring of all the tribe is the india-rubber tree (*ficus elastica*), with its long glossy leaves and crimson capsules. It was strange, whilst looking up at its gigantic limbs, to recall the little plants of the same description, furnished with half a dozen leaves, often so carefully tended in England; still the great rosy shoots had a familiar appearance. One of the remarkable points of this tree is its manner of throwing out prodigiously long spurs, which stretch along the ground in ridges of more than a foot in height.

The ficus glomerata was another very considerable tree, which bore a profusion of fruit, in appearance much resembling the small English fig; but though its flavour is unpleasant, it is eaten by the natives. In the bearing season it gives forth a strong, sickly perfume, which is most disagreeable.

There were numbers of tamarind-trees, particularly two giants in our own garden. The skeleton bears some resemblance to that of a large elm, but as if for the sake of contrast, its gnarled and far-stretching limbs are clothed with leaflets of the most delicate fern and tenderest green, fine as those of a sensitive plant, which they much resemble. The huge corrugated bole teems with animal life, and its lofty crown is the delightful abode of numerous birds, whilst orchids and ferny plants cling to the rough bark, and plant themselves in its interstices. The blossom is insignificant, and the pod is many months before it reaches maturity. The wood is beautiful, but it is not often

used by cabinet-makers, for its exceeding hard-
ness makes it difficult to work. It yields a gum
called kuteera. The bole is often hollow, which
I should not have observed, had I not occasionally seen trees pierced by neatly scooped little
arches, which allowed the eye to penetrate into
their interior. This was the work of the Hindoos, who enthroned their divinities within
them. I could not but picture to myself the
strange appearance which the copper idol, surrounded by lights and garlanded with flowers,
would present, squatting in this shrine of
Nature's own handiwork. That curious phenomenon, the sleep of plants, was first observed in
India in the tamarind-tree, by Garcias de Horto,
in 1567, but it was not understood until de-
monstrated by Linnæus. The natives have an
idea that the tamarind renders the neighbourhood of the spot where it grows unwholesome,
but many plants which we planted about its
roots grew luxuriantly.*

---

* Plants are very innocent, and easily taken in. By
throwing a bright light upon those of a sensitive nature
during the night, and placing them in darkness during the
day, the botanist, Decandolle, succeeded in changing
their habit so far that they closed up their leaflets, and
slept the sunny hours away, while they opened them to the
artificial light thrown upon them, when others of their kind
were slumbering.

VOL. I.   Q

The tree which was our boast, in point of height, was a cotton-tree, said to be the tallest for miles around. When first I saw its ungraceful limbs they were bare; the cylindrical bole had a smoothish bark, thickly studded with sharp thorns, broad at the base, and nearly an inch long. Nature had taken extra care to guard its produce. The great blood-red flowers came forth with a glow of colour, but the blossom, pulpy and coarse, will not bear examination. The long thick pod, which in due time burst and poured forth an amazing quantity of soft, silky, cream-coloured cotton, appeared to be composed of a flat circular membrane, with a tiny hole in the centre, from which a seed had fallen; but it was not easy to capture this substance, which was so light that it fled before the outstretched hand. The hedges and fields were covered so thickly with it that they looked as if the old woman had been plucking geese for a month. This cotton is unfortunately too short in the stopple to be worked up, and is therefore of very little value—a remark which is equally applicable to many other cotton-producing shrubs and plants which grow in the Deccan. The women make pillows of it, and bring them about for sale, offering a large one for a shilling. It is also quilted into the garments which the natives wear during the rains. It has a handsome leaf, composed of five deeply indented fingers, which spring from a main rib.

The jamun, a very ornamental tree, producing large timber, has bright glossy leaves, something like those of the beech. It bears bunches of purple fruit, something like grapes, but with a stone in the middle; but in spite of their tempting appearance, they were abandoned to the boys and birds. We had also the so-called Belgaum walnut (*Aleurites Triloba*), introduced into India from the Society Islands. The fine-coloured large leaves are three or five lobed, and the young foliage is covered with a mealy substance, which gives it a peculiar metallic appearance. It bears spikes of white flowers, and when the fruit is full-grown, it resembles a large unripe, white-dusted apricot. Two nuts are contained in the husk. I have often picked them up, but have never tasted them. The natives say that when ¦fresh they are very unwholesome, and require to be kept for a year before they are eaten. The tree, however, is valuable, on account of these kernels, which yield above fifty per cent. of fine clear oil.

There were some young but tall trees, which we took to be mangoes, until suddenly one of them put forth a quantity of petallated flowers of the purest yellow, when it proved to be the champac (*michella champaca*), a species which is highly estimated by the Hindoos. They celebrate its charms in their poetry, and will beg, steal, and even buy the blossoms at a high price; for they believe that their overpoweringly sweet perfume is particularly acceptable to their gods. I was obliged to discard a handful brought into my room, and the scent still clings to a blotting-book into which I put one of the flowers. The Buddhists also hold this tree to be sacred, and reserve its wood to make from it images of Sakiya (Buddha).

We possessed a cluster of the cocoa-nut palm, the most elegant of all the tribe. We were proud of the half-dozen nuts they bore, for their production proved that we were within the influence of the sea breeze. Scattered about were many Palmyra-trees, but several of them were past their prime. The cylindrical stem, a little wide at the base, was set so firmly upon the ground, without visible roots, that it always reminded me of a Doric column—all the more so as it grew in joints of about a foot high, which might well have been taken for smooth-tooled stones. The strings of seeds which burst from the huge pods, sweeping down until they attained a length of more than ten feet, were their greatest beauty. At first the threads were very delicate and green, as they swayed about, making me think what mermaids' hair might be like. The seeds, set in groups of three on alternative sides of the thread, were at first very small, but they swelled until they were as large as marbles. The trees then became black and ugly, and were hacked down. So heavy had they then become, that it took three men to lift one of them into the refuse cart.

We were fortunate enough to have a soap-nut tree (*Sapindacea*), which had a soft, bright green leaf, with a downy brown stem, and bore spiked heads of little pale flowers, which fructified into nuts, sold by the ounce in the bazaars. The husk of these nuts is the valuable part. Soaked in tepid water, it forms a lather, which is employed with good effect in cleaning silks, washing flannels, and restoring the colour of woollen garments.

The sandal, growing in every hedge and compound, is a thin, straggling tree, with distorted limbs, and is described as a species of myrtle. The leaves, which are small, pointed, and shiny, are symmetrically arranged on each side of a slender stem. The fragrant branches fetch a high price, as all classes desire the sweet-scented boughs for the celebration of their funeral rites. Notwithstanding this, however, the tree bears an evil reputation with the fanciful natives. I met with the following description of it in the translation of a remnant of an ancient Hindoo treatise upon timber: " The root is infested by serpents, the blossoms by bees, the branches by monkeys, the summit by bears—in short, there is not a part of the sandal-tree that is not occupied by the vilest impurities." In spite, however, of this list of evils, the sandal-wood is so remunerative that the Forest Commissioners of this Presidency are about to make regular plantations of it on a plan which has been tried with success in Madras.

Under the names of Acacia Arabica, or Babool of India, I was not prepared to meet with my old friend, bearing the tiny powdery yellow balls, which at Cannes sell for forty francs the pound; yet there it was, set with sharp thorns, and growing wild in our compound. It was by no means so luxuriant as its better cultivated sister in the south of France, yet the flowers had even a sweeter perfume, and nothing could exceed the delicacy of the sensitive leaves. I could not succeed in pressing them with any good result, for, like those of a true Mimosa, they shut up the moment they were touched. The blossom in this country is appreciated only by the natives, to whom every sickly perfume is agreeable, and who offer them up in the temples. The rough crooked branches overflow with gum, which is eagerly collected in the jungles, and its pods of tree are greedily devoured by sheep and goats.

In addition to those I have named, we had two trees and a shrub of unrivalled beauty, a glorious trio. The first in the year to flower was one of many champac, a kind of magnolia, about twenty feet high. When bare, the stiffness of its skeleton is remarkable, the boughs, which branch out at right angles, being incapable of a curve or an inclination. The flowers, which are delightfully fragrant, come out in clusters, thousands of the narrow-petalled, vellum-like blossoms, white at the tips, but gradually assuming a hue which I can only liken to that of a golden sunset. The long, pointed, lance-like leaves soon mingle with the flowers, and when the latter pass away the foliage is very fine.

In the month of March the whole country is ablaze with the flame-coloured blossoms of the golden Mhune, a tree which is a native of

South America, and has not been acclimatized in India above fifteen years. I have not yet become acquainted with its proper name. Its growth resembles that of the cedar, but its horizontal limbs, which have a slight dip, are covered with the most exquisite foliage, fine as that of the sensitive plants, and large as the plumes of an ostrich, waving about, in varied tints of green. The leaflets fold themselves together, and sleep away the dark hours; the candelabrum, whose blossoms produce a most splendid effect, maintains its beauty all the year round. The Poinsettia, a very large, spreading shrub, which bears during the cold season, is a native of Mexico. The cluster of little yellow balls, which first appear, are soon surrounded by bags of pointed crimson-scarlet leaves, of unequal length. Nothing can be more superb than this flower, seen by the light of a tropical moon, when its lurid colour is bathed in the luminous atmosphere. This is the plant which adds so greatly to the splendour of the gardens of the Tâj at Agra, where it grows to perfection. Further north than that it does not flourish. It is a sticky plant to touch; its foliage of fine pointed pale green leaves is very handsome, and it is full of a white milk, which yields gum. It is not unusual to see whole

avenues of this shrub. We had a number of
Eucalypti in our garden, and all about the neighbourhood, planted with the idea of purifying
the air. In Algeria they were cultivated with
success. I have seen many of tolerably large
growth, which had been planted where lakes
had been drained, and where ground which had
lain fallow for a thousand years had been put
under cultivation, but they will not flourish in
the high table-lands of the Deccan. The only
specimen in the fort which appeared to be
healthy was one in our garden, so placed as to be
constantly irrigated, and consequently growing
with amazing rapidity.

The eucalyptus has been extensively planted
by Government in the Cannara jungles, but
I was told by one of the Forest Commissioners
that the experiment had failed. It is an ugly
tree, with small oval blue-green leaves, which
grow so close to the branches that they
cannot be separated from them without being
torn, in which case they emit a powerful aro-
matic odour, the medicinal qualities of which
are considered to be valuable in cases of fever.
The eucalyptus is the true monarch of the
forest kingdom. In the almost untrodden
regions of Australia trees have been met with
that surpass in size even the Wellingtonia

Gigantea.   Ferdinand Müller, the botanist,
says that trees of the species eucalyptus amyg-
dalina, four hundred and eighty feet in length,
were met with lying on the ground ; a fact perfectly confirmed by the statement of Mr. George
Robins, who saw in the mountains of Berwick
one of those trees standing, which had, near the
ground, a circumference of eighty-one feet, and
the height of which he estimated at five hundred
feet.   This eucalyptus, therefore, could over-
shadow the great pyramid of Egypt, and the
spire of Strasbourg Cathedral, for the former is
only four hundred and eighty feet in height, and
the latter four hundred and sixty-six.

CHAPTER XI.

Our Bungalow—Building in India—Anglo-Indian Words
—Beautiful Floral Display—Tameness of Bird and
Beast—Buffaloes—Our Establishment of Servants—
Butler and Cook—The Puttah Wallee—The Malee,
or Head-Gardener—Frequent Demands for Holidays
—Want of Privacy—Pretended Christians—Expenses
of the Table—Grafting of Mangoes—Provisions, Fruit,
and Wine.

OUR bungalow, a charming residence, consisted entirely of a ground floor, the construction of which always reminded me of a French
church. The lofty drawing-room had a rounded
end, the long dining-room crossed it, and
through the vestibule were seen the stout pillars set upon square bases, which supported the
southern verandah and the lofty porch. The
sacristies were numerously represented by the
bedrooms, which ran along the sides of the
house. The building was almost entirely enclosed by wide verandahs, delightful places of
resort, always shady, but never gloomy; and
the whole was packed under a high-pitched

roof of tiles, which swept down to within some ten feet of the ground.

Large as the house was, we had to add to it, and I watched the erection of what were to be my own quarters, with much interest. The new rooms were built of great square blocks of calasite, and every morning there came some wonderful old women, with metal ornaments, and blue savis with red borders, who had pestles two yards in height, with which they pounded away at a quantity of lime and fine sand, which was to form the flooring. This the builder called chunam, but the true chunam, which is much used in Eastern houses, is made of white shells, reduced to an almost impalpable powder, which is made into plaster, and produces a most brilliant effect.

The old ladies, who always arrived with the dawn, reminded me of Michael Angelo's three fates; and as they worked they used at first to chant in parts, probably some old history, which effectually scared away my slumbers. I was obliged to learn the magic word which meant in English " Hold your tongue !" which, after it was hurled at them, silenced them for ever. I trust, however, that it might have had a milder signification in Máhratta.

In my ignorance I was all astonishment at see-

ing two dark brown boys, clad in little beyond
the sacred thread, but decked out in silver
bracelets, anklets, earrings, and relic-boxes,
perched on my skeleton roof, and putting on
the tiles. A canvas ceiling was spread, but
not until there had been much delay in consequence of the unpunctuality of the dersei (tailor)
who had to stitch it together. This man, in
consequence of a death in his family, had a
half-grown beard, and G—— used periodically
to threaten to shave him if he did not get on
with his work, a penalty the infliction of which
would have entailed upon him dire disgrace.

Then the builders cleared out, and were succeeded by a band of women who brought large
bundles of prepared palm strips which they
wove into smooth, sweet-scented matting,
forming a pattern by introducing strips of
different colours. They brought with them
black babies with unnaturally large eyes,
who rolled about in a corner, and sucked
guavas. I used to watch these women, who
were very young (possibly not above thirteen
or fourteen), wonder at the dexterity with
which they used their flexible toes, and
admire their pretty round arms, which were
tattooed so completely that they looked as if
covered with fine lace. The sight of them

seemed to make intelligible the words of Goethe, when he said, " The painting and tattooing of the body is a return to animalism."

When they vanished, I took possession of my pleasant chamber, with its dressing and bath-room. It had a large glass door, opening into the verandah, a French window, with a low seat, and two cottage windows, which gave upon the garden. I felt it strange to leap out upon the tropical vegetation. Some of the great arum leaves, bronzed, or soft as velvet, lobed and pointed, were a yard in length ; and there was a palmesettia, covered with crimson blossoms, through which the fine-pointed green leaves were seen. There was also the amaran-this, with its superb golden flower, which I had only previously seen in store-houses. The stephanalis was near, for its sweet perfume was wafted into the chamber. Then there were large pyramids of the double geranium, and ferns, from the Nilgherries, the Cannara jungles, and the pathless ghâts ; and through them I could see the waving plantain-trees, and a great banyan, with aerial roots, and tall Palmyra-trees, backed by light green clouds of the sensitive foliage of the tamarind-tree. My easy-chair was a place to dream in. The book in my lap lay neglected, I could not help following the flight of the bright birds and glorious butterflies as they glinted by, or watching the changing hue of the chameleons as they darted about.

The house stood in about two acres of ground—the Compound, as it was called, a name so indicative of its various divisions that I was tempted to use it, for I was ignorant that it was a corruption of the Malay word Kompany, and imagined it to be one of those Anglo-Indian words to which I have a great aversion. (Why cannot people, for instance, say luncheon, instead of tiffin?) To the north lay the stables, the kitchens, and other offices, the poultry houses, the sheds for the milk-giving animals, sheltered by trees,and hidden by a building erected by G——, and a rabbit-house, which looked exceedingly like a family mausoleum. In the midst of the enclosure rose the old arched tomb, where a certain cobra was known to keep watch over the bones of Afzool Khan's prime minister.

On one side, near the front of the house, there grew a great round-headed rámplul, which yielded an immense quantity of fruit, esteemed as sacred by the Hindoos. It was large, heart-shaped, and netted, and was full of custard, in itself a perfect meal, but by no means one which was digestible. This tree was enclosed by trellis-work, which was covered by fine creepers; and within the bower were set such flowers as loved the shade. On the other side was a Badminton ground, where benches and seats were arranged; and there were flower-beds and a splendid collection of caladiums. One very tall fir-tree rose near this spot, with peculiar foliage, as fine as horse-hair, and round its great trunk there clung a night-blowing cenus, a long-pointed plant, which climbed until it attained the height of sixty feet, and then threw out great straggling sprays.

One day we discovered that these were covered with dull yellow buds, which pointed upwards; and when, in the evening, we had lights brought under it, never could I have imagined so glorious a specimen of the floral world. The flowers, above a foot in length, had turned over in opening, and hung suspended above us in exquisite beauty. We counted two hundred and ten of the great star-like cups, but no doubt there were many hidden by the stems and branches. A long ladder was brought, and some half-dozen flowers were cut off. Although so large, nothing could exceed the delicacy of their texture; the wax-like leaves, white at the tip, were lemon-colour at the bore, and the deep fringe of exquisite fine petals was of a rich deep golden hue. We had been told that, if the flower was deprived, when plucked, of its long stem, it would last much longer. We did not, however, find that the operation made any difference in this respect. All faded in a few hours, and lost their sweet perfume. The blossom, though much finer, bore some resemblance to that of the water-lily. In this great rush of vigour, Nature had for this season exhausted itself, and we looked in vain for succeeding buds.

The confiding tameness of bird and beast is one of the pleasures of Indian life. All the butter and the ghi used for cooking was made at home. The two great buffaloes, called, from the rivers that watered their native plains, Krishna and Malparba, came up morning and evening to be milked, at the side verandah, into shining brass vessels. Their little ones accompanied them—tame things, with budding horns and lucid eyes, who were pleased to have their heads rubbed, and to follow one about for bits of sugar-cane. Buffaloes' milk is very rich, and produces the thickest of cream. Then the small Deccan cows came up with their calves. With the exception of the hump upon the neck, they bear a great resemblance to certain Swiss cows.

They are black and ash-colour, and very wicked.
M. eventually got rid of our old friends the
goats, which required constant attention, as
they must browse whilst in milk. With one
exception, the poultry were confined to their
own quarters. The favoured bird was a turkey
cock, who had a history, having been singled
out for his merits to grace the festive board
upon the anniversary of G—— and M.'s wed-
ding-day. On the very eve of the joyous occasion, however, he sickened with a severe attack
of small-pox, which was the means of preserving
his life for many months. He was very fond of
following me about, but not altogether out of
friendship. My feathered friend ultimately disappeared, and I was too prudent to ask any
questions regarding his absence. The great
twin brothers had their kennels close to the
house, and would occasionally steal into it, to
the vast indignation of Bustle, who would never
cease barking until, with their tails between
their legs, and drooping ears, they, for the sake
of peace, took their departure.

The human creatures about us formed a mot-
ley population—Protestant and Roman Catholic,
Mahomedan and Hindoo. In consequence of
the sub-division of labour in an Indian establishment, wages are the greatest item of ex-

pense. On the first of every month quite a crowd flocked up to the office to receive their money, on which occasions G—— had never less than thirty-three pounds to disburse, and often above that sum. These people were highly and regularly paid; they were well cared for when sick; their wages were never cut (a common and convenient way of punishing domestic offences); but they were kept up to their work, and no sauntering about, or peeping round corners, was allowed. Many of them had followed their master from Sattara, and there was seldom a change. The children had an English nurse —a dear old woman, whose one standing grievance was the difficulty of renewing the poke bonnet of her youth, which she insisted upon retaining. She had an ayah under her, who spoke our language, and was strictly enjoined to teach no word of Máhratta to her charges, and not to be eternally petting them, and picking up their toys.

The conversation of the most respectable natives is very impure, and though children at the time may not understand what is said, the meaning of a coarse speech often dawns upon them when they are older. The second rule was laid down because M. and G—— desired their children to be thorough English children, and disliked the half-Indianized, fretful little beings so often to be met with. It is not uncommon to see two native women and a man anticipating every whim of some querulous little thing, who would have considered it a hardship if required to lift up her own doll from the floor. I have seen an ayah and three Sepoy orderlies engaged about a couple of little children, the soldiers even assisting in tubbing them. Our ayah, though possibly not more than five-and-thirty, was so stiff and shrivelled that she had an air of positive old age; she was very small, and very black, and as she sat in her low chair, or on the ground, with her skinny arms round the fair child, she looked exactly like a monkey wrapped up in white muslin. She wore mysterious pockets and leather bags under her external garment, and was the slyest of old women. She used to steal out in the grey of the morning, and drawing a long bamboo from its place of concealment in the hedge, she would knock down the ripest mangoes and guavas, conceal them about her person, and creep back again, quite unconscious of the amusement which I had derived from watching her stealthy movements.

The butler, a young man, with a face like a bronze lion, was a Portuguese—at least, he came

from the Portuguese settlement of Goa, which
sends forth numbers of servants, who are
necessary, for a Hindoo would not place beef
upon the table. He had a young wife in the
compound, and when any particular ceremony
took place in the Goanese chapel, she used to
steal G——'s flowers, I was going to say to his
*un*utterable indignation, but I recall the first
part of the word.

In India, a butler is a very important personage (in G——'s household only such duties
devolved upon him as would have been his
business in England), but he is not to be envied.
He represents all the other domestics, and is
scolded for their faults and omissions; he orders
the dinner, he gets in the stores, and sees that
the babies and the horses are properly fed. It
often happens that the master is tired, or lazy,
and that the mistress speaks no word of Hindustani; the weather is hot, and they are both
thankful to have a deputy who keeps the heterogeneous household together. Our second man was
a Mahomedan, and a respectable one, although
he did not object to our eating ham with turkey.
Our housemaid, as we called him, was a mild
Hindoo, a favourite with G—— and myself, but
not so with M., who declared that he was capable of pulling an iron bar in two. It is astonish-

ing what this race can do with their subtle, gristly fingers. He had a woman under him whom we never saw. He was a man of good caste, and to touch anything in the bath-rooms might have cost him a trip to the Ganges. G——'s waiter was Portuguese, his puttah-wallee a Mahomedan. Like all his race, he was sharp, active, and hard, but tolerably trustworthy. He had charge of the office, wore a long coat, with a band crossing over one shoulder, which was fastened on one side by a metal badge, on which was engraved his master's names, &c. It is the puttah-wallee's duty, if required, to accompany the children and nurses when they walk or drive, but that was not permitted in this model household. Had I submitted to it, he would have followed me in my walks, and carried my books to and from the library. If there was a party, it was he who ushered in the guests, and on such occasions, to the great amusement of M. and myself, he arrayed himself in a straight garment which came down to his heels, and was made of brocaded pink satin. His smart red turban served him as a pocket, and in its folds he carried all notes confided to his care. Like all the other servants, he never entered the house save with naked feet (the nails, both of the hands and feet of the natives, are carefully tended by professional persons, who know also something of surgery, and there are female barbers for the women), but out of doors he wore sandals worked with gold, which might have excited the envy of an ancient Roman. We had two derseis, or tailors, who sat in the verandah, made our dresses, brushed them, put them away, and ironed all our muslins. They were very nice quiet men—Hindoos—with the dreadful eye between perpendicular lines upon their foreheads.

Of course the cook was a very important person, and as beef and bacon were again a consideration, a Portuguese reigned over the department. As usual, this functionary had a mate under him, and as M. could harangue him both in the tongue of the country and in Spanish, which did duty for Portuguese, they got on very well. It is astonishing what these men can do with small means. M. insisted upon the use of a dresser and rolling-pin, but paste in general is made upon a board placed on the floor, and smoothed out with a bottle. On one occasion a ball-supper was in preparation, and M. thought that some pies in cones would look very well, but how to ornament them was the question. The babbajee pondered till a bright idea struck him, and he looked up with a radiant face; he could mould the designs, and, if Madam would only lend him her paints and brushes, he could manage to perfection.

The málee, or head gardener, was a strange-looking man, with a thing like a cap of liberty on his head, a splendid silver waist chain, several earrings, a necklace, and a relic box, that is to say, a box containing the emblem of his sect. The greater part of his ill-shaped head was shaved, but down the centre a straight narrow line of hair was allowed to grow, ending in a circular patch, by way of representing the dreadful eye, and his would-be whiskers were trimmed into patterns. Hindoos bestow the utmost care upon their hair, which is exceedingly luxuriant, and their barbers trim it and arrange it in all sorts of fanciful fashions. G—— had two orderlies, one of whom was from a native regiment, who sometimes had their shining tresses braided into innumerable plaits, and folded up at the back of their heads. I wish that I could have sketched our dobies (washermen), father and son, both such handsome, stately-looking men. This occupation is peculiar to people of good caste. The beestie, with his great cream-coloured bullock (its hump wreathed with flowers on festival days), was a picturesque object.

There was one man in the establishment to whom I had the utmost aversion, for he was cruel to his cattle. He had in his charge a little buffalo, who had been given to me as a pet. The poor thing used to yearn for the green grass, which was almost under his nose, and which it might have had with very little trouble; but it was only by resorting to bribery that I could obtain for it proper attention and a little indulgence. This man would sometimes point out to me wounds which had been inflicted upon him by his animals. I felt myself obliged to look commiserative, as I wished to conciliate him; but I used to think to myself that I was very glad that he was hurt. The appearance of this individual was most remarkable; he had large nostrils, but scarcely any nose; his hard, bright eyes were perfectly round, and he wriggled his lithe body about when he walked. I do think that this man must have been a snake in some former state of existence, and this reptile had a kind of sympathy for him. The bite even of a cobra, he declared, he found to produce no ill effects. It is certain that he caught several in our compound, and that G—— saw one of them (not a cobra) produce blood by its bite. He was alarmed, but the uncanny creature laughed, and went on his way unharmed, and apparently unconcerned. We always called him " the missing link."

The domestics were occasionally very troublesome in asking for holidays, and that under such plausible pretexts that it was difficult to say no. One man would desire a few days in which to marry his daughter and feast his friends; another would announce that his father, or some other near relative, was dead and that he must attend to the funeral ceremonies. When G—— was from home, the death-rate increased to an alarming extent, and at last became so seriously inconvenient that we had to assemble the household, and announce that none of their relations were either to marry or to die until their master returned. Our friend the brigadier told us that he had set up a register of such events, and that upon his butler's saying that he must go and bury his father, he pointed out to the man that the relative in question had departed this life seven months previously. The butler never attempted to argue the point, but grinned, and appeared to be pleased rather than otherwise that the event should have been recorded.

In general, the trying part of an Indian establishment is its want of privacy, for there

are very few houses in which the servants are
not all over the place. If there happen to be
visitors, they cross through the rooms on the
slightest pretence, merely to look at them.
Perhaps the dersei will take the opportunity of
bringing in some torn garment, having all of a
sudden grown most conscientious as to the
manner it which it is to be mended. The doors
and windows being of necessity open, there are
eyes and heads everywhere, if allowed, but not
a sound indicates the presence of their owners,
who steal round the corners with naked, noise-
less feet, their garments never rustling. Natives
are very curious, and dearly love to gossip
when their masters are out, gathering together
in the roads, and discussing the affairs of the
family over the garden hedge. Great mischief
has arisen from this custom, and from the habit
which some ladies, who would scorn to do so at
home, have of talking to their ayahs, who, in
such cases, collect all the personal gossip they
can, and, of course, colour it highly; but ayahs
are rapidly going out of fashion, and ladies, if
possible, secure European attendants in their
houses and about their persons. Still the
native servants, more especially the Hindoos,
have very good points. During a great afflic-
tion with which God, for some inscrutable good

purpose, was pleased to visit us, they showed their sorrow and sympathy in a most simple and unobtrusive manner.

I cannot help saying a few words respecting those servants that called themselves Christians. It may seem to be a startling assertion, but it was a fact: they were a most unprincipled set of people, for they were hypocrites, who professed any religion to serve a purpose. The missionaries declare that this class work infinite mischief, for they mislead many of the English with whom they come in contact, by inducing the unreflecting to believe " that the heathen, when converted, only make bad Christians, and are better left alone." Such is the speech in many a mouth. Respecting the best means of winning over the Hindoo race to true Christianity, people differ greatly. I do not presume to offer an opinion upon so momentous a subject—indeed, I am not sure that I have one (how lightly people talk of their opinions!) ; but to my mind the following lines, written by one who was competent to judge, are very significant :—

" It cannot be doubted that the endeavour to diffuse Christianity amongst the higher classes of the natives is one of very great importance, for the institution of caste gives the higher classes greater influence in India than in any other country; but it was found that they could not be reached by any of the agencies formerly at work, and up to the present time it is only by means of an English education of so high an order as to prove an attraction to them, that those classes have, in any degree, been brought within the range of Christian influences. The number of persons actually converted to Christianity from year to year, by means of these schools, has never been considerable, and seems smaller of late years than ever. On the other hand, the converts of this system, though few in number, belong to an influential class; and it is an interesting circumstance that, through their influence and example, Christianity has spread, in some degree, amongst persons belonging to the same class who have never been at mission schools at all, or who have attended schools from which Christianity has been carefully excluded. The good effected by these schools cannot be safely estimated by the number of conversions that has actually taken place in connection with them, for it is universally acknowledged that they have done much good incidentally. Many Hindoos, who still adhere to their ancestral faith, value these schools highly on account of the high moral tone by which they are pervaded. It is chiefly

owing to the influence of these schools that we
see amongst the Hindoos such a spirit of inquiry,
and the germs, at least, of so many moral and
social reforms."

To a Hindoo the most attractive form of
Christian religion is that of the Roman Catholic
Church; but, strange to say, the missionaries sent
to India occupy themselves very little with the
conversion of the heathen; they rather seek to
make proselytes from other Christian communi-
ties. Our ayah was one of their converts. I
used to wonder what her ideas upon the subject
could really be, for, from all I could gather, they
appeared to be most cloudy, and certainly, if
she had any religious convictions, she did not
bring them to bear upon her moral conduct,
and I have observed that Christianized ayahs,
in general, fall back upon caste if they have any
task allotted to them which they are unwilling
to perform. But is it surprising that such
should be the case? This woman had inherited
the fatal legacy of a hundred generations of
heathenism, had to rid herself of the evil ten-
dencies handed down to her, to forget the gross
converse of her youth before she could become
a Christian at heart. The Lenana Mission is
widely spread, and is supposed to produce good

fruit, but it has many stumbling-blocks to encounter, one of which is the aversion which the native lady has to the idea of learning to read; her narrow mind associating learning, in a female, with vice, for the only Indian women hitherto so instructed were the dancing girls belonging to the temples. Moreover, the generality of Hindoo men are against the movement. A highly enlightened native said to me, "Before our women and girls are educated, we must have a new literature."

The ordinary expenses of the table were moderate, as we had abundance of cream and vegetables of our own. Mutton was but three halfpence the pound. Nothing could look more delicate than the joints, but it was necessary to use the meat whilst unpleasantly fresh, and it had a strong, oily, woolly flavour to which I never became reconciled. M. entered into a speculation with regard to mutton, which ought to have enriched the family, but it was a failure. She bought a small flock of sheep, and took base advantage of a meadow which G—— had hired for the cows and buffaloes. Though they were full-grown, these sheep did not cost more than fourteen shillings the half-dozen. Beef was plentiful and tolerably good, and was the same price as mutton, but there is a prejudice against

the flesh of this animal, which is said to induce
certain maladies of a painful nature. It is
generally buffalo beef, and these animals, being
very impure feeders, are often fed upon stable
refuse, and for the same reason the milk and
ghi sold in the bazaars are often unwholesome.
Occasionally, however, a fine one would arrive
from Bijipur or Gokák, and then a notice, word-
ed in the most peculiar manner, was sent round.
G—— generally managed, amongst other parts,
to secure the hump, which is excellent, if carefully salted; when near its end, it grates like
hung beef, but when it first comes to table it looks
like a great red cloven foot. Veal was good,
but not common, and fresh pork we never saw.
The poultry, a little tough in consequence of its
freshness, was otherwise good, being fattened
at home. It was reared in the Portuguese territory, and brought from thence in great round
baskets, balanced upon the heads of wild dark
men. The birds were very tame, and whilst
their masters and the butler were striking their
bargains they were let out to take a walk and pick
up what they could. If not bought, they were
guided back to their cages by a twig with a
bunch of leaves at the end. I came to look upon
Goa as a land flowing with milk and honey; all
the best mangoes come from thence, as well as

oranges and other fruits. From thence G——
used to get up casks of excellent pure wine,
which entered Goa from the mother country, free
of duty, but a heavy tax had to be paid at the
British frontier. Still the wine, which was rich
and rather strong, cost him less than a shilling a
bottle. The Branco was made from the white
grape, and somewhat resembled good raisin
wine; the Tinto was a kind of port, a little
rough, but well-flavoured. Coarse lace, made
very effectively by hand, was also brought from
the same quarter. Some people had it dyed to
match the colour of their dresses. Occasionally game was brought round—snipe, wild
duck, teal, a kind of bustard, partridges, &c.,
with painted plumage, but their flesh was remarkably hard and white. A fine hare could
be bought for a shilling. At certain seasons the
fresh-water fish made a pleasant addition to
the table. The marsal, which somewhat resembles a pike, is much esteemed. There were
eels in abundance; and a certain fry, which,
when sent up with slices of brown bread and
butter, deluded people into the idea that they
were eating whitebait. Prawns, which were
plentiful, were generally served up on toast,
without which no Anglo-Indian dinner is considered complete. The green chilli makes an

excellent toast; when young it is not so hot, and the flavour is most refreshing. Oysters would occasionally arrive all alive, but not good enough to be served up uncooked, having lost a good deal of their sea flavour from being kept artificially on their journey from the Malabar Coast.

People differed much in their appreciation of tinned provisions. With some exceptions, such as salmon and bacons and hams, which they got out whole from Aberdeen, they had a prejudice against them, considering them to be neither good nor wholesome. A good cook will send up an excellent dinner with little recourse to their aid. The great expense at a dinner-party is the champagne, which flows in abundance, many touching no other kind of wine; and at the messes it is now handed round at dessert. Our vegetable garden was so productive that we very seldom availed ourselves of those attached to the station, which, however, to many people are a great boon. We had all sorts of salads and ordinary vegetables grown from English seed, which must be renewed each season, as it deteriorates. The exotic sorts were sweet potatoes, a variety of marrowy guavas and pulpy productions, green sugar-cane, very young, which is cooked in various fashions, and the spike of the maze when tender. This is a favourite dish, but it is only presented *en famille*, as it has to be gnawed. What is called the thirty days' rice, grown during the rains, is nice, and much given to invalids. Fruit, to the European, is a great Indian luxury, and very wholesome, some half living upon it. Many varieties are of a very substantial nature, for in this latitude it was evidently intended to be the staple food of the inhabitants. Its cultivation, however, is somewhat neglected in this part of the Deccan, as there is not now sufficient demand for the finest sorts. When communication with other parts of the country was slow the case was different. Many people remember our compound a luxuriant grove of orange and lime-trees; but a solitary specimen alone remains now, and that is strangled and hidden away by a great creeper. Doubtless the fruit of the mango stands first. If uncultivated, the tree spreads into a forest, with far-stretching branches and noble foliage; by cultivation it is dwarfed. It bears an endless quantity of fruit, and is most luxuriant near the sea. In its early stage the fruit resembles a large unripe plum, and is suspended from the parent in branches, each on its long green thread. It gradually assumes an oval, flattish, and not very symmetrical form, and becomes golden yellow, green with a flush of red, or russet, according to its variety. Some of them taste so strongly of turpentine as scarcely to be eatable. One sort, which is rare, resembles an apricot, and is only served in perfection by the native princes, who moisten the roots with libations of fresh camel's milk. It cannot be bought, but G——, who has often eaten it, pronounces it to be delicious. Mangoes are grafted by the arching-in process, and in this country two devices are practised in order to render it, or other large trees, graceful. One consists in punching out here and there on the stem pieces of bark; the other in driving a large nail into the stem of the tree where the branches fork out. This, it is supposed, prevents the sap from descending, and concentrates it in the fruit-bearing branches. In some respects this fruit is inconvenient. It is said to tinge people yellow; its juice stains the hands, and woe be to your dress if the slippery stone falls upon it. The tree was introduced into the West Indies by Sir Joseph Banks, but has never attained such perfection there as in India.

It was a pretty sight to see the great baskets of fruit uncovered in the verandah—the large golden pines (principally from Goa) were much superior to those produced in the West Indies, and very nearly as good as our English hot-house productions. We had some in the garden, but there was scarcely any motive for growing them, as in the season we could get three for a shilling. Sometimes we bought plantains, but at others the great konds ripened so rapidly that we had to give them away. The long, narrow, green leaf, as it waves about, is very beautiful; they are often cut into shapes, and serve to convey certain articles in place of paper. There were numberless varieties of this fruit, but none of them, to our mind, so delicious as those we had eaten in North Africa. It was curious to watch the purple glow unfold. I have seen leaves a foot and a half long. Concealed under each leaf is a fringe of yellow threads, which force the covering off, and swell into the fruit. Sometimes there were great round pomelos, ornamented like the great globes hung suspended from the tree. The perfume of the blossom is delicious in the open air. They are not, in my opinion, good to eat, but I need not dwell upon their excellence when made into sherbet—that is a matter of history. The small-netted carland apple is both good and pretty.

One day a fresh fruit was brought for me to try—a fruit about which there can be no middle opinion, for it is either liked or disliked exceedingly. When the great spongy rind is cut open, it presents to view a number of raw-looking bags, the colour of uncooked veal. This is eaten in various ways, and is so glutinous that if mixed with sugar and put into a mould it will turn out in a shape. The large nut which each bag contains is, when roasted, said to be very like the chestnut.

We were fortunate enough to have a number of guava-trees, much esteemed not only for their fruit, but for their foliage, which is always green. Children are very fond of the raw fruit, but I must confess to liking it best when stewed. The soft furry rind alone is used when thus prepared, but when jelly and port are made, the seed which fills the interior like that of a fig is also employed. Stewed citron is very nice; and the shrub with its glossy, myrtle-like leaves is highly ornamental.

Some like the loquât, the fruit of which grows in clusters, and look like little yellow pears. What pulp it contains has a pleasant, sharp flavour, but the large and numerous stones are a drawback to its merits. The tree bears a beautiful blossom, and the foliage is fine. We had pomegranates, valuable for the beauty of the flower; but the fruit is poor in Western India, unless the tree, like ours, be well irrigated. It seems scarcely our sister-tree, which bears the enormous ruddy brown heads, bursting with the richness of their ruby contents, which G—— brought from Sind. We had an ornamental culinary plant, called the roselle. The part made use of is the husk of the berry, which contains the seeds—it makes the most delicious tarts, and a jelly finer in colour than currant jelly, for which it makes an admirable substitute.

Some deluded people, G—— included, were proud of their strawberries, but I never saw any in Belgaum that were worth eating. We had, however, a profusion of the so-called raspberry, a large downy bramble from the Nilgherries, which bore a fruit like a hoary blackberry, but red inside, and with very little flavour. The Cape gooseberry, or Peruvian cherry, the fruit of which makes an excellent preserve, is worth mentioning. Its bright yellow ball is concealed by angular leaves, and has a pleasant acid flavour. Of course I can only make mention of some of the good things with which our table was supplied, but I think that I have mentioned such a variety as to show that we did not starve in Western India.

G—— spared neither expense, time, nor personal labour upon his garden, and it was far the finest in Belgaum. During the dry season a number of hands were required morning and evening to water the plants in pots and tubs, which could not be irrigated. There were many beautiful creepers, trained upon trellises and frames of bamboo. I think that the bright pink sprays of the antigonon stood first. The leafy plants grew with the greatest luxuriance, and some of them were rare specimens. There were above five-and-twenty varieties of the caladium. The show of roses was almost as good as in a garden at home; the plants were sent over in tin cases by the best English growers. The vegetable growth was prodigiously quick, and required constant pruning and renewal of soil. I have seen a rose in bloom which had only budded three weeks previously.

Among the annuals the balsams attained the greatest perfection; the blossoms of the pink and white variety were as large as those of the variegated camellia. The balsam grows wild all over the country, but the exotic seed only answers for one season; planted a second time, you have the simple flower, which grows wild. It is the same with the chrysanthemum, which is also indigenous. The latter is ornamental even if carelessly cultivated, coming out in a profusion of small yellow blossoms. It was odd to see it blossom by the side of what in England would be called Summer plants.

A delicate, sensitive plant, which grew along the ground, was one of my favourites. The delicate leaves were of a fine green, but if swept over by the hand their beauty vanished, and a few dry sticks were alone visible. In this country Nature appears to delight in contrasting her colours; the tall bright yellow acacia, overtopped the gorgeous crimson poinsettia and clouds of pure blue convolvuli, grew by its side. It was a treat to open the windows in the fresh early morning, and look upon the hundreds of azure eyes which were drinking in the colour of the sky. Sometimes at night, when the very air seemed aglow, I used to step out to see the pure white moon-flower; the blossom was at least eight inches across, and emitted a delightful perfume. It is a kind of convolvulus. The juice of the moon-plant is mentioned in ancient Hindoo poetry as fit for the sustenance of hermits. Gardening in India is a great and very wholesome pleasure.

CHAPTER XII.

Difficulties of Driving—Red Dust—Venerable Groves—
Temples and Dharam Sálás—The Dheer's Well—The
Edgar—Churches and Chapels—Refuges for Lepers—
The Jack-tree—Jungle Creepers—Drives about the
Camp—Uses of the Acacia-tree—The Commissariat
Lines—Intelligent Elephants—Cultivation of Cotton
—Camping Parties—Fashionable Resort—Scene at
the Band Stand—Dogs Military and Civilian—Jam-
bottee.

UNTIL I got accustomed to the constant
turmoil which went on, I found driving
very fatiguing. To begin with, there was either
the insufficiently protected viaduct over the
fosse to be crossed, or we had to face the dark
way, the light in Durga's shrine, the sharp turns
of the main guard, and the earthworks. Then
the roads, although remarkably good, were
constantly blocked by herds of cattle going to
and fro to water, bullock-carts, tumbrils, and
waggons laden with cotton. As for the natives,
they appeared desirous of being run over, or at
least to consider that it was not their duty to

avoid an accident. It was the duty of the Gora-wallers to clear the way—black, keen-sighted men, who even in the dark could distinguish small objects. (In consequence of their perfect vision, Sepoys beat the English soldiers in firing at long range.) They were as active as monkeys, and were continually jumping up and down, shouting, running beside the horses, or waving white dusters, which I came to understand meant rocks ahead.

Fortunately, Arab horses are very courageous and steady; not even the fierce lightning, the glow of the blacksmith's or the baker's ovens, the flaming piles which on festive occasions are set by the roadside, or the torchlight processions accompanied by the shrieks and groans of barbaric music, daunting them. But in India horses get accustomed to the vicinity of flames, for every evening a heap of brushwood is kindled in their stables, in order to destroy mosquitos and other flies.

Belgaum is situated upon ferruginous clay stone, and no one who arrives there in the hot weather, before the rains, can fail to be astonished at the red hue which pervades the landscape. The top soil is completely pulverized, and everything—hedges and trees, roads, and houses—is covered with it; and when lit up by the glowing rays of a setting sun, the effect produced is quite weird-like. This red dust is destructive to wearing apparel.

Two roads led to the camp and downs, which were above two miles from the fort. One or the other was generally our destination. If we passed out by the smaller gate we crossed a charming piece of broken ground, dotted over with groups of palms, and solitary trees of prodigious growth. There was, for instance, the mango, so like the Spanish chestnut, the banyan, and others of the fig tribe, but most beautiful of all were the great trembling clumps of bamboo, vestiges of the thick jungle from which the place takes its name, Belgaum signifying Bamboo Town. These canes are so hard that they can with difficulty be cut, and some of them contain so much silica that upon striking them with a steel sparks are produced. They serve a hundred purposes, amongst others those of physic-bottles and pens, and replace the whalebone used in ladies' dresses. Beyond the town the plains are upon a larger scale. The single trees were replaced by venerable groves, with gnarled and far-stretching branches, which the the natives call topes. Sometimes their boles are hollow, or curiously twisted and distorted. In their solemn shade rose Hindoo temples and

altars, Mahomedan mosques, and here and there
a Dharam Sálá (Dharam is a Sanskrit word of
many meanings, in this instance signifying hall).
These places of refuge are open to travellers of
every rank and creed, who have nothing to do
but to mount the wide steps, throw down their
few possessions under the groined corridor, or
seek the deeper gloom of the Sálá. Some of
them are handsome buildings, either erected by
the neighbouring townspeople, or built by private individuals, who thus endeavour to work
out their salvation in another state of existence
into which they are to be introduced by a new
birth. There is always a well near at hand,
often a tank, and sometimes they are very
picturesque objects. In Indian romances the
Dharam Sálá is the theatre of all sorts of strange
events and queer encounters, and when I looked
upon the different groups of people I used to
wonder if they too had pathetic tales to tell, or
stirring events to recount. In unfrequented
places the Dharam Sálá is a mere mud hut.

Before the camp is reached we pass the
Dheer's well, which, although now dry, is carefully preserved as a relic of ancient times, when
the present town of Belgaum was not. It is to
this spot that the secret passage from the fort
is said to lead—why, no one can tell. Behind it

were some comfortable bungalows, with handsome gardens, shaded by some trees. To the right rose the Edgar, where on certain days the Mahomedans worship; and then the large Protestant church. The latter is built of brick, and not badly designed, but, alas! its foundations are imperfect. Yet it is quite a new building, and cost a vast sum of money. A Scotch church, a small establishment of teaching sisters, and two Roman Catholic chapels, cluster together in amity, the latter being a branch from the establishment at Bombay, and the officiating priests, who are English gentlemen, exceedingly painstaking.

At a short distance from the town, in an obscure spot, good men have established a small refuge for lepers, in which the unfortunate creatures, who have generally very large appetites, are fed, cleansed, and taught a little. Such institutions are now springing up in many towns, but it is not long since many of these miserable beings were secretly burnt, and even buried alive by their fellow-men, and even now numbers of these pariahs drag their weary limbs to some sacred stream, the Ganges, if possible, and drown themselves, fully persuaded that by so doing they ensure themselves a healthy body in the next sphere of existence. At some distance there was another Roman Catholic edifice, under the sway of the Archbishop of Goa, the priests of which were very jealous of their English brethren. We were told by our Portuguese servants that it would be considered an offence on their parts if they held any communication with the English Roman Catholic clergy.

The camp is backed by long lines of magnificent barracks, a region of bungalows and mess-rooms—a kind of Indian St. John's Wood, a labyrinth of fine broad red roads, beautiful gardens, and green compounds, to scarcely one of which the entrance was not guarded by a fine pair of curiously carved Jain pillars—alas! whitewashed—which had stood for centuries side by side in some sacred temple, until it had been despoiled by the iconoclast Mahomedans. These bungalows are the property of private individuals, but are subject to certain regulations, being under the authority of military rule, and no civilian can set up his household gods in one of them, if it is required for an officer. When a new regiment arrives great are the heart-burnings, and the frequent changes always reminded me of a game at " My ladies' toilette."

Some of the steep roads about this region were shaded by beautiful timber-trees, which frequently met overhead. At certain seasons

their beauty was enhanced by the parasites which
cling to them, among which were many orchids.
The vegetation is somewhat different from
that in the fort. The wood of the useful teak,
which here spreads its great leaves, is as dur-
able as that of oak, which it resembles in grain,
but the colour is much paler. It bears a remarkable blossom, the flowers growing in long
spikes, and giving a grey hue to the tree. There
was also the jack-tree, most valuable for its
hard wood, which attains a great height, and
roots itself firmly in the earth, with the evident
intention of standing for centuries. The fruit
grows upon stout foot-stalks, and projects from
the trunk and thickest branches. Oddly
enough, the position of the fruit varies with the
age of the tree, being borne first on the
branches, then on the trunk, and in old trees
on the roots. When the latter is the case, the
fruit bursts through the earth and discloses
itself, and is considered to possess superior
flavour. When half grown, the fruit suspended from the branches is of a ruddy brown,
and at a little distance resemble foxes' brushes.
When full-grown, the coarse rind becomes
green. An average-sized jack fruit weighs
forty pounds. There were many splendid
jungle creepers, slightly coarse in substance, if

examined, but remarkable for their vigour and glorious colour, such as the trumpet-creeper, an orange red; one with a beautiful lilac flower, the name of which I never learnt; and the more delicate red purple bougainville, more leafy, however, and not so vivid in hue as in Algeria, where the climate appears to suit it better.

The drives about the camp were charming; we gave home names to the bits of blue country, which, framed at the end of long avenues, looked so far away. There was the hill of Jellergur, rising all solitary from the plain, like the lone Soracte—that was our Italian view. To the east was disclosed a blue ridge of hill, with rich, far-stretching woods at its feet—Malvern from the Ledbury Hills; and, turning to the west, the rising forest and the purple peaks made us sigh for the old halls of our kinsfolk.

With all its beauty and fresh breezes, a residence in the camp has some drawbacks, particularly in being exposed to the utmost fury of the monsoon, and because the houses, built when Belgaum did not belong to the Bombay Presidency, are all turned the wrong way, as far as the weather is concerned, in order to suit the Madras monsoon. Worst of all, there is a deficiency of water. Many compounds have no wells, and when water has to be fetched, adieu to all idea of a really good garden, unless much money is spent upon it.

The broad road which led from the main gate, after passing the tank, crossed the moor. Looking back, a fine view of the fort, with its massive outworks, gates, and ruined towers, was obtained, along with jungle-clad hills to the east, famous for panthers. There were hedges of aloe, not the fine large aloe, or striped or blue tinged, so handsome in many countries, but the sharp, prickly plant known by the name of Adam's Needle; and there were numberless varieties of the acacia, some of them with spikes of white flowers, others yellow, one a small-leafed tree, bearing bunches of gold, like buttercups. The most remarkable variety was a tree which bore clusters of a cream-coloured vellum-like substance, shaped like great claws. Another kind, which was very insignificant in appearance, was very fragrant. Many of these acacias go to sleep so early that at first I imagined that they were dying for want of water, so shrivelled did they look; but on passing them next morning, they were as fresh and green as possible. All the acacia tribe yield gum, and the wood being very hard, it is used for carts, and for the primitive plough of the country. Shaped into the necessary form by the hand of Nature, man has but to cut down a stout branch which has an angular crook, fasten it behind his bullock, and guide it across the field, so that it rips open the earth. The great pods, which render the acacia ugly when it has dropped its leaves, and tend to destroy the beautiful effect of the fresh foliage, are very useful to the country people, whose skeleton cattle greedily devour them when they can obtain no fresh food.

The commissariat lines were soon reached. Sometimes when driving alone, I got out to look at the animals. A few horses, but many mules, are employed; handsome creatures ranged together in open sheds. There were rows of patient bullocks of the Brahman type, some of them of a beautiful cream colour, with glossy skins and very large, handsomely-formed horns, which in these animals are considered a great point. They came from the north of India, and were worth, at least, sixty guineas a couple. Then there were camels, very picturesque to look at, but as peevish and perverse as these creatures are all the world over. I have, in the Sahara, seen camels whom their owners have, for the time being, been obliged to abandon, in consequence of their determination not to move on. When this occurs, and it is frequently the case, some indications of the tribe to whom they belong is affixed to them, and if found alive by another tribe, even if enemies, they are bound to succour them and forward the animals to their masters. Such is the etiquette of the desert.

Of course, the elephants were the most interesting. One old fellow with great tusks, clamped round with iron rings, was known all over the country. On one occasion, the Commander-in-chief came, bringing with him an addition of twelve large animals, which were all tethered in an open yard. Most sagaciously did they twinkle their cold, grey eyes, but woe to anyone who touched their cakes or sugar-cane. One of these very elephants had killed his driver because the man had cheated him of a couple of cakes, of which they get a certain number each day. These elephants, so exacting as to what is their due, will not take more than they consider themselves entitled to. The cakes that remained, when we saw them, they lifted into a basket or some other receptacle, storing them for the morning meal, as they were about to march. A good elephant costs £100, and its yearly keep is reckoned at £120.*

---

* Why it should have been introduced I do not remember, but in one of Professor Max Müller's lectures, there is an

Past the commissariat the road split into forks, one of which turned towards the camp, another crossed the breezy downs, and a third led to the point, a pleasant spot where people met to enjoy the invigorating wind which invariably set in as the sun declined. I was fond of these swelling wolds, dotted over with large trees, principally of the fig order. Nothing could look more picturesque than the great camping parties which gathered around them on their way with cotton from Dharwar to Vingorla, where it would be shipped. Many and many a bale we saw there on its way to Manchester. A great deal of cotton is grown in the district, but not in the immediate neighbourhood of Belgaum, the soil not being sufficiently rich. It flourishes best

---

amusing anecdote respecting an elephant. A monk thus writes to one of his brethren at home, describing many wonderful things he has seen in Rome. " You may have heard how the Pope did possess a monstrous beast called an elephant. The Pope did entertain for this beast a very great affection, and now behold it is dead. When it fell sick, the Pope called his doctors about him in great sorrow, and said to them, 'If it be possible heal my elephant.' Then they gave the elephant a purge which cost five hundred crowns, but it did not avail, and so the beast departed, and the Pope grieves much for his elephant, for it was indeed a miraculous beast, with a long, long, prodigiously long nose; and when it saw the Pope, it kneeled down before him and said, with a terrible voice, ' Bar, bar, bar !' "

in the deep black earth around Dharwar, which is forty miles south of Belgaum, and close to the frontier of Madras. Until lately, the cotton in our part of the Deccan was raised from New Orleans seed acclimatized. At one time Egyptian seed was sown, but the quality produced was too fine to be remunerative. The cultivation of exotic cotton is now found to be a mistake, and its use was everywhere diminished. The first crop from the fresh seed comes up well, but after that the quality deteriorates. There are 300,000 acres under cultivation in the southern Máhratta country. The same soil will only produce good cotton once in three years.

The long narrow waggons or tumbrils were drawn up so as to protect the bullocks from the wind. Many of them were handsome animals, in good condition, eating their hay with serene satisfaction. Some of them had collars of tinkling brass, or, possibly, necklaces of cowrie shells, put round their necks, either to ensure good luck, or to scare away any malignant goblin who might approach them in the deep shade of the spreading trees. I dearly loved to pass these encampments at night, when the blazing fires cast their lurid light around; and large caldrons, set on stoves with red-hot embers under them, were throwing off clouds of white steam from the seething rice or other grain, whilst groups of wild-looking men sat down in circles, beguiling the time by chant-ing some very popular legend in a melancholy minor key. Sometimes we caught the fragrant odour of spices from a cargo of ginger, pepper-pods, or cardamum seeds on its way, like the cotton, over the great ridge of the Western Ghâts, and down into the Concan to the sea.

The favourite evening drive was to the point (there is a scandal-point at every station), where all the beauty and fashion of Belgaum assem-bled, in order to discuss the news of the day, arrange their plans for anticipated gaieties, and drink in the cool evening breeze. The point commanded an extensive and diversified view. The wide expanse of down and moor was broken by valleys, strips of wood, and little pools, which, like mirrors, reflected the beauty of the sky, smiling patches of blue, rosy red or orange, purple or black, as might be. We always turned our faces to the west, in order to catch the lingering daylight. In the far distance rose the spectral ghâts, which cut us off from the fertile Concan and the Arabian Sea. On the nearer hills we could mark the rough jungle by which they were crested. These hills abound with game, big and little, but they are not only famous for the sport they afford, they produce the garnet, or carbuncle, as the stone is called when over a certain size; and in the beds of the mountain streams gold-dust is found, not, it is true, to any large amount; but a man searching for it is sure of gaining at least a shilling a day. My informant—and he was a good geologist—told me that from the nature of the strata, so similar to that of Golconda, and the crystals it contains, he doubted not that diamonds also existed in it.

Cheeta Hill, as one of this chain is called, is a very paradise for the naturalist, abounding in beautiful birds, curious insects, lovely ferns, rare orchids, and curious pitcher-plants. Alas! snakes are also plentiful, and at certain seasons the deep jungle is most unwholesome. There is a race-course near the point, but nothing had been stirring on it lately. In an Indian station the amusements vary according to the pluck and purses of the officers stationed in it. A year or two ago a good pack of hounds was kept up. The sport was excellent, the country open, and there was plenty of foxes, to say nothing of the jackals, which afford good running.

During the previous monsoon, a gentleman met with a strange adventure near the point. As he was passing along in his dog-cart, to his surprise he saw something splashing about in a puddle by the side of the road, and on examination found that it was a young alligator. He got it carried to his quarters, where it was quickly provided with the largest tub the camp could supply, where, however, the creature only lived for two or three days. Alligators have been known to travel overland for considerable distances, and this specimen was supposed to have come from the Falls of Gokák, forty miles off, where they abound. But we afterwards heard that there were several in the tank, so perhaps after all he was only out upon a short exploring expedition.

The climate of Belgaum is delightful. In the middle of the day, during the cold weather, it was quite exceptional if the thermometor rose above seventy degrees; and it was equally so if it rose above ninety degrees during the hot season. The evenings and nights were almost invariably cool, occasionally cold. I am speaking of the temperature of a large room shaded from the sun, but never closed. Still the climate is undoubtedly trying, on account of the sudden change which takes place shortly before sunset, when the hot wind which travels over the great plains of India ceases to blow, and is succeeded by the cool breeze, sometimes

very strong, which has passed for thousands of
miles over the Indian Ocean. In five minutes
there will sometimes be a difference of seven-
teen degrees. During the three months' monsoon there were occasional breaks of a few
days, when the weather was perfect, the
temperature being cool, the air clear, and tenderly bright. We used to liken it to that of a
North-country September in England ; but even
in Western India there was no escaping the
dreary influence of sullen November. This was
our Winter. Then the trees looked dead, and
an east wind set in, not exactly cold, but so
searching that it found out every sensitive part
of the body, and dried the skin like frost. This
wind is very fatal to animals, especially to
horses and dogs ; nor is it less dangerous to
man. "A stroke of the wind," as it is called,
produces paralysis, from which many people
never recover. At this season all windows
which look towards the east are closed. The
days were certainly unpleasant. The angry
sun was seldom seen save when, huge and
fiery, it sank down in a horizon of dull, but
fervid orange red.

By way of compensation the heavens at night
were, beyond expression, grand. Returning
home in an evening, we had "sultry Sirius,"

the largest star in the sky, flashing with ever-varying colour. Orion, reclining on his side, calmly regarded us. Venus almost outshone the moon, and when the moon was full, it rose with a flush of silvery rose-colour, fainter, but as fine as the glow which heralds in the sun. As time went on, Orion rose upon his feet, and the Southern Cross came slanting above the horizon; but when Orion was sprawling at the zenith, then that most striking and brilliant of constellations stood erect. In this part of the world the latest sunsets occur at the end of June and the beginning of July, when, for several days, the luminary sets at forty-one minutes past six. The earliest are at the end of November and the beginning of December, when the sun sinks below the horizon at twenty-two minutes past five (Bombay time).

There is no evening like the evening which succeeds an English Summer's day. In the North of Europe they are deferred too long. It is unpleasant to go to bed like a naughty child, with the light in one's eyes, but the Indian night closes in too soon. There are no violet eves, there is no gloaming, the great orb disappears behind the distant hills whose out-lines sharpen and grow black, cut for a moment against a glowing background, some large star struggles to appear, the sky grows green, the fells purple, and the landscape grey. You are taken by surprise, for you are scarcely able to distinguish the features of the friend you are talking with. You hurriedly shake hands with him, there is a general flutter, horse-cloths are rolled up (all the year round the horses wear their fules whilst standing still), lamps are lighted, and away you go over the dark moors.

The band-stand, where the regiments take it in turns to play, is another general gathering-place. For one half of the year the effect of the Grecian building in which the performance takes place is marred by the matting with which it is necessary to shelter it from sun and storm. It is set down on a pleasant moor, with long lines of barracks in the background. Twice every week the little world repaired to this spot. Bullock-carts come full of children, little things in different stages of growth, the lowest being a tiny creature in robes of white, who get out with their tall, robust ayahs, gay in scarlet vests, white savis, and gold ornaments, talkative and bold. They file off with the elder children under their wings, to have their gossip, whilst the muslin bundle follows, carried—oh! so carefully—by a tall, dark man, who keeps the lace veil over its face, and re-

gards it tenderly. Meanwhile the little folks
kiss and quarrel, and talk over their magic-
lantern parties, whilst their parents dwell upon
the past delights of ball or Badminton.

And then the dogs, they composed a society
of their own, and I have no doubt that their
reflections were as sensible, if less artificial, than
those of their so-called betters. There were
the military dogs, many of which were of the
bull-dog order. The younger the master the
more hideous the pet; some of them being,
indeed, of priceless ugliness—perfect gems in
their way. There was the collector's dog, long-
legged and lean, looking mildly at the world
through half-closed eyes. He was a gentle-
manly dog. The judge's animal was broad-
chested, round-headed, and clever, a good fellow, although he growled, and now and then
responded to a pat by a snap. He never meant
to hurt, it was his way. The Padré's dogs
were intellectual and hungry. The canine
civilians varied in appearance and character,
some of them being stumpy and obese, with
projecting teeth, and white trimmings to their
faces, and were inclined to be uppish; but Mabel
—I ought to have mentioned that distinguished
member of the Royal Geographical Society first
of all—she was military. Though young in

years, Mabel's brow was wrinkled by travel and by thought. When her black lip curled with scorn at the ignorance displayed by her companions, it disclosed sharp fangs; but would not the gentlest temper ever possessed by man or beast have been soured, had its owner been obliged to trot in puppyhood two thousand miles over the burning sands of Africa. As for Grouse and Drake, they also had seen the world, and sitting down in the attitude of sphinxes, they looked on and marvelled at the airs and graces of their juniors. Bustle snuffed about with a divided mind. He delighted in the society of ladies, but then there were chameleons to hunt. Once upon this very spot had he chased and eaten one of these creatures, and never had he forgotten the exquisite morsel. Let none of my four-legged friends be angry at this allusion to them. Had I not regarded them with favour, I should have left them unnoticed, for I had nothing to do with curs.

Occasionally one or two native chiefs honoured the band with their presence. There was Jambottee (called, like a highland proprietor, by the name of his territory), who belonged to the Jeunesse Dorée of Western India, and aped the European. He came upon the ground in an equipage which he had purchased from a departed brigadier—a dirty carriage and ill-groomed horses; but he did not drive them badly. He was quite a youth; so much that his face, had it been white, might have been called chubby; but, as it was, its dusky hue was relieved by the great, soft, intelligent eyes. His costume was most remarkable, consisting, to begin with, of his dandy half-high patent leather shoes, of grey-ribbed stockings, of so precise a fit that he must have sent a model of his calfless leg to Nottingham, gartered under the knee, and mounting up, until they disappeared under the folds of a small cotton sheet (a Duthie cloth), which was wound round his body; his white waistcoat and jacket, resembling those of a *garçon* in a *café*; and lastly his Eastern turban, sometimes made of soft pink woollen, of the hue which is always associated with raspberry ice, at others consisting of enormous lengths of soft muslin, red, chocolate, or blue striped with gold, artistically wound into innumerable folds, and put on with a slight inclination to the left ear. This young gentleman was tolerably educated, and could read and write with facility. He was not very rich, his estates being said to bring him in about £5000 a year. I was somewhat curious about this youth, and one day asked a friend who was a little acquainted with him why he did not reside at Jambottee, which is a tolerably large town. "Probably because he is afraid of being poisoned," was the reply. "If you inquire, you will find that most of the chiefs in this part of the country are young; a family of means like, above all things, to have charge of a youthful heir, by whom they manage to get pretty pickings. I was in a native state only a few months ago where there is no doubt that the boyish chief, who died suddenly, and was burnt before the British authorities were informed of the event, was poisoned." Poor Jambottee! I looked with commiseration at his smooth round face.

"What does he do all day? What is his home life?" I demanded.

My friend laughed. "Probably a couple of hours ago he was sitting all but naked upon the floor, ladling melted ghi into his mouth with one hand, and throwing rice into it with the other." I looked horrified. "And when he goes home he will most likely shut himself up along with his prime minister, and drink arrack until the small hours. Such is the life of many a chief." Alas for Jambottee!

Sometimes the moon would rise before we were scattered by the " The British Grenadier,"

and the succeeding strains of the National
Anthem. First it was but a tiny crescent,
scarcely visible in the after-glow, but as it
waxed larger and larger the more delightful
grew the homeward drive, which lay for the
most part under tall trees. Such a soft light
fell upon the swelling hills and dark groves
that one could count every trembling leaf in the
great bouquets of bamboo. The moonlight,
indeed, we agreed, was, in this latitude, not
so positively bright as in our own country;
the shadows thrown were not so black; the
lines which marked out landscape, mosque, and
temple not so sharp; but the whole atmosphere
was alight with a gentle glow, which was
exquisitely beautiful.

On the eve of one full moon, book in hand, I
left the drawing-room, and sauntered into the
maidan, where the Pir's tomb stood, and, out of
curiosity, I looked at the print, which I found I
could read with ease. The old fort by moonlight was wonderfully picturesque; and sometimes in these glorious evenings we mounted the
ramparts, or crept through the ancient Jaina
temples, in which the shadowy gods appeared
to regard us sternly.

CHAPTER XIII.

Old Mosque—The Nág, or Cobra Tank—Shárpur—Population—Jewellers—Curiosities—Sacred Stones—Ancient Pedigrees—Thugs—Garden Parties—Travelliug Merchants—Men from the Cannara Jungles—Plants and Tame Animals brought for sale—Conjurers and Snake-charmers—Indian Jugglers puzzled—A Charm against Violence — Mahomedan Burying-places — Amusements of the Soldiers—Native Troops—My First Christmas in India.

WE occasionally visited some interesting spot in the neighbourhood, and one day drove to a place with a very long name, which I have forgotten. The hard metal road, up and down hill, was a severe tug for the horses. Our object was to see an old mosque, and one of the underground reservoirs peculiar to India. In some parts of the country they are works of considerable magnificence, but this was a very humble specimen of the kind. Although it was said to be very ancient, and had once been the nucleus of a town of some local importance, the only remains were a cluster of mud hovels. An elderly man, pointing to the well, remarked to G—— that it was very old. A wide flight of steps, covered in, conducted us to a broad landing-place, with a stone screen, and a double set of steps led to the deep black pool, while overhead were the remains of an arched roof. It was an oblong building, with two stories of galleries running round it, ornamented by deep niches formed in the wall, the largest of which faced the stairs. When these were set with idols, it must, in the shadowy twilight, have been an awe-inspiring place, and the effect still more curious if brilliantly lighted up, and filled with worshippers.

The mosque, which was time-worn, had, in our opinion, originally been a Jain temple. The Mahomedans were in the habit of taking possession of such buildings, and adapting them to their own points of the compass, to fit them for the celebration of their own worship. Many people may remember the crooked matting and oddly-placed pulpits in St. Sophia.

On the other side of the present Belgaum, there was an open tank, called the Nág, or Cobra-tank, near which some irregular mounds marked the site of the older town. The country here was flooded during the rains, when it became brilliantly green with the springing rice. A raised road led to Dhorwar, a military station about forty miles south, on the confines of the Madras Presidency, and near it began the great Cannara jungles, which stretch along for upwards of three hundred miles.

Sometimes we drove on this solitary road for the sake of the dogs, when the great twin brothers, and Bustle (busiest of all) were in their element, splashing in and out of the lakes and pools after rats and bandicoots. The town of Shárpur* lay in this direction, unseen, but very near the road, its low sloping roofs quite hidden by trees, which swept down to the very ground. Shárpur is a place of some interest, and belongs to a native chief, whom we sometimes encountered, driving a ricketty old carriage, with two gora-wallees behind, one of whom was tall, and wore a white turban, while the other was small, with a red covering to his head. On State occasions he was followed by a guard of seven or eight men, with blunderbusses, arrayed in dirty white cotton, who scrambled along on tattoos. The walls of the town, which at no distant period had been in complete repair, had at each end an arched gateway, flanked by stout round battlemented

* Shárpur means King's-town.

towers, pierced with narrow slits for jangals. I used to fancy that the town establishment of the Balowtry and Alowtry would be found very perfect in Shárpur, the place had such an old-world look. There were some wide, suburban-looking streets, lined by houses, which were nearly completely closed, though one occasion-ally caught a glimpse into a large dim court-yard. Under the verandahs, which were very wide and long, the women were employed in weaving savis, and sorting and winding the bril-liant silks with which they were to be striped. A few children, with entire caps of fresh flowers, and ornaments strange to me, would roll about in the dust along with the dogs and a few scraggy fowls (natives have a prejudice against keeping poultry).

Along the principal street there flowed an endless stream of men with very large turbans, and all in white. The primitive population of this Hindoo town were Lyngates, and there was none of the restless mixture of races which compose that of Belgaum. Even my unprac-tised eye could perceive that the tall handsome men, who walked calmly along with dignified gait, and complexions of tender brown, were of higher caste than those I had been in the habit of regarding.

The people of Shárpur, which is a rich place, deal in pearls and precious stones, and work in gold and silver, making not only personal ornaments of handsome design, but supplying half Western India with gods and goddesses, and driving a gainful trade as bankers and money-lenders. The improvident Hindoo, though he will not part with his land, will mortgage it to its utmost value, and the expenses incurred at marriage festivals and on the numerous holidays frequently plunge him into difficulties which not only last for his own life, but embarrass his son, who, by ancient Hindoo custom, is answerable for his father's debts. It was the habit of the sowars, as the goldsmiths are called, to bear their wealth upon their persons; and those who wish to see pearl earrings and gold bangles, must go to Shárpur, where I envied many a young man his wristlets.

One of the curiosities of the place is a mosque, a handsome building, which has never been roofed in, and was commenced just when the Mahomedan power received its death-blow. There lie the clean-cut white stones, just as they were left by the masons, the pillared aisles, weather-stained and falling into ruins. The sacred Hindoo buildings were assembled together in one particular part of the town. On one side of the street was a lofty, open Linga shrine, and on the opposite side, at a little distance from each other, were three long and lofty halls, into which the light of day was only admitted through the curiously-carved high and red-stained doorways, which opened from under verandahs. We gazed into these, but did not attempt to enter. In one of them we observed a Lingham, a symbol of the power of Shiva, at least twelve feet high, covered with brightly-burnished metal—probably a mixture which is common in a country where there is abundance of copper and brass. A large black stone figure had sole possession of the second hall; and the third was lighted up and filled with worshipping devotees, who were adoring a many-limbed black and gilded idol.

The palace of the chief was a large, three-storied wooden erection, exceedingly dirty and dilapidated, but about which there was some handsome carving. In driving, I often noticed the painted and whitewashed stones, set up in the fields, some of them boundary stones, others placed about in order to ensure good luck to the growing crops. During one particular month, in returning home through the gathering darkness, the bright light of a small lantern, swung from a pole, was always to be seen, evidently so placed as to shine upon some object concealed in the ditch.

A trifling accident to one of the horses near this spot enabled me to gratify my curiosity as to what it might be. I found three black stones, placed one upon the other, well greased, and encircled with flowers, the sacred filets placed round them by some procession of peasants—sacrificial filets, prescribed by the gods of boundaries, one of whom is called by the long name of Yajñavalkya. The melted libations of ghi, which deluged these particular stones, had perhaps been rendered still more acceptable to the powers above by the addition of a little salt. Salt is often used in the temples, but it must be made by solar evaporation. The gods will not be propitiated by the article which Liverpool exports to their shores at so cheap a rate. I have been told that the ryot, or peasant, if questioned as to his feelings on sacred subjects, will declare that his idea of the proper way of carrying out his religion is to do right, and to worship the village god and the sanctified stones. The owners of land have the greatest objection, to part with it, considering such a step a religious offence, and maintaining that it is not theirs to dispose of—

that they are mere tenants of the god to whom it was made over centuries ago. It is often found that the very servants in your house have a pedigree in land which many a rich man in England would give half his wealth to possess. A servant of G——'s, in Sattara, once asked for leave of absence in order to settle some family claims upon a portion of land which he had inherited, and the judge who had examined and given his decision upon the affair, told him that the land in question had been granted to the family for military service done nearly three hundred years ago. We knew that the puttah-wallee was a gentleman possessed of landed property, because he was always in hot water with regard to the money he had borrowed upon it; and our malee used to run away to his own village periodically, in order to sow his land, leaving G—— lamenting; but he was generally pursued and brought back by the patel of the place.

We often passed the long, low, white jail, built on the spot occupied by the English during the siege, and in which I believe some older building is still embedded. Close by, on ground torn, cut, and disturbed, rises an obelisk, and some table-tombs, the marble slabs of which, that would have told their tale, had been stolen for curry-stones. The inscriptions cut upon the pliable stone have been worn away by the action of time and the weather, but one name survives, that of Lieut. Dormer, with the date—1820, or 21.

Some years ago this jail was full of Thugs, who had been the scourge of the country from Belgaum to Mysore. One old man among them confessed to upwards of three hundred murders, and it was from his mouth that "The Confessions of a Thug" were taken down. Some of these wretched worshippers of the cruel Bavani used to work in the garden of the officer who was then at the head of the district police, and he was quite fond of relating their various deeds of villainy.

One evening, as we were returning home, we met a procession of people bearing lanterns, and carrying a kind of pagoda, covered with white calico, trimmed with bows and streamers, the occupant of which, a dead Lyngate, was taking his last ride, seated cross-legged, the position in which he was about to be buried.

The society in Belgaum was tolerably extensive—a great advantage—as, after visits of ceremony had been exchanged, it left people at liberty to choose the companionship of kindred souls. The garrison was composed of a battery

of artillery, one European and two native regiments, besides a certain number of military men
holding special appointments, and a good many
civilians. The knot of people gathered together
in the fort might be looked upon as residents,
as they were independent of regimental changes.
When I first arrived there were a good many
garden-parties, pleasant gatherings, where
people met together to play at Badminton, or
lawn tennis, or to talk, and sip cool beverages,
whilst listening to the band. Sometimes these
entertainments would conclude with a little
dancing. One gallant bachelor colonel, whose
compound was furnished with magnificent trees,
spent a small fortune in hanging their gnarled
boughs with lanterns, the effect of which
was very pretty. When the rains came on,
this kind of society passed away, and the
afternoons were often enlivened by the arrival
of travelling merchants from the interior of
India—cunning fellows—who knew that, when
a second deluge seemed to be impending, people
were sure not only to be at home, but would be
tempted to look at their goods, and buy from
sheer ennui. Those who dealt in the more costly
wares would arrive in covered carts, drawn by
reeking bullocks, from which they brought forth
great bundles, which they would open in the

verandah, spreading about their contents until it looked like a fancy bazaar. They had goods collected in every part of India—shawls and coloured embroidery, silks and satins, useful washing silks, inlaid boxes, and balls painted over in the most delicate patterns, the parent one as big as a pummalo, and containing a progeny which gradually dwindled in size until the last one was little larger than a pea. These balls were irresistible attractions, although perfectly useless. Among the other heterogeneous articles were jewels, silver filigree, fans, neck scarfs, Cora silk, tempting toys, and boxes of ivory letters neatly cut, and brightly-coloured objects, some of them curious and strange. Oh! the temptation of such a dazzling collection upon a wet day! How different was their liquid Hindustani and soft voices, when compared with the harsh Márathi I was accustomed to hear! Rough people would bring bison and buffalo horns, twisted into many shapes—though the natural form was the best —so highly polished that one's distorted image was reflected from their surface. Some of them were delicately engraved with fanciful designs. To be of use, however, they require to be mounted, and they are sometimes set in chased gold.

More interesting were the savage-looking men who arrived with ferns and orchids from the Cannara jungles, which stretch their vast length along the Malabar coast. Canarese, Tamil, and Telugu are all spoken in Máhratta, though quite distinct languages, and not derived from Sanskrit. These Canarese people were small and thin, and as black as it was possible for men to be. They are believed to be the descendants of the unconquered aboriginal tribes driven into the jungles by the invading Aryan settlers. It is reckoned that the pre-historic races now scattered over mountains, or living in far-spreading forests and deep jungles, number twelve millions. In every part of India where the soil has not been reclaimed, are found relics of the aboriginal races, more or less barbarous. I never saw these wild beings without indulging in endless speculations as to their history.*

---

* The code of Manu, supposed to be written 900 B.C., gives laws as to the property the conquered aborigines may be allowed to possess :—

"Their abode must be out of towns. Their sole property is to consist of dogs and asses. Their clothes should be those left by the dead. Their ornaments rusty iron. They must roam from place to place. No respectable person must hold intercourse with them. They are to perform the office of executioner on all criminals condemned to death by the king. For this duty they may retain the bedding, the clothes, and the ornaments of those executed."—"Land of the Vedas." By the REV. R. PERCIVAL.

The water-ferns they brought attain the height of ten or twelve feet, and it was necessary to put them into pots, and sink them in the ground: They had also delicately-swathed little bunches of the gold, silver, copper, lace, palm and other ferns. One of them, the true oak-fern, is a very curious production; its root, a great bit of mouldy-looking wood, throwing up large, dead-looking leaves, which shelter the green fronds. The orchids, lilac and white-blossomed, G—— bound, along with moss, upon the trees, and they flourished well. Other people brought trained animals—monkeys, dogs, and goats, the former generally got up to represent Rajahs and their wives, and to act little scenes. These little creatures were, to all appearance, well treated, and seemed fond of their masters. We were also visited by snake-charmers and conjurers, who came with long bamboos on their shoulders, from which dangled mysteriously-filled baskets. They were accompanied by musicians, who played on a fife, struck the tom-tom, and clashed the cymbals. Some of their feats were neatly done, but I never myself witnessed anything wonderful.

A friend of G——'s puzzled a band of these people, who came to his house, by playing them a trick which surprised them not a little. It so happened that he had a glass eye, and at the end of the performance he cried out—" Bah! you shall see what I can do. You know nothing!" Whereupon he dexterously slipped out the artificial eye, and held it towards them, they looking on dumb, transfixed with astonishment. With another sweep of the hand he restored the eye to the socket, and regarded them with an air of conscious superiority. " Wha! wha! wha!" they cried, tumbling their possessions anyhow into the baskets, in their haste to be gone. " Wonderful!" and off they set.

It did not rain incessantly, as, three or four times a week, we were able to snatch a drive. The gentlemen amused themselves in many ways, with whist, pigeon-shooting, and cricket, a tent being erected at the latter for the benefit of lady spectators. We frequently drove to the ground where the shooting was going on, in order to bring G—— back, and if he was not ready, we walked about the breezy down. At a short distance from the spot, sheltered by some very old trees, were a couple of ancient buildings, one of which, with a low dome, was probably the resting-place of some holy Pir. Like many a Mahomedan building, it was freely marked with impressions of the human hand, just dabbed with red or white paint, and laid on the wall—the hand, with its five fingers, being the symbol of despotic power. On the outside of dwelling-houses this figure is supposed to act as a charm against violence, the dwelling and its inmates being placed under the power of an invincible hand. Its companion building was also a Mahomedan burial-place, but it had probably once been a Hindoo temple, for it had a pyramidal roof. Some say that the architecture of the Hindoos originated with the pyramid, in which form it is certain that the oldest pagodas are built. Near the door there cropped out of the sward a half-buried stone, on which the soles of two feet were marked; and I afterwards found that it was the custom formerly to place a memorial so engraved upon the spot where suttee had taken place.

The soldiers' sports, in which some of the officers joined, were very amusing. One of these was riding at the ring, in which no great success was attained. The Yorkshire farrier, who was quite a character, and used to get prodigiously cheered, rode at it as if he were going to carry off a ton's weight by sheer force. Some of the young men jumped with much agility, but I do not fancy that the highest jump registered, four feet eleven inches, was anything remarkable. No one succeeded in picking up the sword at full speed, but many were skilful in cutting into halves the oranges placed on bamboo posts as they rode by. The gunnery was the most interesting spectacle. On one occasion a gun was taken to pieces, put together, and fired in one minute and twenty seconds, which I believe was considered to be good work. The game of polo was frequently played upon their maidan by the young officers of the Royal Fusiliers. Some of their little Deccan Tats were wonderfully quick and knowing.

On moonlight nights the gallant Colonel of this regiment would allow his band to play, when the Christy Minstrels belonging to it would sing some of their amusing songs. At these merry gatherings, the Irishmen brought their floor and danced jigs, and the evening's entertainment would conclude with blind-man's buff, played with a will, and led off by the Colonel, the young officers being blinded by grotesque caps, which were drawn over the face. Picnics also took place by the same magic light; but these entertainments were, somehow or other, not quite so successful. The elders could not double up their legs comfortably upon the ground, and next day there was sure to be trouble among the matrons, forks and spoons and plates having gone astray, fine napkins having been exchanged for those of Dhorwar cotton, and the junior members of the assembly were certain to have caught cold. Sometimes Penny Readings, which it was necessary to patronise, took place in the barracks, and plays were performed, deep tragedies being followed by screaming farces. "Lady Audley's Secret" was performed, the heroine's part being taken by a handsome sergeant's wife, and the kick with which she sent her groom husband down the well was a sight worth seeing.

Society in general went in for innumerable dinner-parties, and occasional balls. Now and then a concert was given in aid of some charity, in which the ladies of the fort distinguished themselves by their vocal and instrumental efforts, pronounced by that great authority, the *Times* of India, "to be worthy of the Italian Opera."

The four months' rains passed very quickly. The largest downfall registered for any single month was twenty-nine inches, and occurred in July. The whole amount which fell during the monsoon was sixty-two inches, a little above the average. The most tiresome duty of the season is the perpetual care which it is necessary to exercise in order to prevent books, prints, photographs,

wearing apparel—everything, in fact—from be-
coming spotted with blue mould, a calamity which
is certain to befall them, if they are put away.
Woe to the young lady who does not air her
ribbons constantly! All clothes ought, at this
season, to be worn in turn. I managed to preserve my gloves by a very simple expedient. I
impounded three French plum bottles (which,
by-the-by, I had helped to empty)—glass bottles
made to screw, and rendered, by the addition of
an Indian-rubber ring, perfectly air-tight. One
of these I filled with new gloves and put it
away in a dry place; another was placed upon
my toilette-table and received those which were
in wear; the third I reserved for the aged and
infirm to use in travelling, for I hold that
wearing gloves keeps the hand cool.

After the rains, another device for killing time
was perpetual Badminton, for which there was
a covered place prepared in the camp. In the
fort, for the occasion, possession was taken of a
large shed, which, by-the-by, had gone through
the Persian campaign. The courts were very
good, and two tiers of empty boilers were so
arranged as to form seats which were covered
with cane matting. As long as people were
quiet they were comfortable enough, but when
any individual began to fidget, the boilers

vibrated, and a thrill ran through all assembled. At these friendly and pleasant meetings, each lady, in her turn, sent down refreshments, and sometimes large luncheon parties were given.

Belgaum was obliged to get up and shake itself when the Commander-in-chief declared his intention of passing through it, during his tour. The troops on that occasion were reviewed; there were sham fights, and all sorts of manœuvres, during which I, for the first time, saw a native regiment, one of the finest in the service—the 2nd Grenadiers, lately arrived from Aden. This regiment held their own against fearful odds. When at Rongaum, in the year 1818, they withstood the Máhrattas, who outnumbered them ten to one. "Tired, hungry, wounded, and parched with thirst, they fought with a gallantry which has never been surpassed," so say the despatches of the day. The Sphinx is embroidered on their colours, in memory of the fact that they were one of the two native regiments who served in Egypt, besides which they were also engaged in the battle of Kinhee, in Persia. Many of the soldiers, too, have medals for the part they took in the campaign of Abyssinia. They were a remarkably fine, tall body of men from the north of India. In full dress they wore a neat little turban, apparently made of the Turkey sugar dear to one's infant heart, and ornamented with a stiff crimson bow. This regiment, for many of its exploits, has well deserved its new title, "The Prince of Wales's Own Grenadiers."

I do not know if it is the case in other Presidencies, but, in that of Bombay, a native regiment is permitted to recruit a hundred of its men from other parts of India, for the once war-like Máhrattas have turned to agriculture, and have deteriorated as soldiers. To me, these strangers appeared to be magnificent specimens of humanity, and I must confess that I compared their majestic gait, shapely heads, fine features, and flashing eyes with those of the European soldiers, and to the disadvantage of the latter. I made a remark upon the subject to an officer in command of these natives. "You are mistaken," he said, "as to their stature; it is true that many of the men from the north and south-east are splendid fellows, but the tallest man in my regiment is but a little above six feet three inches—their wide pigamas, flowing drapery, and picturesque puggrees deceive you as to their stature." These men are allowed to wear their native costumes out of hours, and many of them were exceedingly picturesque. I delighted in seeing the different races, and after a time I fancied myself able to tell from whence a man came, and that principally from the mode in which his hair was arranged. Those from the Punjaub wore it long, and turned up into a kind of chignon; the Sikhs parted theirs behind, and banded it round the head. The Jews shaved the hair from off their temple, and wore short crisp curls behind the ear, with no gloss upon them. There are numbers of Jewish soldiers, and being generally men of education they are pretty sure to rise in a regiment.

One day when the 7th Royal Fusiliers were reviewed, Grouse and Drake chanced to be with us, and, seeing the soldiers about to fire, they rushed in behind a company, a position from which no calling could induce them to return. There they stood with their tails straight, and as stiff as if cast in bronze. Poor doggies, they were quite confounded, and evidently disappointed when they found that, after the firing, their eager anticipations of sport were rewarded by the sight of not even a single bird.

The face of society changed almost as much as that of nature. Our three regiments marched off, playing pathetic airs of adieu; and familiar faces were replaced by those of strangers. The resident society also broke up in the

Autumn, but only for a time. The collector
went on his way with a long train of baggage-
waggons; the judge, the "up-country judge,"
disappeared; the engineer officers were off to
their tanks, roads, and bridges. The forest
department spread their wings and flew to the
deep jungles, where they would see many a
wild beast before they met with Europeans
again. Education struck its tents, and the
chaplains exchanged duty with brethren from
afar, and, worst of all, G—— was off with
hundreds of miles before him—long days upon
the Indus and its banks, with Aden in prospect.
For M. and myself, who were stationary, roses
bloomed, and the garden blossomed, but Christmas, when it stole on, appeared, at least to me,
very strange. We filled great baskets with
flowers and ferns, and sent them to the good
teaching sisters, for the adornment of their
little chapel (our own churches being abundantly
supplied), and endeavoured to make the season
as pleasant to the little ones as it could be
without their father.

On Christmas Eve we had a display of such
fireworks as were permissible in the immediate
neighbourhood of a powder-magazine and an
arsenal. There were Bengal lights, and crackers, and wheels; but the prettiest of all were

the bouquets of golden spray, with green and red flowers, which shot up from earthenware chatty pots. It was a balmy Summer's night, the soldiers' children came to look on, and we had chairs taken to the meadow where the display took place. During the evening, highly-coloured wooden toys, representing rajahs and ranis, in cloth of gold, wild animals, and tropical fruits, kept arriving—some of them presents from the servants. They were not shown to the children, who were instructed to hang their stockings up, that Father Christmas might fill them during the night; and as soon as they were asleep a pretty scroll, representing a rosy-red robin, singing with all his might out of a snow-flecked holly bush, was hung over their breakfast-table.

Christmas morning, with all its surprises and good wishes, began very early. We elders had to undergo the ordeal after breakfast of standing in the verandah whilst all the servants came up to make their salaams; and M., with Dick in her arms, thanked them in an eloquent speech. We also came in for our share of good things. The Parsis sent tall, circular cakes, in form very much resembling their own towers of silence; some one else sent a rare present of rosy apples; the brigadier a dish

of peaches grown in his garden ; and in the course
of the morning came a great *mendiant*, consisting of dried figs, dates, almonds, and raisins,
arranged in quarters upon a dish large enough
to have contained a leg of mutton, taking me
back to my Paris days. For the sake of "auld
lang syne," I (with a little help from the
children) ate steadily through that *mendiant*.
We had a merry dinner, when the chicks were
gone to roost (what a pleasant time it is when
they are asleep), but could not enjoy it
thoroughly in G——'s absence. There was a
dance on the last evening of the year, and so
ended my first Christmas in India.

END OF THE FIRST VOLUME.

LONDON: PRINTED BY DUNCAN MACDONALD, BLENHEIM HOUSE.